DEADLY LITTLE VOICES

Also by Laurie Faria Stolarz

DEADLY LITTLE VOICES

A TOUCH NOVEL

Laurie Faria Stolarz

HYPERION

NEW YORK

First Edition

10 9 8 7 6 5 4 3 2 1

G475-5664-5-11258

Printed in the United States of America

Library of Congress Cataloging-in-Publication Data
Stolarz, Laurie Faria, 1972–
Deadly little voices : a touch novel / Laurie Faria Stolarz.—1st ed.
p. cm.
ISBN 978-1-4231-3161-8 (alk. paper)
[1. Psychic ability—Fiction. 2. Aunts—Fiction. 3. Pottery—Fiction.
4. High schools—Fiction. 5. Schools—Fiction.] I. Title.
PZ7.S8757
[Fic]—dc23   2011012308

Reinforced binding

Visit www.hyperionteens.com

THIS LABEL APPLIES TO TEXT STOCK

Jack and Jill ran up the hill, both for a little fun.
Jack's plan was deception while Jill sought affection.
And Jack wouldn't quit till he won.

I

A VOICE STARTLES ME AWAKE. It's a female voice with a menacing tone, and it whispers into my ear.

And tells me that I should die.

I sit up in bed and click on my night-table lamp. It's 4:10 a.m. My bedroom door is closed. The window is locked. The curtains are drawn. And I'm alone.

I'm alone.

So, then, why can't I shake this feeling—this sensation that I'm being watched?

I draw up the covers and tell myself that the voice was part of a dream. I remember my dream distinctly. I dreamt that I was in my pottery studio, using a spatula to perfect a sculpture I've been working on: a figure skater with her arms crossed over her chest and her leg extended back. I began the sculpture just a few days ago, but I haven't touched it since.

I look down at my hands, noticing how I can almost feel a lingering sensation of clay against my fingertips.

That's how real the dream felt.

I take a deep breath and lie back down. But the voice comes at me again—in my ear, rushing over my skin, and sending chills straight down my back.

Slowly, I climb out of bed and cross the room, wondering if maybe there's someone else here. Standing in front of my closet door, I can feel my heart pound. I take another step and move to turn the knob.

At the same moment, a voice cries out: a high-pitched squeal that cuts right through my bones. I steel myself and look around the room.

Finally, I find the source: two eyes stare up at me from a pile of clothes on the floor. I'd recognize those eyes anywhere. Wide and green, they belong to my old baby doll, from when I was six.

She has twisty long blond hair like mine and a quarter-inch-long gash in her rubber cheek.

I haven't seen the doll in at least ten years.

Ten years since I lost her.

Ten years since my dad scoured every inch of the house looking for her and, when he couldn't find her, offered to buy me a new one.

My arms shaking, I pick up the doll, noticing the black X's drawn on her ears. I squeeze her belly and she cries out again, reminding me of a wounded bird.

I rack my brain, desperate for some sort of logical explanation, wondering if maybe this isn't my doll at all.

If maybe it's just a creepy replica. I mean, how can a doll that's been missing for ten years suddenly just reappear? But when I flip her over to check her back, I see that logic doesn't have a place here.

Because this doll is definitely mine.

The star is still there—the one I inked above the hem of her shorts when I became fascinated by the idea of all things astrological.

I pinch my forearm so hard the skin turns red. I'm definitely awake. My backpack is still slumped at the foot of my bed where I left it last night. The snapshot of Dad and me in front of the tree this past Christmas is still pasted up on my dresser mirror.

Aside from the doll, everything appears as it should.

So, then, how is this happening?

In one quick motion, I whisk my closet door open and pull the cord that clicks on the light. My clothes look normal, my shoes are all there, my last year's Halloween costume (a giant doughnut, oozing with creamy filling—a lame attempt to rebel against my mother's vegan ways) is hanging on a back hook, just as it should be.

Meanwhile the voice continues. It whispers above my head, behind my neck, and into the inner recesses of my ear. And tells me that I'm worthless as a human being.

I open my bedroom door and start down the hallway, to go and find my parents. But with each step, the voice gets deeper, angrier, more menacing. It tells me how ugly I look, how talentless I am, and how I couldn't be more pathetic.

"You're just one big, fat joke," the voice hisses. The words echo inside my brain.

I cover my ears, but still the insults keep coming. And suddenly I'm six years old again with my doll clenched against my chest and a throbbing sensation at the back of my head.

I look toward my parents' closed bedroom door, feeling my stomach churn. I reach out to open their door, but I can't seem to find it now. There's a swirl of colors behind my eyes, making me dizzy. I take another step, holding the wall to steady myself; the floor feels like it's tilting beneath my feet.

On hands and knees now, I close my eyes to ease the ache in my head.

"Just do it," the voice whispers. It's followed by more voices, of different people. All trapped inside my head. The voices talk over one another and mingle together, producing one clear-cut message: that I'm a waste of a life. Finally, I find the knob and pull the door open, but my palms brush against a wad of fabric, and I realize that I haven't found my parents' bedroom after all.

It's the hallway closet. A flannel sheet tumbles onto my face.

Instead of turning away, I crawl inside, and remain crouched on the floor, praying for the voices to stop.

But they only seem to get louder.

I rock back and forth, trying to remain in control. I smother my ears with the sheet. Press my forehead against my knees. Pound my heels into the floor, bracing myself for whatever's coming next.

Meanwhile, there's a drilling sensation inside my head; it pushes through the bones of my skull and makes me feel like I'm going crazy.

"Please," I whisper. More tears sting my eyes. I shake my head, wondering if maybe I'm already dead, if maybe the voices are part of hell.

Finally, after what feels like forever, the words in my head start to change. A voice tells me that I'm not alone.

"I'm right here with you," the voice says in a tone that's soft and serene.

An icy sensation encircles my forearm and stops me from rocking. I open my eyes and pull the sheet from my face, and am confused by what I see.

The hallway light is on now. A stark white hand is wrapped around my wrist. It takes me a second to realize that the hand isn't my own. The fingers are soiled with a dark red color.

Aunt Alexia is crouching down in front of me. Her green eyes look darker than usual, the pupils dilated, and the irises filled with broken blood vessels. Her pale blond hair hangs down at the sides of her face, almost like a halo.

"Am I dead?" I ask, rubbing at my temples, wondering if the red on her hands is from a gash in my head.

"Shhh," she says, silencing the other voices completely.

"Am I dead?" I repeat. My throat feels like it's bleeding, too.

She shakes her head. A smear of red lingers on my forearm. I see now that it's paint. "Come with me," she whispers.

I blink a couple of times to make sure she's really here—that she's not some apparition straight out of my dream. Dressed in a paint-spattered T-shirt and a pair of torn jeans, Aunt Alexia leads me out of the closet and back into my room. She helps me into bed, taking care to tuck my doll in beside me. And then she starts humming a whimsical tune—something vaguely familiar, from childhood, maybe. Her lips are the color of dying red roses.

I pinch myself yet again to make sure I'm not dreaming. The time on my clock reads 4:43.

"Has it really only been a half hour?" I ask, thinking aloud.

Aunt Alexia doesn't answer. Instead she continues to hum to me. Her voice reminds me of flowing water, somehow easing me to sleep.

Dear Jill,

    I'll bet you were flattered to learn that
I'd had my eye on you long before I first
stepped into the coffee shop where you worked.
I'd sit in the parking lot during your shifts
and watch you through the glass. Some days
I'd park just down the street from your house.
Other days, I'd watch you walk home from
school.
    When I finally did show my face, I noticed
that you liked to watch me too. I'd see you
checking me out as I pretended to do homework
at one of the back tables of the coffee
shop. One time I spotted you applying a fresh
coat of lip gloss when you thought I wasn't
looking. I'd never seen you wear any before,
so I assumed it was to impress me.
    For months your hair was always the same—
in a long dark braid that went down your
back—but after I'd started coming around,
you wore it down and loose. Am I correct in
thinking that wasn't a coincidence?
    It was a while before we said anything more
than coffee talk—a large mocha latte one day,
a double-shot espresso the next—but I knew a
lot about you. That you were sixteen and had
never been kissed (cliché, but true). Are you
wondering how I knew that? Or is it possible
that you already know?
    You remember, don't you? That time, in
your room, when your father called you to
the kitchen? When you left your diary out

on your bed? When your balcony door was left partially open? I fantasized that you'd left the diary there on purpose. That you knew I was lingering right outside. That you wanted me to read it.

Did you miss not having your diary for those days that I kept it? Or maybe you'd fantasized about me reading it too?

I also knew that you used to skate (I'd seen the trophies in your room). And that aside from the spray of freckles across your face, you couldn't have been more different from the rest of your family—especially your mother: the one who got away.

I'd never let you get away.

The first time I saw you was one day, right after your school had let out. I'd been sitting in my car, waiting for the final bell to ring, when you came stumbling up the sidewalk with a giant backpack over your shoulders. I watched you in my rearview mirror, noticing the defeated look in your eyes. Like a wounded dog, resigned to death.

It was the most beautiful thing I'd ever seen.

You were already dressed in your coffee shop attire: black pants, white blouse, and a long bib apron to cover it all. There were groups of kids walking in front of and behind you. One of them had shouted something out—something about the fact that you'd chosen to wear your work uniform before you'd even punched the clock. But you just kept moving

forward, sort of hunched over and looking
down at your feet, failing to acknowledge that
someone was making fun of you.

That's how I knew that people probably
didn't understand you the way I would. And
that's when I decided to make my move.

. . .

Dear Jack:

I remember the first time I saw you. It was just after I'd gotten trained to work the front counter. You were sitting at a table at the back of the coffee shop, taking sips of the mocha latte I had made for you, with extra whipped cream and a smiley-face drizzle of chocolate syrup (I wonder if you noticed), and trying to do your homework.

I thought it was kind of peculiar that someone who was studying didn't mind being wedged in between a table of mothers with their food-throwing kids and a quarreling couple on the brink of breaking up.

But there you were in my direct line of vision, with sandy-brown hair and deep blue eyes, with dark-washed jeans and a sun-faded sweatshirt.

Beautiful.

Which is why I never questioned anything.

You were older than me, definitely in college. I knew because you made reference to a class you were taking: "I need the fuel to pull an all-nighter. I have a huge exam tomorrow." You gestured to your book entitled Romantics in Literature. It was exciting to imagine you reading love stories at night.

I wondered what your name was, and if you'd ever go out with someone still in high school. But part of the beauty of it was the fact that I didn't know these things.

And that you didn't know me.

You had no idea who I was, or what the kids at school said about me behind my back.

Or straight to my face.

I remember the day we made physical contact—when I handed you your coffee and your finger brushed against mine, but in a totally obvious way. You gazed into my eyes, causing my pulse to race.

"Sorry," you said, with a smile that didn't show any hint of remorse. "What's your name?"

I opened my mouth to tell you, half excited (the other half shocked) that someone like you would ever want to talk to someone like me, let alone ask my name.

"On second thought, don't tell me," you said with a grin. "It might be more interesting if we keep this game going for just a little while longer."

"This game?" I asked. My face was on fire.

You winked and told me that it was my turn. "I've already made my move. Now it's all you. As soon as you're ready, you know where I'll be." You motioned to your usual table at the back of the shop. And that's where you sat for the next several months straight.

. . .

2

I DIDN'T TELL ANYONE about what happened last night, when I was hearing voices, because the truth is that I'm scared to death of what it might mean.

Kimmie, Wes, and I are sitting at the kitchen island at my house, surrounded by empty Dairy Queen bags and munching the sort of processed, grease-laden, and overly sugarfied snacks that'd be sure to make my health-freakish mom shrivel up, melt down, and evaporate into a *Wizard-of-Oz*-worthy cloud of smoke quicker than you can sing "We're Off to Eat a Blizzard."

If my mom were home, that is. But she's at work, teaching a class full of preggos how to do a downward-facing dog in a way that *blooms* the hips and *flowers* the pelvis, thus preparing the body for childbirth (or for a centerpiece arrangement; take your pick).

For some reason, Kimmie's being super reflective today, insisting that we talk about my recent breakup with

Ben. "Do you think you've given yourself sufficient time to mourn?" she asks, ever dramatic.

"Excuse me?" I pause from popping another fry into my mouth.

"Because if not, you could one day wind up a victim of your own subconscious's desire to sabotage your every relationship." She pulls an issue of *TeenEdge* from her backpack, flips open to a bookmarked page, and reads aloud: *"The end of every great relationship is really like the end of a life, because with it comes the death of something that used to be, followed by a mourning period."*

"Since when do you read that swill?" Wes asks.

"Hardly swill. It's *genius*," she says, correcting him. "Consider yourself lucky that I decided to share such genius in your presence."

"Except I'm not sure I'd call anything that comes out of *TeenEdge* 'genius,'" he says, pointing to an article titled "How Duct Tape Changed My Life."

"Well, I think it's a fairly accurate assessment," I say. "About the end of relationships, I mean." Because with most endings, there also comes a loss. And I feel I've lost my best friend.

I realize how dumb that probably seems, especially considering that Ben is neither lost nor dead. I mean, I see him all the time. He's in my lab class. And in the back parking lot after school. He's down at the east end of the hallway when I go to pottery. Not to mention in the corner study carrel in the library during every single B-block.

Sometimes I catch him looking at me, and I swear my

skin ignites. It's as if a million tiny fireflies light up my insides, making everything feel fluttery and aglow. It's all I can do to hold myself back and turn away so he doesn't see how achy I still feel.

Because we're no longer together.

I know how pathetic this sounds, which is why I don't utter a word of it to Kimmie and Wes. But still, as deflated as I feel, I refuse to spend my days and nights brooding over our breakup. I don't write his name a kajillion times on the inside covers of my notebook, nor do I check and recheck my phone in hopes of a call, message, or text from him.

The truth is that Ben wasn't the only one who wanted to push the pause button on our relationship.

"I wanted to take a break as well," I remind them.

"At least that's what you keep telling us," Wes says, giving me a suspicious look.

"Of course, how am I ever supposed to get that break, when Ben's so obviously present, and at the same time absent, in my life?" I continue.

"Elementary, my dear Chameleon," Kimmie says. Both she and Wes insist on calling me reptilian names whenever they feel like it, which is reason number 782 for why I hate my name.

Camelia.

"You need to rebound with a bloodhound," she says. "Preferably an immortal one with the power to shape-shift into a really hot guy."

"You want me to date *a dog*?" I ask, half tempted to

flick one of my fries at her face.

"Not a *dog*." She rolls her eyes. "Hook up with your preferred type of predator."

"Shall it be werewolves, vampires, angels, demons, or zombies?" Wes says, painting his lips with a ketchup-loaded french fry to make his mouth look bloody.

"Haven't you heard?" Kimmie asks, lowering her cat's-eye glasses to glare at me over the rims. "Immortals are the hot new accessory of the season. Everyone's trying to score one before they go out of style."

"So true," Wes says, pushing his ice cream to the side. "As if us guys don't have enough pressure trying to look good, be charming, wear nice clothes . . . Now we have to run around on all fours and gnaw at people's necks to be considered sexy."

"Stop it, you're turning me on," Kimmie says, using a napkin to fan herself.

"Thanks," I say, "but I prefer my men human."

"Yeah, I suppose I do, too. I'm old-fashioned that way." She lets out a sigh.

"Adam is human," Wes says, perking up, curiously excited to point out the obvious.

"So nice of you to notice." I pick a strand of curly blond hair (fingers crossed that it's mine and not the cook's) out of my pool of ketchup.

"Yes, but being a mere mortal does not automatically make him rebound material," Kimmie says.

"Excuse me?" I ask, utterly confused.

"Adam's the kind of guy you fall in love and live

happily ever after with," she explains.

"In other words, *not* the kind of guy you get caught macking with behind your boyfriend's back . . . But obviously, that happened anyway." Wes covers his mouth at the horror of it all, clearly trying to be funny.

But I'm far from amused.

"Honestly, Wesley Whiner, are you trying to get this ice cream dumped over that crusty coif of yours?" Kimmie positions her Blizzard over his new haircut, which is basically a modified version of a Mohawk (buzzed on the sides with an inch-wide landing strip down the center of his scalp).

"I'm sorry," he says, meeting my eyes, his face even graver than when Mr. Muse threatened to confiscate his bottle of hair gel in gym class.

"That's better," Kimmie says, putting her ice-cream weapon down.

"I promise not to joke about Adam," he continues, "or any of your other hedonistic love trysts again." He takes an overenthusiastic bite of ice cream, and even I can't help letting out a laugh.

In a nutshell, Adam is Ben's ex–best friend. About three years ago, a lot of drama went down between the two of them—drama that involved Ben's then-girlfriend Julie. Apparently, Adam had been dating Julie behind Ben's back, and after she died, Adam blamed Ben. A lot of people did. The rumor going around was that Ben had gotten so angry when Julie had tried to end their relationship that he pushed her over a cliff. In the end, it turned out that Ben wasn't to blame for her death. And thankfully, a jury of his peers agreed.

Like me, Ben has the power of psychometry—the ability to sense things through touch. When he touched Julie on their hike that day, he sensed the truth right out of her: basically, that she and Adam had a secret relationship going on. And so he touched her harder, eager to know more. Julie got spooked and started to back away. That was when she fell backward off the cliff and died almost instantly.

"Might you and Adam ever make things official?" Wes asks.

"We're officially friends," I say, hearing the irritation in my own voice.

"Yes, but are you officially putting your tongue down his throat?" He checks his profile in his pocket mirror, giving a stroke to his Elvis sideburns.

"I haven't seen Adam in a couple of weeks."

"And did that encounter involve an exchange of saliva?" he persists.

"I think I'm done with this inquisition," I say.

But it's not that I don't deserve it.

Adam and I started getting close a couple of months ago, when I thought his life was in danger. It's worth pointing out that my power of psychometry works a bit differently than Ben's. He's able to picture images from the past or future through his sense of touch. Meanwhile, my love of pottery allows me to sculpt prophetic clues— clues that have some sort of relevance to the future. And sometimes, though this may sound nuts, I hear voices when that happens.

In the case involving Adam, my senses proved right. He *was* in danger. Luckily, with Ben's help—and after Ben saved my life for the fourth time, nearly getting himself killed in the process—things ended up safely for Adam.

But as Adam and I were working together to keep him out of harm's way, he admitted to some pretty shady things—things he seemed completely transformed by and at the same time remorseful for.

Things that were pretty amazing to hear.

Adam was being so open and honest about his past. Meanwhile, I felt as if the secrets between Ben and me just kept getting bigger. And in the end, those secrets—that lack of trust—were basically what tore us apart, more than any kiss between Adam and me ever could have.

It's been exactly six weeks since Ben and I decided to "take a break." Six weeks of watching Ben's superhero popularity grow, especially among the female population at our high school. And six weeks of Adam's coming around on occasion, wanting to spend time with me.

"Well, at least you haven't heard any voices or sculpted anything psycho lately," Kimmie says.

Part of me feels guilty for not telling them about last night. But I'm not quite ready to hear them draw parallels between my aunt Alexia and me.

My aunt Alexia, who's been labeled by doctors as mentally disturbed, with suicidal tendencies.

Who's been in and out of mental hospitals for as long as I've known her.

And who claims to hear voices, too.

Aunt Alexia has been staying with us for a couple of weeks, but last night was the first time she ventured out of the guest room for more than five minutes. My parents assure me that giving her space is the right thing to do, that someone with a past like hers needs time to adapt to her new surroundings.

But my theory—and one I've only ever shared with Ben—is that Aunt Alexia is psychometric, like me. That she's able to predict the future with her art. And that if I don't come to terms with my own psychic ability soon, I may one day end up like her.

*T*HE FOLLOWING DAY IN SCULPTURE class, I try my best to concentrate on Ms. Mazur's lecture about avoiding excess water in our works-in-progress, but I really just want to sculpt.

"By adding grog, your pieces will have less of a chance of shrinking as they dry out," Ms. Mazur explains.

"It's all about the shrinkage prevention," Kimmie jokes, waving a sad little wand of clay at me.

I ignore her comment and make an effort to refocus on what Ms. Mazur is saying. She's in the middle of explaining something about plasticity now. I gaze down at my ball of clay, imagining what I might sculpt.

After a few moments spent spacing out, I notice that Ms. Mazur is no longer talking. The students in class, Kimmie included, have already added their groggy bits to their hunks of clay, and begun to wedge them out.

I do the same, noticing right away how much easier it is to work with the grittier texture.

"Big difference, wouldn't you say?" Ms. Mazur asks, returning to her desk at the front of the room.

I close my eyes and a series of images pops into my head, including the skating sculpture I've been working on—the one from my dream last night.

I start to replicate the skater's silhouette when all of a sudden I feel hot, like my skin is burning up. I touch my forehead. It's soaked with sweat.

"Camelia?" Kimmie says. "Um, no offense, but why does it look like you just got jiggy with Mr. Floppy here?" She hands me the paisley scarf from around her neck and then confiscates her clay wand.

I let out a breath, feeling more overheated by the moment. My shirt sticks against the sweat on my chest.

"Camelia?" Ms. Mazur asks. She stands up from her desk and places her hands on her hips. A pencil falls from behind her ear.

I want to answer her—to tell her that my insides are absolutely on fire—but instead I make a beeline for the door. I hurry down the hallway, en route to the bathroom. When I reach it, I find that the door is locked.

I move across the hall to the girls' locker room, noticing a pair of ice skates in front of the door. I step right over them as I fling the door open, expecting to find girls changing for class. Instead it's empty and dark.

I feel around the wall, knowing there's a light switch somewhere. Finally I find it and switch it on, but only the

21

lights in the back—by the sinks and stalls—come on.

A good ten yards away.

I start off in that direction, noticing a trickling noise, like running water. It sounds as if it might be coming from one of the sinks. The fluorescent light strip makes a harsh buzzing sound and flickers with each step I take—as if it might be on the verge of going out.

Still sweating, I pick up my pace. The smell of mildew and something sweet, like rotted fruit, is thick in the air, causing my stomach to churn.

A moment later, I hear something else—a whispering sound. I peer over my shoulder to look.

It seems even darker now. I can barely make out my hand in front of my face, never mind the door through which I entered.

I'm just about to turn away when the whispering sound comes again. "Who's there?" I ask, trying to be brave.

My pulse racing, I resume in the direction of the lighted area, but then a voice whispers, "Do you know what you are?"

I back away against a locker, hoping the darkness will hide me.

"You're such a joke," the voice says. It's a female voice, with an angry tone, reminding me of the voice from last night. It's only inches from my face.

I thrust my hands forward, prepared to knock aside anyone in my path. To my surprise, no one's there.

I hurry toward the lit area, still able to hear the trickling water, but now those lights have gone out, too.

"You're trapped," the voice says, followed by an evil giggle.

I move into the area near the stalls and feel around for the windows on the far wall. Both windows are closed, so I can't call out. I struggle to find one of the levers that open them, wondering why no light's coming in. Meanwhile, footsteps continue at a slow pace behind me. I can hear heels scuffing against the cement floor, just a short distance away.

Finally, I find a lever and try to crank it open. But the window is locked. I move to the side, somehow managing to find another lever. That one's locked, too, and remains locked, even when I pull, twist, and pound it with all my might.

"No," I hear myself cry out. I smack my fists against the glass, eager to break right through it.

"There's no way out now," the voice says. "You should've quit when you were told."

"No!" I repeat. My heart hammers. Bright lights flash across my eyes, until I feel physically sick. I stumble back, holding my hands over my ears, just as a flashlight beam shines against one of the mirrors above the sinks.

It takes me a moment to focus, to notice that the mirror is broken, that giant pieces of glass have collected in the sink, and that the water from the faucet is running over the broken pieces, somehow producing a dark red color.

There's a message scribbled across the unbroken portion of the mirror.

"*Die already, will you?*" a female voice says, reading it

aloud and then letting out another giggle.

At the same moment, I find a shard of broken glass clenched in my hand. "No!" I hear myself scream, so loud that my throat burns.

A moment later, I feel a hand settle on my shoulder, snapping me back to reality.

It's Kimmie's. We're still in sculpture class.

Her face is a giant question mark: her eyes wide, her mouth hanging open. But she grips my shoulder harder, as if preparing me for what will come next.

"Camelia?" Ms. Mazur asks. She stands from her desk and places her hands on her hips. A pencil falls from behind her ear, and suddenly I'm overwhelmed with an enormous sense of déjà vu.

The other kids in the class stare at me, awaiting some sort of explanation. But I have no idea myself what has just happened.

I reach up to touch my forehead. My hairline is dry. My shirt isn't sticking to my back or chest. And I no longer seem to be sweating. I doubt I ever was. It was probably part of a hallucination of some sort.

I must've zoned out shortly after I began to sculpt.

My fingers thoroughly saturated with clay, I look down at my work, half expecting to find the skater silhouette I started earlier. But instead, I see that my hand is gripping something.

"What is it?" Kimmie asks, following my gaze.

I open my hand, fully aware that I've yet to answer Ms. Mazur or address even one inquisitive stare.

A wad of clay sits in my palm. At first, it seems like a meaningless glob. But then it suddenly occurs to me: the shape of the clay, the way it fits in my palm, and the jagged hook at the very top.

It's a sculpture of a broken piece of glass.

I clench it in my palm, almost able to feel the cutting of my skin, the severing of my nerves.

"What's wrong?" Kimmie whispers. Her paisley scarf is still tied around her neck, exactly as it was before class. She lets out a nervous cough.

"*Issues*," Davis Miller sings, somewhat under his breath.

The comment ignites an explosion of snickering.

"I have to go," I say, getting up from the table. I apologize to Ms. Mazur, telling her that I'm not feeling too well.

She nods, more than happy to give me a pass to go see the school counselor. As if somehow that will save me.

4

I HEAD TO MS. BEADY'S OFFICE, eager to be dismissed from school for the day, but she insists that we talk first. She has us sit in the two comfy chairs in the corner of her office. It's a setup she's designed to try and fool unsuspecting students into thinking they're just there to chat. But I already know the drill.

I decline her offer of a cup of tea, and remain staring at the wall above her head—at her PhD from the University of Texas, and her newly acquired certificate in Adolescent Development.

"So, tell me about what happened in sculpture class," she says. Obviously, Ms. Mazur has already called to tip her off.

"I guess I sort of freaked."

"What do you mean by *freaked*?" she says, making lame-o air quotes as she talks.

"I mean just what I said," I tell her, unsure how much

clearer I can actually be, or how much I want to reveal.

Ms. Beady nods as if what I've said were utterly fascinating. "And do you know *why* you *freaked?*" More air quotes.

I bite my lip, wishing she would just let me call my mom to come pick me up.

"Well, I'm actually glad you stopped by," she says, when I don't answer. She crosses her legs at the knees; there's a run in her nurse-uniform-white panty hose. "I've been meaning to check in with you. You've been through a lot these past several months."

I nod, thinking about the last time I was in here—not long after I was kidnapped, when I'd just begun to hear voices, and when Ms. Beady attributed both to post-traumatic stress of the stalker-ex-boyfriend-Matt kind.

She tucks a strand of mousy brown hair behind her ear and gazes down at my hand. "What have you got there?"

I loosen my grip, surprised to find the clay replica of broken glass still clenched in my hand. "Just something I was working on. I left class so fast . . ." I don't even bother finishing the excuse; I can already hear how dumb it sounds.

Ms. Beady scrunches up her face for just a second before going therapist-neutral again. "You like pottery a lot, don't you, Camelia?"

I shrug, almost surprised at how little she seems to know me. I mean, we've been through this stuff before. We've talked about my job at Knead, and how I want to open up my own pottery studio one day.

"Do you find that it helps you relax?" she continues.

I clutch the clay piece again, feeling a slashing sensation

tear through my palm. The pain sears my skin and shoots up my arm.

Ms. Beady's lips are moving. She's telling some happy story; there's an animated flair to her speech.

But I don't hear any of the words. It's like someone turned down the volume, pressed the mute button on her voice.

"Ms. Beady?" I say, reassured that at least it seems *she* can hear *me*.

She furrows her eyebrows, finally acknowledging the troubled look on my face. She leans forward in her seat, clearly asking me what's wrong. There's a confused expression across her round face.

Still I can't hear her.

Instead, I hear the whispering again inside my ear, which makes my head ache. The voices tell me that "there are two."

"Two *what*?" I want to cry out.

I try to tell myself that the whispering is coming from Ms. Beady, but her lips aren't moving. She gets up from her seat and scoots down in front of me. Her expression is full of concern.

Finally, she starts talking again. I'm tempted to pretend I understand what she's saying, but instead I shake my head and cover my ears, fighting the urge to shout over the voices.

Ms. Beady gets up to make a phone call. I drop the glob of clay and huddle down in the chair, desperate for someone to help me, even if that means her.

5

FINALLY, I CAN HEAR AGAIN—can hear that Ms. Beady is leaving a message. I assume it's for one of my parents. I assume she'll try contacting both of them (if she hasn't already).

"Just one more," she says, talking aloud to herself. She searches her computer for what I imagine to be the number of my in-case-both-parents-are-unavailable emergency contact person.

"I'm actually starting to feel a bit better," I say.

It isn't a lie. The voices seem to be gone. My heart's beating at a normal rhythm. And my head is no longer aching.

Ms. Beady turns from her desk. "Can you hear me, Camelia?"

I nod.

She covers her mouth so I can't read her lips, and asks me my favorite color.

"Dark blue. Like the sky, just before nighttime."

She looks relieved. A tiny smile crosses her lips. She comes and sits in the cushy chair opposite mine, studying my face as if trying to decide whether to believe me about feeling better. "Any chance you want to talk about what just happened here?"

I nod again, somewhat willing now to give her a chance.

But instead of asking me what *I* think, Ms. Beady starts prattling about how *she* thinks I have had a panic attack. "It was most likely a panic attack in your sculpture class, too," she says. She goes on to insist that I'm still suffering from the repercussions of the past several months, and that I'd benefit from consistent therapy and/or prescription meds. "I'm going to recommend to your parents that you start seeing someone in town," she says. "I have the names of a couple of really great doctors. I'll be calling your parents to give them the information."

I look down at the floor. My hunk of clay is still sitting where I dropped it. Could the fact that I'm not holding it be part of the reason I'm feeling more together?

Less crazy.

"How does all of this sound to you?" Ms. Beady asks; her tiny gray eyes go squinty.

"That depends," I venture, choosing to take charge. "How do these doctors feel about people who claim to have psychic abilities?"

"Psychic abilities?" Her left eye twitches.

"Forget it," I say, feeling self-conscious.

But Ms. Beady continues to study me; I can feel the heat of her stare on the side of my face. "Hold on," she says, returning to her desk. She spends the next several minutes looking something up on the computer. She writes the information down and then hands it to me on a sticky note.

"'Dr. Tylyn Oglesby at Hayden Community College,'" I say, reading it aloud.

"Maybe she'll be able to help you."

"Why?" I ask, eager to know if it's because I used the word *psychic*.

Ms. Beady's eyes lock onto mine. "Dr. Tylyn and I worked together on a case a few years back. She's very good at what she does."

"Will you be telling my parents about her as well?"

"Is there a reason why I shouldn't?"

"I don't know," I say; my voice trips over the words. "It's just that I'm not quite sure they'll like the idea of my seeing a doctor who's into that kind of stuff."

"The final bell's about to ring," Ms. Beady says, ignoring my concern. "Why don't you go along to your locker?" She hands me a hall pass and then tidies up a stack of papers on her desk, seemingly ready for our conversation to be over.

INSTEAD OF WAITING AROUND for the final bell, I bolt out the side exit, cross the main road in front of the school, and hop on a bus that takes me to Knead.

My boss, Spencer, is here, as well as Svetlana, his most recent hire and current girlfriend. Svetlana has zero talent in the pottery department, but she's supermodel-gorgeous and speaks with a cute accent, making her the perfect candidate for the job—at least, according to Spencer.

Spencer reminds me of a pirate today, with a bandanna wrapped around his head and his dark, kinky hair hanging loose. He and Svetlana are cleaning a bunch of greenware (clay that's been pulled from its mold, usually in the shape of a bowl, a mug, or some random tacky thing).

"Hey, there," Spencer says to me. He holds up one of the pieces of greenware: two playful bunnies, one pouncing on the back of the other, though on closer inspection it looks as though they might be humping.

"For Easter," Svetlana explains. "Cute, yes?"

"You can't be serious."

"Say what you will," Spencer says, "but the seniors at the community center love this kitschy crap."

"*Crap* being the operative word." I set the bunnies back on the table, feeling awkward for even holding the busy bunnies in the first place. I move over to my work-in-progress at the end of the table, grateful for the diversion.

Unlike the sculpture of the figure skater that I've been working on at home, this sculpture has continued to baffle me ever since I first laid hands on it months ago. I lift the tarp and pull away the rags that keep it moist, revealing a vaselike bowl. It started out as an abstract piece—something to keep me distracted from all the drama going on in my life. But every time I look at it, more drama surfaces.

Because it makes me think of Ben.

I was working on this piece at the time of our breakup. It's different from anything I've ever sculpted before. The sides twist inward, resembling entangled limbs, and the top curves out to look like a mouth. I've been working on it for a while now, seeing where my impulses take me, but I can't seem to get it right.

"She's obsessing you, isn't she?" Spencer asks, standing at my side now. "I get obsessed with my pieces, too." He nods toward his work area in the back, where he's been plugging away at a life-size bronze ballerina. "Sometimes I find myself awake at three in the morning, pacing the hallways of my apartment, unable to stop questioning my work. I go over the process in my head, wondering whether if I'd used a different casting method maybe she'd look less forced."

"Your work is brilliant," I tell him, hoping he knows it's true.

Spencer shrugs off the compliment, preferring instead to focus on me. "So, what's the problem?" He takes a closer look at my piece.

"I don't know. I mean, I don't even know what I'm doing here." Why would I even think of coming within a thousand-mile radius of a pottery studio after what just happened in sculpture class?

"Care to share?"

I take a deep breath, feeling lonelier than I have in a long time, and more fearful than ever before. "Not really," I tell him.

"You're just trying too hard," he says, still assuming that my sucky mood has to do with my sucky sculpture. "I can see where your efforts are going, but you're falling a bit short on technique."

"As if I couldn't feel worse."

"Are you kidding?" he asks, stroking his facial scruff. "Technique can be learned. But talent and obsessive compulsiveness like ours . . . that has to be innate."

"And where do you suppose I learn better technique?" I ask, wondering if he's going to teach me.

"What you need is a life drawing class. More care needs to be taken with respect to body, form, and awareness of the muscles and joints."

"It's a bowl," I remind him.

"A bowl with a whole lot of body," he says, pointing out the area beneath the handle, where it looks like there might be a knee. "I've got a friend who works at Hayden. Are you up for a little Life Drawing 101?"

"That depends. . . . How much does it cost?"

"Don't worry about it," he says, stepping away to grab his cell phone. "Dwayne owes me a favor or two. I hooked him up with a hottie a couple weeks ago, and he's been begging to pay me back ever since."

While Spencer calls his friend to see if I can serve as hottie payback, I glance over at Svetlana. She's abandoned the bunny figurines and is trying her hand at rock sculpture now, by experimenting with Spencer's mallet and chisel.

"You're in," Spencer says not two minutes later, sliding his phone shut. "Dwayne's expecting you Thursday night at six o'clock sharp. Apparently, you've already missed a few classes, but he'll treat you as a drop-in."

"Thanks," I say, trying my best to sound enthusiastic, because I know I should be grateful.

"Sure, just don't let me down."

"In what way?" I ask, surprised by the comment.

Spencer looks away, toward the table of feisty bunnies. "I just think you have an amazing amount of talent, and I don't want to see it go to waste."

"It won't," I say, suspecting that Spencer may be feeling a bit sucky, too. Before I can ask him about it, a loud clanking bursts in on our conversation.

"It's okay?" Svetlana asks, noticing our attention. Bits of soapstone lie strewn about the table.

"Not okay," Spencer says, most likely referring to the fact that she's not wearing the requisite pair of safety goggles to protect her eyes. She's placed them on one of the bunny statues instead.

I'm just about to tell her that failure to take safety precautions is a huge no-no in Spencer's Big Bad Book of Studio Rules, but then I reconsider. Because, while it appears that the bunnies may indeed be humping, at least they're trying to use some form of protection.

Dear Jill,

Do you remember the day you wore a skirt
to work? It was black, and went about three
inches above the knee. I remember trying to
appear engrossed in my work, but I couldn't
help noticing the way your backside stretched
the fabric of the skirt, the way the length
rode up every couple minutes, and how you
kept trying to tug at the hem, most likely
regretting your choice of outfits. You
probably could've chosen a size or two up,
but I was really glad that you didn't.

It was getting late, just a few minutes
before closing time. Could you tell that I
was nervous? Did you see me fumble in my
pocket for the trinket I'd brought along for
you? The piece of sea glass. I'm sure you've
heard what the media is saying—that I'd given
similar pieces to girls who came before you.
It's disgusting the way that people try to
cheapen what can only boil down to a lack of
creativity. Why does no one question it when a
guy gives all his past and current girlfriends
roses or candy? Why are such gifts not
considered devices as well?

Regardless, please know that I could never
have compared you to any of the other girls.
You were—and will forever remain—far more
special than any of them. Which is why I knew
you'd love it. Which is how I knew you'd
love me.

. . .

Dear Jack:

It was a Monday. I remember because it was also a holiday (a long weekend) and I was off from school, working the morning shift.

I wore a skirt that day, and I kept checking my reflection against the stainless fridge, wondering if it made my hips look wider than they already were, or emphasized my chunky knees.

You sat at your usual table at the back of the coffee shop, studying from that <u>Romantics</u> book. I held my breath and ventured to imagine you were thinking about me as you read it.

Finally, when the crowd at the shop had thinned out and my line had gone down, you glanced up from your notebook and smiled in my direction before coming up to the counter and asking me what I thought you should order.

I remember how self-conscious I felt, hoping you didn't notice all the freckles on my cheeks, or that my nose was way too long for my face. "What do you like?" I asked.

"You know what I like." Your grin was lethal—straight white teeth, pale full lips, startling blue eyes.

I turned my back and started to pour a glass of iced coffee, almost wishing that you'd just sit back down. But then you muttered that you got me something, and I swear my heart all but stopped.

You reached into your pocket and pulled out a piece of sea glass. "I was combing the beach this morning and spotted it," you said, handing it to me.

Turquoise, diamond-shaped, and brilliant, it took up half of my palm.

"I couldn't believe it myself," you continued. "I mean, it was just sitting there, sticking out from a pile of kelp. I almost didn't see it, but something told me to take a closer look. That's when I noticed what a beauty it was."

"A beauty," I echoed, hearing the question in my voice. You must've heard it too.

"So beautiful," you said, closing my fingers around the piece, and then taking my hand in yours.

Did you notice how my lips parted? And how I took a step back? I couldn't imagine you were truly saying what it sounded like you were saying. Because why would you ever say that?

"It reminded me of you," you said, still holding my hand. I wondered if you could feel the sweat in my palm. "Can I ask you something?" you continued.

I nodded, wanting desperately to believe you—to believe the moment, to believe your sincerity. But I honestly didn't know how.

Before you could utter another syllable, Carl ordered me to help Dee out in the storage room. "It's a real mess back there."

When I turned to answer him, I felt your hand slip away. "Can it wait a second?" I looked back in your direction, but you were no longer there.

Your back toward me, you collected your books from the table, and then headed out the door without saying good-bye.

. . .

7

*K*IMMIE CALLS WHILE I'm at Knead, desperate to know where I am and why I went all psycho-and-demonic in sculpture class (her words, not mine). Part of me wants to hang up, but instead I agree to let her and Wes pick me up, which is exactly what they do. Less than twenty minutes later, they're parked and waiting outside the studio.

Luckily, we don't really talk much to one another in the car. Kimmie is too busy on her cell phone, telling her dad why he can't expect her to change plans on a moment's notice. Kimmie's parents separated recently, and Kimmie and her younger brother, Nate, have been spending some weekends at her dad's new apartment in the city.

"Just because you want to play house with your fourteen-year-old girlfriend on the weekend of the twenty-first doesn't mean that I have to rearrange my whole entire social schedule," she tells him.

"The highlight of which involves eating curly fries, playing video games, and driving around aimlessly with me," Wes snickers.

Kimmie moves the phone away from her ear as her dad speaks, enabling us to hear his garbled voice. He's demanding that she give him more respect, and reminding her that his girlfriend, Tammy, is actually *nineteen* years old, not *fourteen.* "And very mature for her age," he adds.

Unfortunately, Kimmie's not the only one whose parents are dealing with drama. Ever since my aunt's most recent suicide attempt about six months ago, my mom hasn't been herself. She's been beyond stressed out, clinically depressed, and ADD-like distracted, which is why she's started seeing a therapist, and why she hasn't been superinvolved in my life lately, despite how messed up it's been. I think she just can't handle it, and I'm pretty sure the feeling's mutual.

By the time Kimmie clicks off her phone, we're in front of my house with exactly one hour before either of my parents gets home. We go inside, and I head straight for the kitchen. The red light on the answering machine practically blinks Ms. Beady's name. I press the play button, and her voice squeaks out, begging for either or both of my parents to call her back *pronto.*

I delete it.

"Okay, are you *trying* to get yourself grounded?" Wes asks me.

"You're right," I say, keeping my voice low, though fairly certain Aunt Alexia is locked away in her room, out of earshot, as has become usual for her. "If my parents have to hear that I had some sort of psychotic episode in the middle of sculpture class, it's better if they hear it while my mother's straight-out-of-a-mental-facility-suicidal-and-possibly-schizophrenic sister is staying with us."

"Point taken," he says, keeping his voice low, too.

"Plus, it doesn't even matter, because I'm pretty sure Ms. Beady left *two* messages earlier, not one," I say, suddenly flashing back to the voice inside my head that told me there were two. Is it possible that it was referring to the two messages? Does that even make sense?

"So, there's at least one other voice mail message out there just waiting to get played," Kimmie says, putting the pieces together.

"Hungry?" Wes asks. His arms are full of bags of Fritos and Starbursts. He's managed to locate my dad's stash of junk food (kept in the baskets over the kitchen cabinets) in less time than it takes most people to pick a wedgie.

We loot the stash, and I lead them down the hallway, almost forgetting the fact that Aunt Alexia's nurse is there.

"Hi," Loretta says, coming out of Alexia's room. She closes the door softly behind her.

Nurse Loretta (a.k.a. Nurse Leatherface, according to Wes) is about sixty years old, but it looks as if she's spent at least forty of those years in a tanning bed. Her skin is pure lines and leather. "Alexia's just gone off to sleep," she tells us, "so if you wouldn't mind speaking in soft voices . . ."

"Will Frito-munching be too loud?" Wes asks, holding the bag out to her.

43

Instead of dignifying the question with a response, Loretta proceeds to the living room to wait for my parents. Meanwhile, Kimmie, Wes, and I head for my bedroom to talk.

"Okay, so I just have one question for you," Kimmie says, flopping onto my bed. "What the hell was up today? Because you totally freaked me out. I was half expecting your eyes to roll up toward the ceiling and guttural phrases to come chanting out your mouth. You know . . . just like a couple months ago, also in sculpture class, I might add, when you flipped out and told me that I deserved to die."

"Maybe you plus sculpture class equals a really bad idea," Wes says.

I take a deep breath and tell them about the voice in my head—how it started whispering at me from the moment I touched my mound of clay.

"And you couldn't just ignore it?" Kimmie asks.

"Nor could you simply stop touching your mound?" Wes grins.

"I actually started feeling better when I ditched the mound," I tell him. "When I dropped it on the floor in Ms. Beady's office."

"Well, there's your answer," Kimmie says. "About putting an end to the voices, I mean. You need to stop doing pottery."

"Cold turkey?" Wes asks. "I mean, shouldn't she try the patch first?"

"In the form of Play-Doh and really malleable gummy worms, maybe." Kimmie giggles.

"I can't stop doing pottery," I tell them. "It's a part of who I am."

"Sort of like how you always insist on dressing like a Gap ad," Wes says, giving my jeans and basic tee a once-over.

"Since when are you one to talk about style?" Kimmie says, coming to my defense. She raises an eyebrow at his sheepskin boots.

"Plus, it wouldn't even matter," I say, interrupting their banter. "Last night I wasn't even doing pottery—just having a dream about it—when I heard voices as well."

"That's actually not so hard to believe," Wes says, rifling through my night-table drawer. He snags a sleep mask and slips it on. "I mean, that's kind of what happens when you dream kinky stuff, too. Your body—God bless it—believes the dream. The next thing you know, you're changing into a new pair of sweats."

"*Ewwww*," Kimmie says, covering her eyes as if that could blot out the less-than-lovely image that Wes has ever so kindly painted for us.

"So, then, if avoiding pottery won't even solve the *there-are-crazy-voices-inside-my-head* issue, is there any way to *adapt* to the voices?" Wes asks, pulling off the sleep mask. "Sort of like how I adapt to my father being such a meddling and narrow-minded prick?"

"I don't know." I pop a lemon Starburst into my mouth. "I mean, today, in sculpture class, I completely zoned out. It was like I was someplace else entirely. Not exactly capable of voices-in-my-head adaptation."

"Well, I *still* think taking a hiatus from pottery might

be a good first step," Kimmie says, pulling a copy of *TeenEdge* from her bag. "You could fake a sprained wrist. I'm sure we could make a legit-looking doctor's note. Because, let's face it, there's way more to life than voice-activated premonitions and seizurelike fits, right?" She flips to an article titled "Pre-prom Planning Made Easy."

"Maybe you could talk to your aunt," Wes suggests.

"I'd like to," I say, finally deciding to fill them in on what happened last night, when Aunt Alexia found me huddled on the floor of the linen closet.

"And we're just hearing about this *now*?" Wes asks.

I shrug and look away, hoping that telling them was the right choice. The truth is that when I heard my aunt was coming to stay with us for a bit, I imagined things a whole lot differently—I thought that *she'd* be the one I'd talk to about this stuff, that we'd be able to help each other in extraordinary ways, and understand each other as no one else could.

"What's this?" Wes asks, reaching further inside my drawer. He pulls out Aunt Alexia's diary and runs his fingers over the cover, where it's been torn and patched over.

"What does it look like?" I point at her name, written across the front.

"Yes, but what are *you* doing with it?"

"I found it," I say, proceeding to explain that I came across the diary several months ago, while putting away holiday decorations in the attic. "It's from when Aunt Alexia was a teen—when people started labeling her as crazy and when she started having brushes with psychometry." At least, I think psychometry was to blame for a lot of her issues.

"And what was it doing in your attic?" Kimmie asks.

"There's actually a bunch of my aunt's stuff stored up there . . . ever since the first time she was admitted to a mental facility."

"Talk about depressing," Kimmie says, flashing me a picture from her magazine of a girl wearing a strapless dress made of duct tape. Whether she's referring to the dress or my aunt's journal, I have absolutely no idea.

"You know what's really depressing?" I say, watching Wes read one of the entries near the end of the journal.

"Even more depressing than fantasies involving a pretty pink dress, sparkly gold shoes, and carbon-monoxide-induced sleep?" he asks. Then he begins to read: *"Dear Diary, I've never felt more alone in my entire life. I feel like a victim of what's going on in my head. Like my head is independent of my body, tormenting me, punishing me, telling me things that I don't understand. I plug my ears up with cotton until they ache and bleed. I blast music, dance around my room, stick my head between my knees when everything feels too dizzy. I also chant to myself:* I can't hear you, I can't hear you. You can't hurt me. No one hurts me. *But nothing seems to work. I need to try something else. I need to end this madness."* Wes snaps the journal shut and shoves it back inside my drawer.

"Well, that was cheerful," Kimmie says.

I swallow hard, thinking that, as crazy as that entry sounds, I can understand what my aunt was feeling. And that's what terrifies me most. "The voices in my head have been hinting that I should kill myself, too," I tell them.

"Hinting . . . because they practice the art of subtlety?" Wes asks.

"Okay, so we seriously need to figure out a way to stop this so-called superpower," Kimmie says, finally closing the cover of her magazine.

"Even if I *could* stop it, would that be the right answer, either? I mean, maybe the voices aren't telling *me* to do it. Maybe there's someone else involved here—someone who's thinking about doing something drastic."

"Give it a little time," Wes says, "and with a few more voices crammed into your head, a couple nights spent reading morbid diary entries—not to mention Auntie Recluse in the next room over—you'll be thinking about doing something drastic, too."

I feed my funk with a three-stack of Starbursts, hoping that what's been happening is indeed a symptom of psychometry, that there's a logical explanation as to why the voices and the visions have been coming to me (if psychometry can even be considered somewhat logical). Because I'm terrified of the alternative: voices plus hallucinations plus me equals crazy.

"Ever think that the voices might have something to do with your aunt?" Wes adds. "Especially if they concern suicide?"

"Doubtful. The voices tell me how talentless I am, how ugly I look, and that I should basically be maggot feed. My aunt would never say those things."

"And you're sure you're not just eavesdropping on the

conversations that my dad has with me?" he asks.

"Very funny," I say, joining Kimmie on the bed and noticing how suddenly sullen she looks—as if she had run out of spandex fabric just stitches away from finishing a dress.

"What were you dreaming about sculpting, anyway?" Wes asks.

"A figure skater," I say, picturing the piece in my mind—the way the skater's leg extends backward, and how her arms cross in front of the chest. "It's something I've been working on, something I began just a few days ago in my basement studio—before I started dreaming about it, that is."

"A female?" Kimmie asks.

I nod, remembering the pair of ice skates in front of the girls' locker room during my hallucination in sculpture class.

"So, does this mean we should be on the lookout for suicidal skaters?" Wes asks, seemingly serious.

I bite my lip, beyond confused. On one hand it feels really good to tell them stuff, but still, no matter how hard I try to explain what's been going on, I can't possibly expect them to understand what I can barely make sense of myself.

"Perhaps here lies the root of your whacked-out dream," Kimmie says, plucking my long-lost doll out from under my covers. Kimmie flips the doll's dress up, revealing dirty rubber knees and a stray pen mark on the belly. "Since when do you sleep with dolls?"

"Hey, don't knock it till you try it," Wes says with a wink. "I've got a life-size Princess Leia pillow that I've been known to cuddle on occasion . . . especially on those cold and lonely nights in front of the fire."

"Miss Dream Baby," I say, ignoring his chatter. "That's what I named her when I was little."

"Miss Nightmare Baby might have been more appropriate," he says.

"She'd been missing for years," I tell them. "But I found her in my room last night."

"*Found* her?" Kimmie's barbell-pierced eyebrow rises. She peers around at my room. Aside from a couple of sweatshirts piled up on my dresser and a few pairs of shoes strewn about the floor, it's actually pretty neat.

"I think my aunt had the doll all this time," I explain.

"So, let me get this straight," Wes says. "Your escaped mental patient of an aunt stole your baby doll when you were little, kept it for some twisted amount of time, and then snuck into your room last night and left it here for you?"

"Okay, first of all, my aunt is hardly an escapee. She was legitimately released into my mother's care. And, secondly, I found the doll by accident—by stepping on it in a pile of clothes and recognizing the familiar squeak."

Kimmie pushes the doll's belly and it lets out a catlike cry. "As if things couldn't get more creeptastic."

"Almost as creeptastic as that noise," Wes says, nodding toward the wall that separates my room from Aunt Alexia's, where we can suddenly hear a scratching sound, like fingernails against wooden panels.

"Ignore it," I say, wondering if Alexia might be trying to listen in on our conversation through the wall. "It comes and goes at various points of the day—ever since my aunt moved in." Apparently she isn't sleeping after all.

"Well, if that isn't enough to drive you nuts . . ." Wes says. "Who needs voices in their head and public displays of convulsions?"

"I know," I whisper, wondering what it would actually take for me to get to that tipping point—another month of voices? Another year? And where will Kimmie and Wes be then? Still by my side? Or tired of my drama? Or maybe even fearful of me? The way I've become fearful of my aunt?

I grab Miss Dream Baby and hug her against my chest, thinking how it was only a couple of months ago that I visited my aunt in Detroit—when we talked a bit, and painted together, and when she showed me her art.

So, what happened?

Why is she like a stranger in my house?

And why can't I get over this anger? As stupid and irrational and embarrassing as it is to admit, part of me— my six-year-old self—can't help feeling angry that she had my doll all this time.

"What's up with the X's?" Wes nods toward the marks made over the doll's ears.

"I'm not sure, but I suspect that the answer might have something to do with hearing voices."

"Do you think she did it recently?" Kimmie runs her finger over the marks, trying to rub off some of the ink.

"Like, maybe somehow she knew you were hearing voices, too?" Wes says, all but frothing at the mouth at his theory. "And this doll is part of some weird and twisted voodoo spell to make those voices go away? You know Van Gogh cut his ear off, right?"

"For the record, it was just his earlobe," I say.

"And is there a point to this random piece of trivia?" Kimmie asks.

"Are you kidding? There's nothing random about it," Wes says. "An artist, rumored to have suffered from major mental illness, cuts off his ear . . ."

"Meaning you think Van Gogh was hearing voices, too?" I ask.

"It's possible," he says, giving a happy tug to his earlobe.

"Just curious, but were you dropped on your head at birth?" Kimmie asks him.

"Anyway," I say, getting us back on track, "it must've been pretty important to Aunt Alexia that I got the doll back. I mean, she hardly even comes out of the guest room."

"That you know of," Wes says, correcting me. "Maybe she merely dropped it while stalking around in your room while you slept."

"But then why tuck me in with it?" I ask, noticing how the doll's eyelids (the kind that open and close) are much droopier than I remember, and how it appears as if the lashes have all been plucked out. I glance in my dresser mirror, picturing the word *BITCH* scribbled over my reflection—when my ex-boyfriend Matt broke into my room several months ago and wrote it across the surface in bloodred lipstick. Is it a coincidence that the words *DIE ALREADY, WILL YOU?!* were scribbled across the locker-room mirror in my hallucination?

"Well, I still think we need to figure out a way to stop all of this touch stuff." Kimmie wraps her arm around my shoulder. "But don't even think I'm going to let you sleep alone tonight."

"Planning a sleepover?" Wes perks up.

"I'll tell my mom we're working on a research thing," Kimmie tells me.

"I, on the other hand, will need no excuse," Wes says. "Dad will be as giddy as a zitless schoolgirl to hear about our threesome. What time shall I bring my pj's? They're Iron Man–themed, by the way, which is totally appropriate, when you think about it." He winks.

"You're so mentally disturbed," Kimmie tells him.

"And speaking of . . . Camelia, what's it going to take for *you* to get some mental help?" Wes asks. "No offense."

"None taken," I say, pulling Ms. Beady's sticky note from my pocket. "I need to call this doctor. Apparently, she works at Hayden and knows a thing or two about all things psychic."

"Hayden as in, where Adam goes to school?" Kimmie asks.

"Nothing like multitasking," Wes says. "A little psychic talk on the shrink's couch, followed by pillow talk on Adam's."

"And what do you think our favorite touch boy would have to say about all this?" Kimmie asks.

"Do you really think Benny Boy needs to know about Camelia's occupancy on Adam's love couch?" Wes asks.

"I was actually referring to Camelia's recent bout of hearing-voices syndrome," Kimmie says. "Don't you think he ought to know about it?"

"Wasn't it you who said I should be mourning?" I ask her.

"Okay, so I didn't want to bring this up," she says, "but since we're sort of talking about him anyway—"

"Rumor has it that Ben's seeing someone else," Wes blurts.

"But it's totally false," Kimmie says, flicking a Starburst at his head. "I mean, let's not forget that he could barely even lay a finger on Camelia without going into a touch-induced tizzy."

"Unless, of course, he only tizzies with Chameleon," Wes ponders aloud.

"We all know that isn't true," I say, thinking about Ben's past with his girlfriend Julie—when he touched her on the cliff that day. "Do we know *who* he's supposedly seeing?"

"Not yet," Wes says, "but I've got calls in to all my connections."

"Within the geek community," Kimmie says, blowing him a kiss.

"Of which you're the current president." He blows a kiss back at her. "Anyway, I should know within the hour."

He checks his cell phone for messages.

I gaze down at my hands, feeling my heart tighten. It's not that I don't want Ben to be happy. It's just that a part of me can't help feeling jealous—the part that wants him to be happy only with me.

"I'm just thinking it might be a good idea to keep the lines of communication open with Ben," Kimmie says. "If not for your heart, then for the sake of your head."

"Not to mention your other body parts," Wes jokes.

"I just mean, considering everything that's going on with you right now," Kimmie continues, "it might not be the best time to stop all communication with Ben."

"No one's stopping anything," I tell her. "And it's not that I don't want Ben to know what's been going on with me. It's just that his power works a lot differently from mine. Don't you think I should be focusing my attention on finding someone who knows exactly what I'm going through?"

"Someone besides your ear-hating aunt, you mean?" Wes says, smooching Miss Dream Baby's ear. "With all due respect, of course."

"Of course," I say, looking down at the sticky note again, knowing full well how crazy my whole story sounds.

And only half believing that I'm not going crazy, too.

WHILE WES DRIVES KIMMIE home to get her stuff, I remain in my room, wondering if Aunt Alexia might be open to talking to me.

I get up from the bed and place my ear against our shared wall, accidentally kicking one of my strewn shoes in the process; the wooden heel knocks into the wall.

My heart tightens and I hold my breath, hoping she doesn't think it was me knocking, trying to get her attention.

A moment later, a clanking noise comes from her room. I huddle in closer, trying to hear something more.

The scratching sound has returned.

"Camelia?" a voice asks.

I start and then turn to look, surprised to find my dad standing just behind me.

"What are you doing?" he asks with a grin.

My pulse racing, I look back at the wall. The scratching sound has stopped now, but I honestly have no words.

He studies me for several moments, then asks if I'm hungry. "Your mother won't be home for another hour," he says, flashing me a bag from Taco Bell. The smell of chicken chalupas calls out to me.

I follow Dad into the hall. He stops in front of the guest room door and knocks a couple of times. It takes a moment for Aunt Alexia to answer; her door creaks open with an eerie whine.

Dressed in a loose cotton dress and a pair of leggings, she stares at me as Dad talks to her.

"Care to join us for a little snack?" he asks her, holding the bag up. "I got enough for all of us."

She hesitates, as if considering the idea, but then shakes her head, still gazing at me. "Maybe some other time."

Dad nods and tells her that we'll be in the kitchen if she changes her mind. I start to follow him, noticing that Aunt Alexia continues to watch me. She tries to be sneaky about it, closing the door most of the way, peeking out through the crack; plus she's switched her room light off.

But I can still see her there: a sliver of white that cuts through the darkness, sending shivers all over my skin.

"Coming?" Dad says, already down the hall, in the kitchen. I can hear him setting up the island.

I take one last look at Aunt Alexia's room, just as the door clicks shut.

"How's she doing?" I ask Dad, joining him in the kitchen. I slide onto an island stool, noting the requisite trash bag he's set out in which to dump any remaining evidence.

Dad pops the lid off a container of salsa and assures me that Aunt Alexia's been taking all her medication, going to therapy twice a week, and receiving high marks for cooperation from Nurse Loretta.

"Yes, but she barely comes out of her room," I remind him.

"At night, she does. She's been sleeping a lot during the day. She's got her days and nights reversed, I guess."

I manage a nod, wondering if her erratic sleep schedule is the reason I've had the sensation of being watched: if maybe she's been skulking around the house while I sleep, and peeking into my room.

We eat in silence for several minutes. I can tell Dad's got a lot on his mind. He keeps gazing up from his trough of guacamole, taking big breaths as if about to say something.

"Is everything okay?" he asks, finally venturing to speak. He looks toward my plate.

"Better than okay," I say, assuming he's talking about the food.

"And what about between you and Aunt Alexia?" he asks. "Is everything okay in that department, too?"

I pause from polishing off the container of nacho dip. "What do you mean?"

"I mean, have you two gotten a chance to chat at all?"

"Not really," I say, choosing not to tell him about last night, because I'm not so sure that being coaxed out of a closet and tucked into bed with my long-lost baby doll constitutes an actual chat. "She seems so much different now than she was at the mental facility—more afraid, less willing to talk. It's like she's taken a step back."

"Well, I think you should at least *try* to talk to her," he says. "Whenever you're ready, that is. I think it might make her more comfortable. Nurse Loretta told us that Alexia's feeling a bit self-conscious about staying here. Your mom and I want her to feel welcome."

I swallow hard; a chip scrapes my throat. "I'd like to talk to her. I think we might have a lot in common."

Dad meets my eyes, waiting for me to elaborate, maybe. But I'm waiting for him to elaborate, too. It feels like there's so much more being said than what's actually coming out of our mouths.

"I think so, too," he says after a two-bite pause. "And not just with your art."

"I agree," I say, staring straight at him, silently challenging him to come clean about what he knows.

Despite the tension between him and Mom these past several months, it was actually Dad's idea for Aunt Alexia to come and stay with us for a while—*Dad*, who approximately two months ago spotted Aunt Alexia's journal in my bedroom when he popped in to say hello. He moved it to my night table, making room for himself on my bed, not even asking what it was.

Is it possible that he didn't notice? Did he not see her name scrawled across the front cover?

Dad falls silent, looking back down at his food again, failing to ask me any more.

"What are you thinking?" I ask, trying to force him back to the topic.

He smiles, then nudges the container of sour cream toward me. "I'm thinking that we haven't even talked about school yet."

I bite my lip to keep it from trembling, disappointed that he doesn't want to discuss Aunt Alexia more. "I take it you haven't picked up your voice mail messages at work?"

"Why?" he asks. "Did something happen?"

I take a deep breath, trying to stay in control, but I suddenly feel like I've absolutely none. My eyes fill with tears.

"Camelia?" He leans across the table to touch my forearm. "Hey," he says, finally getting up and coming to sit beside me.

I snuggle up into his chest the way I did when I was five, wishing that I could go back in time and be a little girl all over again.

Dad strokes my hair. He smells like coffee and chili peppers. "What is it?" he asks.

I break our embrace to look at him again—at his swollen eyes and the furrow lines on his forehead. He looks almost as scared as I feel.

"I had a panic attack in sculpture class," I lie, wiping the tears from my eyes, "and Ms. Beady recommended that I start seeing someone . . . a therapist, I mean."

I don't expect him to believe me. I'm almost sure he's

going to interrogate me and demand to know the truth. But instead he lets out a giant breath, relieved by the news; I almost spot a grin on his face.

"Did you think it was something else?" I ask, still hoping that he'll open up and that he'll want *me* to open up as well.

But he eats his grin with a side of denial, and then hops on Beady's bandwagon, telling me how unsurprised he is by the suggestion—not to mention the alleged attack—considering everything that's happened these past several months.

"I think talking to someone is an excellent idea. You've been through a lot, and your mother and I want what's best for you."

"I know," I say, proceeding to fill him in about Dr. Tylyn. "She works at Hayden, and Ms. Beady says she's good."

"Do you want me to give her a call to set something up?"

"Sure." I hand him the sticky note from my pocket. "Just make sure the appointment is on a Thursday. I'll be at Hayden for an art class anyway. Spencer wants me to take a life drawing course. He says I need to put more *body* into my work."

"And what do bodies have to do with bowls?" he asks, finally unleashing his grin.

"Honestly, I have no idea. But hopefully I'll find out."

9

*F*OR THE NEXT COUPLE DAYS at school, people look at me as if I were some kind of freak. And I can't really say I blame them.

My episode in sculpture class was far worse than I thought. Kimmie finally breaks down and tells me that I didn't just call out "no" a couple of times; apparently I *shouted* it out at the top of my lungs and did some weird convulsive thing while clawing the air with my hands.

I'm assuming the convulsive thing was because I was so completely stuck inside my head, picturing the windows in the locker room and grappling to get out through one of them.

Not that it even matters, because every time I walk down the hallway now, I part the sea of onlookers as if I were a science project come to life. A far cry from the last several years of school, when I was barely even noticed; when I blended into my surroundings, ironically like my namesake, the chameleon; and when that was perfectly fine by me. Teachers, on the other hand, have been giving me special treatment, talking to me like I'm on the verge of a nervous breakdown and opting not to call on me when I clearly don't know the answer. You'd think it'd come as a perk, but it's actually been more of an annoyance.

Case in point: yesterday, Mr. Swenson, a.k.a. the Sweat-man, my chemistry teacher, got all are-you-sure-you-can-handle-doing-the-lab-this-week?-because-if-you-need-some-extra-time-just-say-the-word-and-I'll-give-you-an-extension. His voice was powdery soft, reminding me of the way a pedophile might sound trying to lure unsuspecting kids into his van with the promise of candy. And he got *this close* to my face, enabling me to smell his burrito breath, which almost made me want to give up Mexican food altogether. *Almost.*

Ben's been treating me differently, too. Instead of keeping his distance and giving me his usual polite nods and smiles in passing, he's been making a point of walking by my locker more often than usual, and looking in my direction en route to his seat in chemistry. It's flattering on one hand, because it shows that he still cares, but uncomfortable on the other, because we're obviously no longer together.

"Hey, there, sexy lady," Kimmie coos, sneaking up behind me at my locker.

It's after school, and I'm trying to cram a bunch of books into my bag, but they keep dumping back out onto the floor.

"New?" she asks, giving my sweater a puzzled look. She reaches out to feel the hem.

"Borrowed," I say. "From my mother's closet."

"Go, Jilly," Kimmie says, using my mom's first name. "One hundred percent cashmere?"

"As if I bothered to check the label." At the same moment, an avalanche of books spills out of my locker.

Kimmie comes to my rescue by picking them up. "Something on your mind?" she asks. "Because you seem just a wee bit distracted."

"It might have something to do with the fact that I've been labeled a full-fledged freak."

"Big whoop," she says, pulling a fan (the paper kind that accordion-folds) from her bag and flicking it open. "I've been labeled a freak since birth, but I'm still as sexy as hell."

I gaze over my shoulder, spotting Davis Miller, my wannabe-boy-band-member neighbor, doing a move that looks suspiciously convulsive, complete with clawing fingers and an obnoxious whine.

Kimmie lowers her glasses to stare at him over the rims—from his tight black jeans and muscle tank, to his Converse sneakers with an inch of vankle (visible ankle, according to Kimmie; basically, when your pants aren't quite long enough to reach the shoelaces). "Seriously?" she asks. "Is there a costume party I don't know about?"

Davis responds with a flailing of his tongue.

"Gene Simmons you are not," she says.

Davis appears thoroughly confused, clearly not a fan

of seventies rock bands, nor of the man with the longest tongue ever.

A moment later, Danica Pete walks by, and Davis lets out an obnoxious sneeze, one that's peppered with the word *loser*. "Hey, Twig!" he shouts, when she ignores him, referring to her less-than-curvy figure. "Running late to a flat-ass convention, are we?"

But Danica continues to ignore him, scurrying down the hallway, clearly on a mission. I want to say something in her defense, but before I can think of anything clever enough, Kimmie whirls me around and asks if I need her to sleep over tonight. "I mean, I totally will if you want," she says. "But if not, my dad's invited me for dinner at his place, just the two of us."

"Thanks anyway," I say, managing to stuff a couple of notebooks into my bag. "But I'll be fine. Go dine with Dad."

"So, no more dreams about sculpting things, I take it?"

"No more dreams about anything," I reply, hoping I sound optimistic, because I don't want to disappoint her.

The truth is I haven't really been sleeping much lately. The thought of my aunt's being awake at all hours of the night, and possibly peeping in on me while I'm asleep, has turned me into an insomniac, as evidenced by the dark circles under my eyes and my apparent lack of coordination.

"Sweet deal," Kimmie says, with a snap of her gum. "Plus, bonus points, you haven't done anything weird in sculpture class in days. So, maybe things are finally getting back to normal."

"Maybe," I say, knowing that it isn't that simple,

and disappointed that she thinks it is. Kimmie's at least partly responsible for my "normalcy" in sculpture class. I've been having her elbow me every five minutes to make sure I don't get too engrossed in my work (which is where I run into problems of the convulsive-and-voice-hearing kind). In one way it's been good, because it keeps me from making a fool of myself. But it's also been bad, because what I've been producing has been utterly empty, which, in turn, makes me feel empty, too.

"So I'll call you later, after my dad's?" she asks. "He promises that Tammy the Toddler won't be there."

"Is that what we're calling her these days?"

"If the diaper fits . . ."

"Best not to give them any ideas," I joke.

"So right," she says, shuddering.

"And I'll call *you*," I add. "I have to go to Hayden later. Spencer got me into a life drawing class."

"Whoa," she says, squeezing her eyes shut; two red roses that perfectly match her fan have been painted onto her eyelids. "Life drawing . . . as in, naked people? Because you know that's what they do in those classes, right? You know there's going to be all kinds of floppy going on . . . and I'm not just talking about the guys. Hi, Ben," she says, without missing a beat. A wide smile stretches across her lips.

I turn to find him directly behind me, mortified to think he might've heard the conversation.

"Am I interrupting something?" He smirks.

"Gotta go," Kimmie says, leaving me to literally *flop* on my own.

66

"How's it going?" Ben asks. He rests his palm against my open locker door, rocking my entire universe.

"Great," I lie.

Still, it's clear he knows otherwise. He squints slightly, as if he could pull the truth right out of me. "Yeah, well, I heard about what happened in your sculpture class."

"Panic attack," I say, lying again.

"Are you sure that's all it was?" His hand brushes against my forearm, causing my insides to rumble and stir.

It's all I can do to take a step back and let his hand fall away. "I'm fine," I try to assure him, hearing a slight quiver in my voice. "How have things been with you?"

I want to hear how miserable he is now that we've broken up. But instead he tells me how nice it is that people are starting to accept him. "I have you to thank for that," he says. "People think I'm some kind of hero."

"Well, you are," I say, almost wishing that he could save me again.

Ben hesitates for a few more seconds, as if wanting to say something else, but I turn away before he can, and close my locker door.

"Well, let me know if you ever want to talk." He smells like the fumes of his bike.

"Sounds good." I turn to face him again, struggling to hold back tears. They burn a hole straight through my heart.

The next thing I know, Alejandra Chavez—ranked number one last year on Freetown High's Most Beautiful People list—sneaks up behind Ben and taps him on the shoulder. "Hey, stranger," she chirps, "I've been looking all over for you."

Ben doesn't flinch, nor does he take his eyes off mine. "Alejandra, do you know Camelia?" he asks.

Alejandra looks at me for about half a second, then shakes her head, even though we hung out last summer at the community pool, when she forgot her towel and I loaned her my extra one.

I consider reminding her but decide it's not really that important. Plus, Alejandra seems far too preoccupied to bother with me. She's completely focused on Ben, asking him where he's been and telling him that she needs a ride home.

"Plus, we're still going for coffee, right?" she asks him.

"Right," he says, finally turning to gaze at her.

She looks supermodel perfect in a short black skirt and tall leather boots. Her inky black hair is swept up in an intentionally messy ponytail, showing off her almond-shaped eyes and angular cheeks.

"But we'll have to meet there," he continues. "I've got a couple errands I need to do first."

"I could come with you." She gives him a flirty little smile, as if she realizes that although she's being too persistent, her good looks make up for it.

"Let's walk to the coffee place," Ben suggests. "It's nice out and my bike's pretty low on fuel."

It's obviously a bogus excuse. He wants to avoid touching her, for fear that he'll sense something he shouldn't.

But I can't really say I mind.

Dear Jill,

I'm sure you noticed that your manager started acting suspicious, like something seedy was going on. I'm sure you saw how he eyeballed me every time I came into the coffee shop, watching to make sure that I ordered something, and that I wasn't just taking up table space.

But did you also notice my efforts? My unwavering concern for your well-being? And my scrupulous attention to detail?

The napkin note, for example: I didn't merely write it on the spot. You'll be flattered to know that I'd actually written that note way ahead of time (the night before), because I wanted to ensure that things played out perfectly.

When I brought it up to the counter, it looked like you'd been expecting me. I remember you were wearing eye shadow and a bold shade of lipstick smeared across your mouth. In some way you reminded me of a little girl playing dress-up, but your attempts were a positive sign.

I ordered a cookie, but you got me a brownie instead. Also positive: I made you nervous. I could tell that you really liked me.

I slipped you my note, making direct physical contact by sliding my finger along your thumb. It startled you—I saw your shoulders tense and your lips stiffen—but you

didn't try to pull away. Also good: you cared
more about my feelings than you did your own.

I left the shop once your manager came
around, but you'll be happy to know that I
lingered outside, hidden in the darkness,
because I didn't want to leave you just yet.

. . .

Dear Jack:

After a while you stopped hanging around the coffee shop as much. But then one day you walked in, scribbled something down on a napkin, and passed it to me as I wrapped up your brownie to go. Once again, your finger grazed my thumb, nearly knocking me off balance.

Carl saw it. The note, that is. But he didn't say anything, because of the brownie purchase (it was our most expensive kind and not a huge mover).

The napkin pressed in my hand, I could feel it wilting in the sweat of my palm, but I didn't want to open it until you were gone, in case it was a note revealing that I'd been the butt of some joke. It wouldn't have been the first time, but I'm sure you already know that.

"What's with that guy?" Carl asked, watching as you collected your books.

I was excited that Carl noticed your attention, that it hadn't just been a figment of my imagination. "He seems pretty nice," I said.

Carl gawked at me, his face as wilted as my napkin note. "You need your head checked."

Carl, in case you were wondering, is twenty-nine years old and in graduate school, working full-time days while taking acting classes at night.

He says he wants to be the next Jim Carrey, but I've honestly never seen that side of him. He always looks like his dog just died (especially when you come around).

Before I could ask him to elaborate, a loud clunk came from the back pantry. Carl headed in that direction, while you bolted out the door.

I remember how my fingers shook as I struggled to open your note. TONIGHT, 9PM, it read. CAN WE TALK? I-M ME AT JACKFORJILL@YAHOO.COM.

I wonder if you saw me rush to the front window, if you were watching as I gazed out into the parking lot. I remember spotting someone getting into a dark car, but I couldn't quite tell if it was you. The driver didn't wave, nor did he pull out of the space. Still, I pressed the napkin-note against my chest, hoping that it wasn't part of a dream, or, if it was, that I'd never wake up.

. . .

10

MY MOM'S IN AUNT ALEXIA'S ROOM. The door is open a crack, and I can hear them speaking in hushed tones. Standing in the middle of the hall, I do my best to listen in, but I can't make out much more than "I'm not hungry" and "I'm just so tired."

Mom continues to ask Aunt Alexia questions—now it's something about her art—but a floorboard creaks beneath my feet, and I know I'm caught.

I retreat toward the kitchen, but it's already too late.

"Hey, there," Mom says, poking her head out into the hallway. She closes Aunt Alexia's door behind her and points me toward the kitchen, where I find a spread of vegan delights set up on the island—from peanut butter cups to flaxseed chips with faux nacho dip.

"What's the special occasion?" I ask, noticing that some of the food looks surprisingly edible.

"Aunt Alexia says she prefers her food cooked."

"Go figure," I say, taking one of the peanut butter cups.

Mom tucks a corkscrewlike strand of her auburn hair back into her bun. "How's school going? No more panic attacks, I hope."

"I take it Dad filled you in."

"Dad, Ms. Beady, your art teacher, the mailman . . ." She counts them off on her fingers. "Okay, well, not the mailman." She smirks. "But you get the point. It would've been nice to have heard the news from you."

"How long have you known?"

"A couple days." She grabs a knife to chop some carrots. "Your dad told me, and then I got a voice message from Ms. Beady. I kept waiting for you to say something. . . ." *Chop, chop, chop.*

"I was *going* to tell you," I say, disappointed that it took her so long to ask me. "I mean, it's not like it was some secret."

"I don't want to lecture you, Camelia. I know that I've been a bit preoccupied lately." *Chop, chop.*

I look back at her array of snacks, trying to put myself in her shoes—having her sister here and still blaming herself for her sister's suicidal tendencies, while dealing with the stress I cause her.

When they were growing up, their mother (my grandmother) believed that Aunt Alexia's birth was the reason her husband left them. And so, Aunt Alexia was constantly punished for simply having been born, while my mother was often doted on, making Aunt Alexia feel even more unwanted.

"You've been fine," I tell her, deciding to cut her some slack.

"Yes, but school for you hasn't been, so why not fill me in? Before the mailman does, that is." She smiles.

I smile back, glad to be able to share some of the lighter details. And so I give her the complete lowdown on Ben. "He looked so happy with that Alejandra girl today."

"But you said you wanted time to yourself, right?"

"Right." I sigh, following up with a halfhearted bite of a peanut butter cup. To my surprise, it tastes like heaven inside my mouth. "Are you kidding me with these?" I snatch another.

"Glad you like them." She stops chopping to push the plate closer. "Edible therapy, wouldn't you say? And, speaking of which, your dad made an appointment for you to see that therapist, but it's not until next week." She eats her worried expression along with a dehydrated flaxseed chip. "Your dad and I think it's good that you'll be talking to someone."

"I guess," I say, not convinced, because, aside from Dad, everyone in this household is seeing a shrink, but no one seems any better off for it.

"It's healthy to have someone outside your network of friends and family to talk to," she continues. "Someone with a different perspective."

I nod reluctantly, thinking how it wasn't so long ago that she insisted I tell her everything. I glance past her at the bottle of pills on the counter. She used to keep it stashed behind the jar of almond butter, but now it's out in the open beside the salt and pepper shakers, like they're suddenly just as common. "How's Aunt Alexia doing?" I ask, curious to know what all the whispering was about.

"She's been asking about you, too." She fakes a smile. "She's doing okay, but she still needs some time. Coming here is a big adjustment."

"To say the least." I nod in agreement while taking a bite of faux nacho dip and wishing I'd stopped at the peanut butter cups.

Later, Mom drops me off at Hayden for my art class. With sketch pad and pencils in hand, I hurry down the hallway, noticing that a bunch of the rooms on both sides of the corridor have the letters *PSY* before the number.

I slow down to scan the names on the doors. Finally I find Dr. Tylyn's office, sandwiched between a water fountain and a supply closet. The light's on, and the door is wide open, but no one's inside.

I lean forward for a closer look. At the same moment, someone grabs my shoulder from behind, completely startling me.

It's Kimmie.

"Okay, what are you even doing here?" I slap my hand over my chest. "Besides trying to give me a heart attack, that is?"

"For your information, I'm trying to ward off depression." She flashes her palm at me. There's a dark brown capital *D*, with a slash mark through it, stamped in the center. "It's henna," she explains. "In other words, temporary. And, before you ask, the *D* stands for 'depression.'"

I'm tempted to ask her if it might instead stand for *dumb*, but I bite my tongue.

"It was Wes's suggestion," she continues, "and Weed, the tattoo artist who did it, said it was sure to do the trick—that even when I'm not thinking about the tattoo, my subconscious will be well aware of its presence, thus ridding my mind of depressive thoughts."

"What happened?" I ask, already suspecting the truth. Kimmie was supposed to be dining with her dad tonight.

"He said he needed to reschedule," she says, her eyes welling up. "He said he had to work late, but it was all a bogus lie. I went by his place and his car was there. Tammy's was there, too."

"What can I do?" I ask, giving her a hug.

"Just be with me. I don't want to be alone, okay?"

"Do you want me to ditch my class?"

She shakes her head and tries to regroup, taking a step back and wiping her eyes with a coordinating scarf (there's a crossed-out *D* at the hem). "Can I come and sketch naked people with you?"

"*Excuse me?*"

"Before you object, I know how much this art class means to you. I know that Spencer went out of his way to get you in, and so I promise not to laugh at any impending floppiness."

"Well, in that case," I say, hooking elbows with her, "how could I possibly say no?"

II

*O*N THE WAY into the art studio, Kimmie explains
that she isn't crashing the course for antidepres-
sive purposes only. "If I'm going to have my own
design business one day, I need to start becoming more
aware of the body."

"Especially if that body is tall, dark, and ripped?" I
ask, suspecting an ulterior motive.

Dwayne, the art professor, spots us right away.
"Welcome to my lair," he says, in a voice as big as he is.
Standing at least six feet seven, he has Einstein-like hair
and tortoiseshell glasses with round frames.

Kimmie introduces herself as an aspiring designer, and
Dwayne eats up every word, telling her about his obsession
with designers like Giorgio Armani and Oscar de la Renta.
"Fine tailoring, fine artists," he tells her. "It's all about
line, contour, and proportion."

"Amen to that," she says, evidently inspired.

"And you must be Camelia." Dwayne turns to shake my hand. "Spencer told me all about those troublesome bowls of yours." He tsk-tsks.

"Troublesome?"

"As you embark upon your sketches," he replies, "I want you to consider things like form, texture, and size."

"Because size is definitely key," Kimmie whispers, grinning at me. "Especially when sketching naked people."

I yank her away so that we can find seats. The easels are arranged in a circle, with space in the middle where the model stands. There are about twelve students in total, including us—a mixture of early-twentysomethings and people who look to be my parents' age.

"I wonder if we'll ever bump into Adam on campus," Kimmie says.

I shrug, having wondered the same, especially since I'll be coming here for the next several weeks.

A moment later, I notice that our model has come into the studio. With his back to me, he stands in the center, dressed only in a robe and flip-flops.

"Passengers, prepare for takeoff," Kimmie says, as he drops his robe to the floor.

I clench my teeth, trying my best to focus—to ignore the fact that there's a naked guy standing right in front of me now. A naked guy with sculpted legs, a muscular back, and perfectly chiseled arms.

"Holy buttocks," Kimmie says under her breath.

"You'll have fifteen minutes to sketch the model in his

first pose," Dwayne tells us, "after which he'll reposition and you'll begin anew."

I take a deep breath and let it out slowly. The model gets into his pose, with his arms folded in front of him. He turns his head ever so slightly.

And I notice.

The way his chin juts out and the line of his jaw.

My pencil drops from my hand, and I feel my heart pound.

"Camelia?" Kimmie asks. She touches my shoulder, perhaps wondering if I'm having another one of my psychometric episodes. "Do you need to go get some water?"

I nod and start to get up, bumping into my easel. It scratches against the floor. My sketch pad topples over with a *smack*.

"It's no big deal," Kimmie says, scrambling to pick it up.

But it *is* a big deal. Because people in class turn to look.

People, including naked Adam.

"Camelia?" he asks, seemingly as horrified as I am. He grabs the first thing within reach—a piece of wax fruit from a bowl near him—in a futile attempt to cover himself.

"Is there a problem?" Dwayne asks; he seems annoyed by the disturbance.

"I'm sorry," I say, collecting my things.

Meanwhile, Kimmie gawks at Adam as he holds the apple over his serpent. "Holy Garden of Eden," she ers, making the sign of the cross. "That Eve's a lucky

12

*J*FLEE FROM THE STUDIO, eager to get away.

Kimmie reluctantly follows. "It's just the novelty of the nudity," she assures me. "By the second pose, you'll be so used to seeing his naked ass you won't even give it a second thought."

"How can you honestly say that?" I whirl around to face her. We're standing in the middle of the hallway, a good six doors down from the studio. "He practically had that ass in my face."

"And the problem with that *is* . . ."

"It's just too weird," I say, shaking my head, feeling my heart beat at triple its normal speed.

Kimmie looks crushed, the way she did the time I accidentally spilled glaze all over the front of her favorite poodle skirt.

"I won't be mad if you want to go back in," I tell her. "I'll even wait for you." I point to a group of sofas in an alcove at the end of the hallway.

"Are you sure?" she asks.

I nod, almost surprised that she wants to take me up on the offer to sketch Adam naked. *Almost.*

Kimmie turns to go back to the studio just as Adam comes rushing out.

Wearing his robe again, he looks relieved to have caught us. "Hey," he says, moving in our direction. His face looks sweaty. His neck is splotchy. Still, all I can picture is that wax apple between his legs.

"Do you have a second?" he asks me.

"Don't you need to be in the studio?"

"I need to be right here," he says, pointing toward the sofas. "Can we talk for a minute?"

"Wait, does this mean that they need another model?" Kimmie taps her chin in thought.

"Don't even think about it," I tell her.

"Actually, they're sketching one of the students," Adam says. "With clothes on."

Even so, Kimmie seems interested. She excuses herself and heads back to the studio. Meanwhile, Adam and I move to the alcove to talk.

He takes a seat on the sofa, and his robe falls open. "Sorry," he says, turning all shades of red. He holds his legs closed, keeping the robe firmly in place. "So . . ." he says, clearly awkward.

But I'm awkward, too. I fidget in my seat, not quite sure where to look.

"Come here often?" he jokes.

"Spencer suggested that I take this course."

"Are you sure that's the real reason you're here?" he asks, still trying to be funny. He pulls up on the robe, revealing a bit of his knee.

"You're such a dork," I say, unable to hide my smile.

Adam bumps his shoulder against mine. "Yeah, but you know you love me."

I swallow hard, not quite sure how to respond.

"And, hey," he continues, before I have the chance, "any time you want to see me naked, just say the word. No need to make up excuses and go to all this trouble."

"I'll keep that in mind," I say, playing along. "So, when did you start modeling?"

"A month ago." He shrugs. "I'm just trying to earn a few extra bucks."

"By baring your bod for cash?"

"Why not? No animals are harmed while I pose."

"My PETA-loving mom would be so proud," I say, noticing the golden-blond hair on his calves. "Are you still working at the art supply store?"

He nods. "But I'm also hoping to transfer to a good architectural program in the fall, so I need all the extra money I can get."

"And now you've lost your gig." I look toward the studio door, wondering if maybe he shouldn't go back in.

"Yeah, but the view is better out here." He's staring straight at me now. "And I'm not just talking about my hairy legs . . . though they're pretty fine, too."

I laugh, but Adam's expression remains serious.

"I've missed you," he says. His dark brown eyes focus hard on mine.

"It's only been a couple weeks," I say, feeling stupid for even saying it. Because deep down, I've missed him, too.

_A_FTER A GOOD THIRTY MINUTES or so spent catching up, Adam goes off to change into his clothes, while I remain in the alcove waiting until the drawing class lets out.

"They should be wrapping up right about now," he says when he comes to join me back on the sofa.

He's dressed in a pair of dark-washed jeans and a long-sleeved T-shirt, but still I can't help picturing him just moments ago: like a Greek god statue in the center of Athens.

"Is everything okay?" he asks, noticing maybe that I can't stop staring.

"It's fine," I say, relieved when people finally start to filter out.

I make a beeline for the door and hurry inside to apologize again to Dwayne. "I shouldn't have run out of the room like that," I tell him.

"It's just that seeing her ex au naturel totally caught her off guard," Kimmie says, calling out from her seat. She's putting the finishing touches on her sketch.

Dwayne smiles, seemingly far more amused by our awkward situation than angered by it, and so he offers Adam the opportunity of modeling for his Tuesday night class and tells me to come back next week.

"Thank you," I say, grateful for his patience.

Meanwhile, Kimmie closes her sketchbook and thanks Dwayne as well. "I learned a lot." She gives him a thumbs-up. "But next week I want to sketch skin."

I drag her out of the studio before Dwayne can change his mind. Just a few steps down the hallway, Adam stops us. "What's the rush?" he asks.

I check my watch. It's almost nine. "I should probably call my mom to come pick me up. Kimmie, do you need a ride?"

"*I* could drive you guys home," he says. "It's on my way."

"Since when?" I ask. Freetown is a good twenty minutes away; his apartment is barely two.

"Yeah, but the Press & Grind is open late, and they have the best mocha-chip brownies in town. I could use a little pick-me-up."

"Perfect," Kimmie says, accepting for the both of us. "And why don't we stop for a pizza en route? All that sketching has got me starving."

The next thing I know, I'm calling my mom to give her the scoop, and then hopping into the front seat of

Adam's old '70s Bronco. The familiar rumble of the engine, coupled with the syrupy scent in the air—from Adam's bacon-scented air freshener—takes me back to just months ago, when, sitting in this very car, Adam leaned toward me to touch my face and I couldn't wait to kiss him.

"This is a sweet ride," Kimmie says, angling herself over the front seat to appeal to Adam's ego. "You do know how much Camelia here loves vintage cars, don't you?" (A big fat lie.)

"Seriously?" Adam asks, practically beaming.

"Are you kidding? Camelia can barely get enough of those car restoration shows on TV. . . . You know, the ones that feature old classic hotrods being restored to their original condition by a bunch of gearheads." (Lie number two.)

"Wow, that's totally cool," Adam says.

I don't have the heart to tell him the truth, and so I merely gaze out the window as we pull into the parking lot of Pizza Rita's.

We order a large cheese pizza, then chat about the class. Kimmie is beyond excited, telling us how inspiring Dwayne is, and how he said she has an eye for balance and proportion.

"Dwayne's a great teacher," Adam says in agreement. "I've learned a lot just from posing—just from listening to the way he instructs his students."

"Speaking of posing," Kimmie says, practically sprouting a pitchfork, tail, and horns, "what does it feel like up there . . . hanging around on the platform? I mean, do you care that people are staring at your junk and stuff?"

"Well, I'm not exactly *hanging around*." He clears his throat. "And I'm not so sure they're staring."

"Trust me," she says, her eyes as big as fishbowls. "They are."

A moment later our food comes, but Kimmie still doesn't let up: "What does a gig like that even pay?"

"It's not such a bad deal," Adam says, trying to remain aloof. "I mean, aside from today's incident, it's relatively painless. Plus, I get to contribute to the world of art."

"By showing your schlong?" she asks, completely straight-faced.

Instead of getting upset, Adam humors her for several more minutes, which reminds me just how generous he is.

And how much I really like him.

We continue to talk, eat, and laugh for another full hour, pausing only once while I call home to give my dad an update. Kimmie seems much happier than when she was in her previous "anti-D" state. And I have to admit I'm feeling pretty human again, too. She even jokes that the D on her hand should really stand for *ditz*.

"Because, let's face it," she says, "this baby ain't coming off for weeks."

"Yeah, but it looks pretty cool," Adam says. "Plus, I'm sure you'll be able to dress around it."

"So right," Kimmie says. "I can also change what the D stands for according to my mood."

"One day, anti-Drama," I suggest. "The next day, anti-Dad."

"The following day, anti-Dolls," she says with a wink.

"Especially creepy ones with eyes that open and close."

"We should probably get going," I say, unwilling to get into my own drama in front of Adam.

Adam agrees, and he drops Kimmie off first. She steps out of the car, but then pokes her head into the passenger-side window to give me a pleading look. "Call me if anything good happens, okay?"

"Will do." I smile, able to read her corrupt and suspicious mind.

Adam drives me home, filling the silence with small talk about his midterm exams and a project he's working on involving the redesign of an elementary-school playground. He asks me questions about my classes as well, but I'm feeling far too nervous for chitchat.

Finally, we pull up in front of my house. Adam puts the car in park and turns to me. "I want to see you again," he says, before I have a chance to say good night. "Can I call you?"

"That'd be nice."

"Really?" he says, seemingly surprised by my response. "So I can take you out sometime?"

"Sure," I say, gazing at the scar on his lower lip. "But just as friends, okay?"

"No sweat." He smiles.

I smile, too, reminded of how happy Adam always makes me and how easy it is to be with him compared to Ben. For a change, that feels really nice.

LATER, IN MY ROOM, I do all my homework and then settle into bed, grateful for the routine and for the fact that things are starting to feel somewhat normal again.

I grab a comb and make an attempt to work it through the kinks in my hair. But the truth is that I've been all kinks lately, because I haven't been pursuing my pottery—not really, anyway.

Part of me wonders if I *should* be pursuing it—if I should be using my pottery to figure out the story behind the voices. But another part of me is terrified of those voices, because hearing them—and getting so caught up in what's going on inside my head that I feel completely confused about what's really happening—brings me one step closer to being like Aunt Alexia.

I look toward our shared wall, hearing scratching sounds again. If I didn't know better, I'd say that she was trying to claw her way out through the wall, right into my room. I'm tempted to scratch back, wondering if she might be trying to get my attention. But instead I press my eyelids shut, cover my ears with a pillow, and try to force myself to sleep.

After a good hour or so spent tossing and turning, I feel myself start to nod off. But unfortunately, it doesn't take, and so finally I head down to the basement to work. My parents are asleep; their door is closed. It's quiet in the house.

I turn on the basement light. Standing about a foot tall, my sculpture of a skater is there on my work board, begging to be touched. And so I do.

I remove the tarp and run my fingers over the figure's leg, perfecting the knee and making the muscles in the calves more defined. I spend an hour or so working on the shoulders, forearms, and hands.

Until I hear something behind me.

A clicking sound.

I turn to look just as the overhead light goes out, leaving me in the dark. I grip my carving knife and start to move toward the stairs. At the same moment, a burst of light flashes in front of my eyes, making them sting.

"Who's there?" I call out into the darkness, telling myself that the flash was from a lightbulb that blew, and that the clicking noise must have come from an electrical problem.

No one answers, but then more light flashes into my eyes, making everything feel hot, loud, confining.

I strain my eyes, trying to see who it is. But it's too dark, and my vision is stained with blotches of bright red and green.

Someone's taking pictures.

"Who's there?" I repeat.

Instead of answering, I hear someone humming a familiar tune that I can't quite recall. From a nursery rhyme, maybe? An old preschool song? It's a male voice, and it has a whimsical quality, as if whoever's singing it is enjoying himself.

The camera flashes continue, making my head spin. Hot tears burn my cheeks.

"You're so beautiful," he whispers, taking a pause from humming.

I shake my head and plug my ears with my clay-covered fingers, driving them all the way in, wondering if his voice is coming from inside my head. I take a deep breath, trying to be brave. The knife pressed firmly in my grip, I start toward the stairs again. But after just a couple of steps, I trip on something. There's a loud clunking sound. I try to keep going, but it feels like there's some-thing wound around my ankles now. I bend down to find out what it is.

A canvas strap of some sort. With something attached. A camera. I can tell from the size, shape, and weight.

I peer into the viewfinder, somehow suddenly able to see, as if there's a nightlight hidden inside the lens.

To my complete and utter shock, my own reflection stares back at me. My wide green eyes: full of fear, burning with questions, tears brimming at the corners.

"There are two," a new voice whispers—a female one this time.

The eyes blink at me a couple of times, while my eyes remain fixed, making me finally realize that the reflection isn't mine after all.

"There are two," the female voice repeats. And then someone shakes me by the shoulders, which rouses me awake. For real this time.

I'm startled to find myself in bed, in my room, with a pair of wide green eyes still staring back at me. Only now it's clear: they belong to my aunt.

15

MOONLIGHT COMES IN through my windows, illuminating Aunt Alexia's face. "Are you okay?" she asks me.

I shake my head, feeling physically sick. I don't even question what she's doing here. Instead, I bury my face in my hands, wishing I were still asleep, knowing I must've nodded off during all of that tossing and turning and merely dreamt about going downstairs.

"I could hear you from my bedroom," she says, tucking Miss Dream Baby in beside me and then stroking my arms. The chill of her hands makes me shiver all over.

"You could hear me?" I ask, sitting up in bed. I wipe the tears that run down my face, then click on the bedside lamp.

She starts humming the familiar tune from my dream—the same tune she hummed after finding me in the hallway closet.

"Is that 'Yankee Doodle Dandy'?" I ask her.

"That depends. Do you like nursery rhymes?"

"Excuse me?" I ask, completely confused, thinking how "Yankee Doodle Dandy" isn't a nursery rhyme at all. And then I suddenly remember the phrase she kept repeating—the one that played in my head when I was in Ms. Beady's office. "There are two," I say, looking at her for her reaction. "Two *what?*"

"I was hoping that you could tell me," she says; her voice is as fragile as snowflakes. "Those words have been on my mind all night."

The comb I've been using to work the kinks out of my hair is still clenched in my grip. I turn it over in my hand, almost able to picture it as the sculpting knife from my dream.

"You were having a nightmare, weren't you?" she asks. "You were dreaming about your art?"

"How did you know?"

"It won't work," she says, ignoring the question. "Silencing your artistic impulses only makes the voices louder. This sickness always finds its way in . . . even if it has to invade your dreams." She's wearing a paint-spattered dress, and her pale blond hair hangs in a braid down her back.

I take a deep breath, thinking about what she wrote in her journal as a teenager: how she tried giving up her art in hopes that her premonitions would stop. But it only made everything worse.

"Don't be like me." Her eyes widen and fill with tears.

I tear up again, too, even though I want to be strong. I reach out to take her hand, but she pushes me away and grabs the doll from beneath my covers. She cradles it against her belly and starts rocking back and forth, her eyes focused on the ceiling.

I look toward my closed bedroom door, wondering if I should call out to my parents. But after a few moments she's able to meet my eyes again.

"I'm sorry," she says, clearly embarrassed. A faint blush spreads across her cheeks. She starts to tuck the doll back in beside me.

"Keep it," I tell her.

"Are you sure?" she asks, straightening the front of Miss Dream Baby's dress. "I shouldn't have borrowed her for so long, but she was a great comfort to me over the years—mostly because she reminded me of you."

"Really?" I ask, curious as to what she means. Aunt Alexia's rare and short-lived visits when I was younger pretty much consisted of my always begging her to show me her art, and her forever shutting me down.

"We have a lot in common, don't you think?" she asks.

I look at her wrists, covered in scars.

"This is where we're different," she says, catching me looking. She takes my hand and guides my fingers over the scars.

It takes me a moment to notice that one of the scars has a starlike shape—just like the star I drew on Miss Dream Baby's back when I was six.

"It's the same," she says, as if reading my mind. "I

thought the star might help protect me, might help make everything right."

"Not if you're dead."

Alexia traces her finger over the X's on Miss Dream Baby's ears. "I spent so many years trying to protect myself, but I soon learned that there *was* no protection. There's only pain. Hopefully you won't succumb to it." She glides her fingers along my wrists, smiling at my unharmed skin. "You're so much stronger than I ever was."

I resist the urge to pull away, feeling weaker than ever before. "How can you be so sure?"

Aunt Alexia continues to pat my arm, lingering over my veins as if sensing something significant. "I feel things," she whispers, glancing toward the drawer of my night table, inside which her journal is tucked. "And, like what happens with you, my art brings that feeling closer."

"So, then you know you aren't crazy," I say, more as a question than a statement, and wishing that I had tried to rephrase it.

Alexia stops patting my arm and looks at me—a cold, dead stare that could shatter glass. "My art *makes* me crazy. It controls me, and I don't know how to handle it. The voices capture me and bring me someplace else."

I swallow hard. My stomach churns. Acid fills the back of my throat. We're so much alike.

"I want to help you," she says. Tears well up in her eyes again. "But I don't know how."

I clench my teeth, trying not to be sick. "You already

are helping me," I manage to say.

Alexia presses Miss Dream Baby against her chest, as if this has all been a little too much.

"Maybe we should talk about this tomorrow," I suggest.

"We need to talk right now," she says, reaching behind her to the foot of the bed; she's brought along some of her canvases. "Would you like to see my latest work?" She turns the first one over before I can answer.

It's a picture of something blue and diamond-shaped.

"Sea glass," she explains. "I was going to paint it washed up on a beach, but something told me that it didn't belong there. Does it look at all familiar to you?"

I shake my head, trying to jog my memory.

"It will," she says, completely confident.

"Does it make sense to *you*?" I ask her.

"I did this during my first week here," she says, still ignoring my questions, "after having spent some time in your surroundings."

"My surroundings?" I ask, curious to know what she means, exactly—if she's been sneaking into my bedroom while I've been at school, or if she's talking about the few times she took my seat at the kitchen island while my mom whipped up something semi-edible.

"And this one is from last week," she says, flipping the next one over. It's a painting of a camera, just like the one in my dream.

"Do you recognize it?" she asks. A knowing grin rests upon her lips.

"Yes," I whisper, suddenly feeling dizzy. The blood

rushes from my head, making the room seem darker and more confining.

"Maybe I should wait to show you this other one," she says. Her face appears slightly blurry now.

"No," I insist, drawing the covers up over me, hoping to stifle this chill.

Aunt Alexia hesitates.

"I want to see it," I assure her.

She places Miss Dream Baby on my lap, then turns the final canvas over.

I recognize the picture right away. It's the glass shard. In the background is a broken mirror, just like the one in the girls' locker room in my hallucination. The words *DIE ALREADY, WILL YOU?!* are scribbled in red across the remaining mirror surface, while a heap of broken glass has collected in the sink.

"How did you know?" I tremble all over. "How do you know these things about me?"

"She's so ugly that the mirror broke," she snaps.

"Who is?" I ask, completely confused.

Aunt Alexia lets out a schoolgirl giggle and starts rocking back and forth again, refusing to answer any more questions or even look me in the eye.

Dear Jill,

    At exactly 8:55 pm your screen name popped up: COFFEESHOPGIRL. I waited a few minutes to see if you'd initiate the conversation. I had a feeling that you would—that you'd be so anxious about keeping me waiting, you'd eventually type some small but telling message. I used to like to test myself like that, trying to predict your actions to see how well I really knew you.

    You'll be flattered to learn that I'd been sitting outside your house that night. That I'd watched you walk home at three o'clock. That around six, you'd had a pizza delivered. And that I knew no one else was at home.

    They'd left you alone once again.

    Aside from your shifts at the coffee shop, you were almost always by yourself. Your father worked all hours of the day and night, and your sister pretty much followed his lead, barely at home, using work and the public library as her paths to escape.

    Are you curious as to how I learned all this? Are you impressed with the detective work I did—all for your sake?

    I wondered if you'd be honest with me about being alone. I doubted that you would. I knew you needed to trust me more, which was precisely what that whole chat session was about.

    . . .

9:00 p.m.

COFFEESHOPGIRL: I don't know how to start, so I
   guess I'll keep things simple . . . hi.

JACKFORJILL: It's good to talk 2 u finally.
JACKFORJILL: It's too hard @ the shop. I feel
   like Im getting u in trouble.
JACKFORJILL: Yr boss seems a little intense.

COFFEESHOPGIRL: Me too.
COFFEESHOPGIRL: Glad to talk to you, I mean.
COFFEESHOPGIRL: And, yes, my boss can be a
   PAIN!!!

JACKFORJILL: LOL. I think he hates me. Which is
   why I don't think I'll be hanging out at yr
   shop much anymore.

COFFEESHOPGIRL: ☹

JACKFORJILL: Don't worry.
JACKFORJILL: What are you doing, btw?

COFFEESHOPGIRL: I just got home.

JACKFORJILL: Not out with a bf, I hope.

COFFEESHOPGIRL: No!
COFFEESHOPGIRL: I had dinner at a friend's
   house.
COFFEESHOPGIRL: No big deal.

JACKFORJILL: Phew!
JACKFORJILL: So, what are u doing now?

COFFEESHOPGIRL: Homework.
COFFEESHOPGIRL: And you?

JACKFORJILL: Same.
JACKFORJILL: I'm putting together a portfolio
   for an art show.

COFFEESHOPGIRL: You're an artist?

JACKFORJILL: I'm obsessed with photography.
JACKFORJILL: That's what I'd like 2 do 4 a career.
JACKFORJILL: I have a couple galleries interested in showing my stuff.

COFFEESHOPGIRL: That's great!

JACKFORJILL: Does that mean you'll come to one of my shows?

COFFEESHOPGIRL: Sure!

JACKFORJILL: What do u like 2 do?

COFFEESHOPGIRL: I used to ice skate. Not so much anymore.

JACKFORJILL: V cool. I tried it once and fell on my ass.
JACKFORJILL: You have 2 teach me some moves.

COFFEESHOPGIRL: That could be fun.

JACKFORJILL: Really?
JACKFORJILL: So, we can get 2gether sometime?
JACKFORJILL: How about next Sat night around 9?
JACKFORJILL: I could meet u after yr shift.
JACKFORJILL: We can just talk for a bit and then I can drive u home.
JACKFORJILL: Helloooooo . . . What do u think?

COFFEESHOPGIRL: How did you know I have to work?

JACKFORJILL: You always work on Saturdays, right?

COFFEESHOPGIRL: I guess.

JACKFORJILL: We could meet across the street

from the shop . . . in front of the bakery. Just dont tell yr boss. I dont want him 2 give you a hard time about it. He hates me, remember? LOL.

COFFEESHOPGIRL: Maybe. I don't know.
COFFEESHOPGIRL: About getting together, that is.

JACKFORJILL: Well, Im going away for a couple wks after that, and then I have 2 work on finals. But we could try 2 squeeze something in then if you prefer . . . maybe in 3 wks or so . . . if we can get both of our schedules straight.

COFFEESHOPGIRL: No, next Sat. should be fine. Sounds good.

JACKFORJILL: Correction: sounds GREAT!

I REMAIN AWAKE FOR THE REST of the night, my insides shaking and my mind unable to shut off. "There are two," I whisper, rolling over and over in bed, trying to figure out what the phrase refers to.

Two days until something horrible will happen?

Two weeks until I lose it completely?

And what does it have to do with a skater? Or with taking pictures?

I smother my ears with my pillow, as if that'll stop the tune inside my head—the one from my dream, the same one Aunt Alexia was humming.

Finally, my alarm clock goes off. While Mom's in the shower, I ask Dad if he can get me an appointment with Dr. Tylyn sooner rather than later.

"Sooner as in, after school today?" he asks.

"Sooner as in, me going in late to school so that I can meet with her this morning."

He takes a seat at the kitchen island, bracing himself for what comes next. "Did something happen?"

"Yes, but it's complicated."

He takes a moment to study me—from my tired eyes and pasty skin to the mismatched clothes I picked from a pile on my bedroom floor. "How complicated?"

"It's just that I'm really confused," I say, wishing he'd either pick up the phone and make the appointment or demand that I go ahead and tell him everything.

"Confused about what?" he asks.

"Please," I say, feeling as though I'm wasting my time. "I'm trying to be responsible here by asking to meet with a qualified professional."

"Who's more qualified than your dad?" he asks, only half kidding.

I open my mouth, almost ready to tell him to forget it—that I'll just keep my regularly scheduled appointment.

But then he reaches for the phone. "I'll see what I can do."

The door to Dr. Tylyn's office is partly open. I peek inside, but no one's in there. Only a doll, with sticks for arms and legs, is there, sitting on the doctor's chair as if staring at the computer.

"It's a voodoo doll," a woman says, sneaking up behind me. There's a cup of something steaming in her hand. "You must be Camelia Hammond."

"Dr. Tylyn Oglesby?"

She's younger than I expected—probably in her

midthirties—with straight dark hair and short bangs.

"Dr. Tylyn," she says. She extends her hand for a shake; her fingers are warm from her cup. "I've heard a lot about you."

"Thanks for meeting me so last-minute."

"Sure," she says, leading me inside with a sip. "This is actually a pretty good time for me . . . before any of my classes start." She gestures to a leather sofa. "Do you like vanilla?"

"In general?" I ask, wondering if we're going to have a snack—if, like Ms. Beady, she offers her clients tea and cookies as a way of getting them to talk.

Dr. Tylyn flashes a stick of what I assume is vanilla-scented incense. "It's subtle," she says. "And it beats the musty smell from the hallway."

"Sure." I nod, taking a seat, watching as she lights the incense and sets it on a wooden holder.

"So," she says, sitting down on the sofa two cushions over, "your father said there was something you needed to talk about?"

"Maybe we could back up a bit." I shift uneasily in my seat, wondering if I should've just waited until my originally scheduled appointment.

"We can back up as far as you like." She scooches away slightly, perhaps trying to give me psychological space.

"I mean, I know my dad might've made things sound urgent," I say, "but I mostly just wanted to get the ball rolling."

"Understood," she says, taking another sip. "When I

spoke with Ms. Beady, she said that you suffer from panic attacks."

I nod, wondering if Ms. Beady also mentioned my interest in psychic powers. "Is that all that she said?"

"What is it that *you* want me to know?" She squints slightly, as if that will help her understand me better.

My lips tremble as I search for words, but I have no idea what to say, or even how to start. I look at the walls, hating myself for feeling so vulnerable.

"Camelia?" she asks, most likely sensing my unease.

Unlike Ms. Beady with her framed pedigrees, Dr. Tylyn has covered her walls with artistic prints: the phases of the moon, a tree with branches that stretch up toward the sky, and a starfish-shaped sun peeking out from the clouds.

"Have you ever worked with someone who claims to have psychic abilities?" I venture.

"It's actually one of my specialties," she says, seemingly unfazed by the question, "and one of my academic interests as well." She points to her bookshelf, where she's got a collection of books on topics such as ESP, telepathy, astral projection, and aura reading.

I take a deep breath, slightly reassured. "Have you ever worked with someone who hears voices?"

"I have." She sets her mug down and leans forward again, waiting for me to elaborate.

But I can't bear to say the words.

"Do *you* hear voices, Camelia?"

I manage a slight nod, feeling my pulse race.

"When you're asleep? While you're awake?"

"All the time," I whisper; my voice quavers.

"And what do the voices say?"

"That I'm ugly and a loser. That I have no talent and would be better off dead." I grab one of her couch cushions and hug it to my stomach.

Dr. Tylyn is far more practiced than Ms. Beady at maintaining a poker face; she doesn't show any inkling of surprise. "So, the voices have only been insulting, then?"

"No. Sometimes they say things that don't make any sense—cryptic phrases, I mean. I think they might be clues."

"Clues about what?"

"I'm not sure," I say, knowing how crazy I must sound.

"And you think the voices you've been hearing may have something to do with psychic abilities?"

"Is that possible?" I ask, wondering if she's ever heard of psychometry.

"It is," she says, looking toward her collection of books. "But it could also be a symptom of something else."

"A symptom of a mental illness, you mean?"

"Some testing would need to be done to give us any concrete answers."

"What kind of testing?" I ask, imagining flashing machines and wires hooked up to my head.

"Just some questions to start." Her voice is as smooth as silk. "What do you say?"

"Let's get started," I say, scared to death of what I may learn. But even more scared of what could happen if I don't try.

17

A T LUNCH, I tell Kimmie and Wes about what happened the previous night with my dream, and how Aunt Alexia was already in my room when I woke up.

"So, that's definitely proof positive that it doesn't even matter if you take a hiatus from pottery," Wes says. "I mean, once again, if just dreaming about sculpting brings on all of this whacked-out stuff . . ."

"So why not dream about something else?" Kimmie asks.

"As if the answer were actually that easy," I say.

"Or maybe we're overthinking the dream," she continues. "Maybe it was just a bad nightmare. I mean, we've *all* had them. Like, I once had this dream where I was being gobbled up by Goldfish crackers. I swear, I *still* have to look the other way when venturing down the cracker aisle of the grocery store."

"And your next shock treatment appointment is *when?*" Wes asks, using a couple of pens as makeshift electrodes to zap the sides of his head.

"Except, that theory doesn't exactly explain why I've been hearing voices," I say, ignoring him. "It also doesn't explain how Aunt Alexia's been able to predict some of what I've been sensing."

"Do you think you and your aunt might actually be having premonitions about the same thing?" Wes asks.

"I guess it's possible," I say, chewing down the thought with a dehydrated kale chip my mom packed in my lunch.

"Well, that could be reassuring, at least," he says. "You could both be on the same supernatural team, working toward the same superhero goal."

"It *is* reassuring," I tell him. Or at least it should be. But in some way, the idea of sensing the same things that my aunt does—of being so completely connected to her—is also beyond terrifying.

"You know what would be hysterical?" Wes asks with a grin. "If your aunt was the only psychic one in this case, able to sense what's been happening in your dreams, your hallucinations, and your day-to-day encounters."

"Meaning that the hallucinations I've been having and the voices I've been experiencing haven't been premonitions after all?" In other words, I'm just crazy. "How is that even remotely funny, never mind hysterical?"

"Okay, so maybe *hysterical* isn't the right word," he says, retreating slightly. "But you have to admit, none of that stuff has happened to you. You haven't been on any creeptastic photo shoots lately, nor have you been harassed in the girls' locker room."

"And no one's called you ugly, stupid, or worthless," Kimmie adds.

"Not yet."

"So, there's still hope," Wes says, still trying to be funny.

I take a deep breath, reminding myself that Wes and Kimmie just don't get it. The voices, the visions, the instances of zoning out: they're all part of a premonition.

They simply have to be.

"I've had premonitions before," I remind them. "Why would now be any different? Plus, maybe this stuff won't *ever* concern or happen to me, but maybe it's happening to someone else—someone who needs my help."

Wes reaches out to touch my hand, clearly sensing how fragile I feel. "We're just playing devil's advocate. You know we're on your side, right?"

"Have you called that doctor?" Kimmie asks.

"I actually went to see Dr. Tylyn this morning. And the good news is that she doesn't think I'm schizophrenic."

"Did you tell her about what happens when you sculpt stuff?" Kimmie asks.

"Or when you just *dream* about sculpting stuff?" Wes adds.

"There wasn't enough time. She mostly just asked me a bunch of questions: if I have trouble keeping friends, if I think my friends might be conspiring against me, and if I've stopped caring about my appearance."

"And you answered yes to all three, I presume," Wes

says, giving my corduroy jeans a curious look.

I fake a laugh.

"So, this is *good* news," Kimmie says. She clinks her seltzer bottle against my container of flax-infused hemp milk (more of Mom's warped idea of lunch).

"It's *very* good," I say, proceeding to fill them in on the artwork that Aunt Alexia showed me last night.

"And you hadn't told your aunt about the hallucination you had in sculpture class?" Kimmie asks. "Or about the dream in which someone was taking your photo?"

I shake my head. "Plus, my aunt had obviously painted the picture of the camera long *before* I'd dreamt about it. I mean, that dream only happened last night."

"So how did she know?" Wes asks. "Just by touching the stuff around your room, or by being in your presence?"

"I guess the same way she knew about the 'there are two' phrase," I say, not even sure what that answer means.

"So, what happens now?" Wes asks.

"I don't know, but there's no point in my giving up pottery. I mean, if what I'm sensing comes through anyway . . ." I look away, remembering what Aunt Alexia said about ignoring my artistic impulses—how it only makes the voices louder. "You know what's really weird?"

"As if all of this hasn't been weird enough?" he says.

"I sort of remember a flash of light in the hallucination I had while in sculpture class," I continue. "The episode that took place in the locker room."

"Like a camera flash?" Kimmie asks.

"So the camera is definitely significant," Wes says.

"And any guesses about the sea glass or the whole skating theme?"

"Not a one," I tell them.

"I just don't get it," Kimmie says, folding her arms. "I mean, I thought things were getting back to normal."

"Do we know any skaters?" Wes asks. "Does this town even have a skating club?"

"We have a rink," I say. "And I should probably pay it a visit."

"Any chance that the camera might be significant because of Matt?" Wes asks, referring to the time my stalker ex-boyfriend was taking candid snapshots of me last fall. "Let's also not forget about the photo that Piper took," he says, reminded of Adam's crazed admirer from earlier this semester; she secretly took a photo of Adam and me kissing, and then sent said photo to Ben.

"Or the photo of me," Kimmie adds, seemingly eager to change the subject. She tells us about a photo that was posted online—a picture in which she's wearing an unflattering pair of underwear. "It appeared on an anonymous SocialLife page."

"Have you actually seen the photo?" I ask. "Or is it just lame-o hearsay?"

"Does this look like hearsay to you?" She chucks a wadded-up piece of paper across the table at me.

I unfold it to find the photo in question: a color shot of Kimmie wearing a superbaggy pair of floral cotton underwear. There's a boldfaced heading over the snapshot that reads: FREETOWN HIGH'S MOST DISASTROUS DRESSER.

"Period panties," she explains, covering her face with her bejeweled hands (she's got clunky cocktail rings adorning every finger). "It's not like I normally dress like that. Or like this," she says, gesturing to her outfit. She's wearing layers of brown and beige in hopes of camouflaging herself amid the school's morbidly oppressive colors.

"Who cares how you dress? This is clearly a violation," I squawk. "Whoever took this photo literally did it behind your back."

It's a sideways shot of Kimmie as she bends slightly forward. There's a tear by the hem of the aforementioned underwear, and the seams look ratty and frayed. As if all of that weren't mortifying enough, the photo also shows her pulling on a pair of gym shorts with one hand, while one finger of her other hand is lodged up inside her nose.

I take a closer look, almost unable to believe my eyes. On closer inspection (which includes squinting), I can see that Kimmie is actually scratching rather than picking.

But still.

"Not a fan of my work?" Wes jokes, pulling a camera from his bag—one that looks frighteningly similar to the one I dreamt about. He's taking photography as an elective this term.

"Please say you're bullshitting." Kimmie squeezes her eyes shut.

"You know I am." He puts the camera away. "Besides, how would I get into the girls' locker room?"

"Good point," I say. "The person who took this must've been female."

"Better point: all publicity is good publicity, right?" Wes winks.

"Tell me that when they've got a picture of your G-string-wearing self posted online for the whole world to see," Kimmie snaps.

"And that would be bad because . . . ?"

Kimmie gazes over her shoulder, where some boys are pretending to pick their noses. One of them has a pair of old and tattered gym shorts on over his jeans to suggest a pair of undies.

"I seriously hate this school," Kimmie says, turning back to face us.

"Did you report the picture to Snell?" I ask her.

"Yes, but the picture had already been taken down by the time I tried to show Principal *Smell*—as had the pictures of all the other ugly-underwear-wearing offenders."

"So, it could've been worse." Wes shrugs.

"Only if I were Danica Pete," she says, nodding toward the front of the lunch line, where Danica lingers, tray in hand, seemingly searching the tables for someone.

"Am I missing something?" I ask, wondering if Danica was one of the other ugly-underwear offenders.

"Besides the obvious?" Kimmie says, shaking her head at Danica's outfit du jour (a pair of pleated navy blue pants, a turtleneck sweater two sizes too big (probably to hide her slender figure), and brown ankle boots. "Though, I'll have to admit, I could've sworn I noticed a cute pair of vintage flats on her yesterday."

"They *were* vintage," Wes confirms. "I recognized the lining when she accidentally tripped going up the stairs and lost one."

"I'm still not following," I tell them.

"Am I to assume you haven't heard about the whole cheating incident that went down in Puke-o's class last week?" Wes asks me. (Puke-o is our name for Mr. Pulco, the calculus teacher.)

"It happened between Danica and a couple of the Candies," Kimmie explains.

The Candy Clique is a group of girls whose names all rhyme with "candy." There's Shandy, Mandy, Andy (short for Anderson, her last name), and Sandy (whose real name is Jen, but whose mother's maiden name is supposedly Sandy).

"For the record, I have no idea what either of you are talking about."

"Tell me, oh, dearest Chameleon," Wes says, "does the rock under which you live have heat and running water?"

"Apparently, a couple of the Candies wanted to cheat off Danica in precalc," Kimmie says, "and Danica told them where they could stick their slice of *pi*."

"But really loudly," Wes adds. "She announced it to the entire class, and then said that their brains, collectively, amounted to the size of a pea. People initially thought it was funny. Supposedly, even Puke-o was caught smirking."

"Good for her," I say, flashing back to an incident that happened in junior high, when I wish she'd been as brave.

And when I wish I'd been brave, too.

"But now the Candies are mad as hell, and the masses have joined their stampede." Kimmie points to the soccer table, where John Kenneally (who just happens to be dating Andy Candy) and his team of lemmings appear to be plotting something evil. They're eyeballing Danica and huddling in close.

"People are treating her like dog dung." Wes sighs. "Even more so than normal."

"Because no one can think for themselves," I say, watching the candy-colored clique (literally, since they're dressed in contrasting pastel colors today) stand up from their table, dump their trash in unison, and move toward the exit.

"You don't seriously expect any of the Candies to have an independent thought, do you?" Wes asks, stifling a laugh. "But I certainly like the way you think." He flashes his bright blue notebook, the cover of which reads: WES'S POETRY JOURNAL. "Sage wisdom such as yours is just one of the reasons why I'm considering letting you be the first reader of my poetry."

"Since when are you a poet?" Kimmie asks.

"Since I needed to find a way to express myself in a manner that doesn't include snapshots of period panties and joining my own candy-coated group."

"Well, just say the word," I tell him, taking a sip of hemp-milk heinousness. "I'd love to read your work." I continue to look around, checking for people's reactions as Danica makes her way across the cafeteria.

That's when I spot Ben, sitting with Alejandra Chavez.

"I'm almost surprised that Danica doesn't take her lunch in the library," Kimmie says. "I mean, it'd probably be a whole lot less painful."

I bite my lip, surprised that Ben isn't in the library, either, that he's elected to be among everybody else, risking the possibility of touch.

And of having me see him with Alejandra again.

Ironically, Danica stops at their table, but Alejandra seems less than excited to see her. She keeps her focus on Ben, practically ignoring the fact that Danica is standing there, looking completely desperate as she shuffles her feet and finally shrugs her shoulders.

"What's all that about?" Wes asks, slipping on a pair of tiny, round, wannabe John Lennon eyeglasses.

"The fact that Danica is standing at Ben's table?" Kimmie asks. "Or that Ben is out of seclusion and lunching with Freetown High's Most Beautiful Person?"

"Both," I whisper, relieved to see that Ben doesn't follow Alejandra's lead. He makes direct eye contact with Danica and nods toward an empty seat.

But Danica turns away and heads toward the soda machines.

"Paging Camelia Chameleon," Kimmie says, using an empty juice cup as a makeshift intercom to get my attention.

The next thing I know, Danica's down on the ground. It appears that John Kenneally has "accidentally" bumped into her, spilling the contents of her tray down the front of her sweater. John tries to stifle his laugh with a lame little cough, then scoots down as if to help wipe up the spill.

Finally, Mr. Muse comes over to see what the commotion is all about. He sticks around for a few moments, making sure that Danica and John have things under control, but then disappears inside the kitchen area, most likely to get his fill of swill.

With the coast now clear, John gets up and tosses a napkin at the glob of spaghetti on Danica's sweater. Meanwhile, kids are laughing and pointing. The soccer-team table cheers John on. "You rock!" someone shouts out.

I grab a stack of napkins and hurry over to help her. Danica's face is almost as red as the sauce stain on her sweater, and she is holding back tears.

"What are you doing?" she snaps, unwilling to trust me. And I know exactly why. She tucks a strand of her shoulder-length dark hair behind her ear, getting a smear of sauce on her cheek.

I gesture to her face with a napkin, then resume cleaning up the mess. It isn't long before I get the floor spic-and-span, but Danica still looks upset. "Let's go get you cleaned up," I say, giving a reassuring squeeze to her forearm.

Danica heads toward the bathroom. I start to follow her, but then I come to a sudden stop.

Ben is standing up at his table, staring straight at me.

It appears that Alejandra is asking him something— begging for him to sit back down, maybe. Her arms are waving, and there's a pleading look in her eyes.

But Ben remains focused on me.

My heart hammers, and my mouth turns dry. I'm tempted to stay and see what he wants. But instead I give him a little wave, and turn to follow Danica.

THE SIGN ON THE GIRLS' bathroom door says OUT OF ORDER, so Danica and I head across the hallway to the locker room. There aren't any ice skates in front of the door, as there were in my hallucination in the sculpture class, and the lights inside are all working. But still, just being in here gives me major déjà vu.

Danica stops short just a few steps inside.

We're not alone: voices come from behind the wall that separates us from the sink area. A moment later, there's a crash.

"Holy crap," one of the voices shouts. "I cannot believe you just did that."

At the same moment, Mandy Candy peeks out from behind the wall, into the locker area, bursting into laughter when she sees us. "Well, at least the cleanup crew is here."

"Let's go," Danica says.

"No way," I say, nodding toward the stain on the front of her sweater.

We wait for the Candy Clique to finish up whatever it is they're doing. After several moments of whispering and giggling, Shandy Candy finally emerges from behind the wall and stops right in front of Danica. Tube of lipstick in hand, she applies a fresh coat of flaming red. Mandy, Sandy, and Andy have all done the same—all of them wearing the exact same shade. "Since you did such a great job cleaning up in the cafeteria," Shandy says, getting right up in Danica's face, "and since you probably don't want us making English class a living hell for you later—"

"And you know we can," Mandy adds.

"We figured you'd be more than happy to tidy up our little mess," Shandy continues.

"We're not tidying up anything," I assure her.

But, surprisingly, Danica doesn't say anything. And Shandy couldn't be less interested in what I have to say.

When Danica still remains silent, Shandy puckers up her red lips and blows an air-kiss at her. Her Candy lemmings follow suit, blowing kisses in Danica's direction before they finally exit the locker room.

"Let's go," I say, leading Danica toward the sink area with barely five minutes left before the lunch bell is supposed to ring.

And that's when I see it.

One of the mirrors is broken. Shards of glass lie in a sink and on the floor. And there's writing across what remains of the mirror. In a smear of bright red lipstick, it says, DANICA PETE WAS HERE. SHE'S SO UGLY THAT THE MIRROR BROKE. P.S.: DIE ALREADY, WILL YOU?!

I shake my head and take a step back, rereading the message, and realizing that Aunt Alexia predicted part of it.

"What's wrong?" Danica asks.

My hand over my mouth, I look toward the windows, feeling the need for some air. But the glass has been covered up with a dark-blue tarp, as if maybe it's being replaced.

"Afraid that you'll be branded by association?" she continues. "Because even talking to me can have reputation-ruining repercussions."

"That's not it," I say, noticing a chunk of red lipstick in the sink as well (a piece that must've broken off). Water from the faucet pours over it, making the inside of the sink look red.

"Then, *what?*" she asks.

I close my eyes, feeling an array of emotions rush through me—the strongest one being relief. Relief because I predicted this, too. Because my dreams and hallucinations must indeed be part of something bigger—something extrasensory. And not merely part of something crazy.

"Well?" she says.

Instead of answering, I dampen a bunch of paper towels, topping them off with a couple of squirts of green gel soap from the dispenser.

"What are you doing?" Danica snaps.

"What does it look like? I'm trying to help you."

"Yes, but *why?*" She folds her arms, trying to appear tough, but I can see the dried-up tear tracks on her face, painted down over her freckled cheeks, almost like a mapping of sorts.

A mapping to track years of heartache.

"Look, I know I haven't given you any reason to trust me," I say, referring to what happened in junior high. "But I want to help you." I force some paper towels into her hand.

Danica starts to wipe a smudge off her cheek, then gazes into the sink full of broken glass.

"It's okay," I say, wishing she'd show me how she truly feels; but I know that's not her style.

Freshman year, she barely showed the slightest inkling of emotion when Steve Hartley thought it'd be funny to show up at the Halloween dance dressed in a "Danica costume," complete with an ugly brown bathrobe (to replicate the tan cardigan she always used to wear), pink tennis shoes, and a bowl over his head for hair. Appearing resilient to ridicule has always been her first line of defense.

"I could care less what those Candies say," she tells me. "What *anyone* says, for that matter."

"Well, they don't know what they're talking about," I say.

But I'm not so sure she's listening. She picks up one of the glass shards. It has a jagged hook at one end.

Exactly like what I sculpted.

She takes a step closer to the mirror. The cracked

surface makes her face appear distorted, cut up into shapes, reminding me of one of Picasso's paintings.

"We don't have to clean this up, you know," I tell her. "We can go to the office and turn them in."

"It's easier this way," she says, perhaps tired of taking their ridicule.

But before we can even start to clean, the door bursts open and the lights go out, leaving us in the dark. The tarp-covered windows block out any sunlight.

"Don't panic," I whisper, assuming we're not alone, that someone else in the room must've flicked off the switch.

The sound of giggling erupts from near the door.

I take a deep breath, trying to ease the palpitating of my heart, and thinking how things are finally making sense—the way Danica's constantly getting ridiculed, the way kids are always putting her down. And the voices inside my head—calling me ugly, telling me I'm stupid, and saying that I'd be better off dead.

There's no doubt in my mind.

Danica is the one in trouble.

*T*HE BELL RINGS before either of us can turn the lights back on, but luckily I remember the mini-flashlight tucked in my bag (a stocking stuffer from Dad). I use it as we clean up the shards of glass and the writing on the broken mirror, per Danica's insistence, and guide us out of the locker room.

"Better?" I say, once we're back out in the hallway. But unfortunately, Danica's sweater is still stained with red sauce. A bit of sauce remains on her cheek as well. "I'm sure if you go to the nurse's office, she'll let you clean yourself up."

"It's fine. I'm fine." She loops the straps of her backpack over her shoulders and turns away without saying good-bye.

I watch her walk down the hallway, disappearing among the sea of students. For just a moment I wonder if

I should try to catch up with her, but I'm not even sure what I'd say.

I try to explain the whole incident to Kimmie after school, but she's far too busy trying to digest the fact that what happened in sculpture class wasn't purely psychotic.

It was psychometric.

"Are you seriously telling me that all that moaning and clawing had a point?" she asks.

We're standing in the parking lot behind the school as a parade of cars screeches by to escape.

"It didn't just have a point," I say, disappointed that she doesn't seem more relieved by the news. "It had a purpose: to warn me."

"That Danica Pete is a loser?" she asks, picking at her chocolate brown nail polish. "Because—newsflash—*everybody* at this dumbass school already knows that."

"Since when do you call *anyone* a loser?"

"Since people like Davis Miller were born," she says, giving him the evil eye as he makes his way to his car. "Plus, I'm merely stating the general consensus. It's not like I have an actual opinion about the girl."

"Do you have an opinion about what I should do?"

"Are you sure you really want it?"

I nod, already suspecting what she's going to say.

Kimmie confirms those suspicions, telling me that I have enough to worry about in my own life without obsessing over Danica Pete, someone I barely ever talk to. "Have you even considered what people are going to be saying about you?" she asks. "Hanging out with Freetown High's Most Socially Unacceptable?"

"And high school social politics became a second thought for you *when?*" I nod toward her Tupperware-container-turned purse. "When did you start caring about what other people think? Plus, wasn't it you who said 'big whoop' to the fact that I've been labeled a full-fledged freak?"

"I'm just thinking about your own sanity here," she says. "I mean, are you seriously going to play Supergirl every time you have one of these psychometric episodes?"

"I don't know," I say, catching Davis Miller looking back at us.

"Plus, I hate to be the one to break it to you," Kimmie continues, "but Danica Pete is hardly capable of skating. If you haven't already noticed, the girl isn't exactly graceful on her feet. She can barely handle walking up a flight of stairs without tripping."

"Am I to assume the *D* stands for *Danica* today?" I ask, motioning toward her palm. "As in, *anti*-Danica?"

"Look, I'm not trying to put her down. I'm just trying to bring some common sense into this picture."

Common sense as opposed to extra sense.

"Did you report the Candies for the locker-room stunt, by the way?" she asks.

"Danica didn't want to. She said she didn't need any more Candy drama."

"That was intelligent," Kimmie says, in a lame attempt at sarcasm.

"It wasn't exactly my choice."

"Look." She sighs. "I know you want to do the right thing, and I *do* believe that you have some sort of extraterrestrial gift."

"Extrasensory," I say, correcting her. "It's not like I'm an alien."

"Right," she says, rolling her eyes at the mistake. "But you have to consider what's right for yourself as well."

"I *have* considered it. And just because I'm not friends with Danica Pete doesn't mean that she deserves to die."

"Who said anything about dying? The girl needs help, so why not get her some? Talk to a teacher, tell Ms. Beady. . . ."

"Tell them *what*?" I ask. "About my premonitions? I owe it to Danica to be involved, to see this through, to try and help her."

"You *owe* it to her?" Kimmie's voice rises. "Why? Did Danica rescue you from a burning building that I don't know about?"

"I just do, okay?" I say, too ashamed to tell her about what happened in junior high.

"Well, maybe I just have to do what's best for me as well," she says.

"What's that supposed to mean?"

"Look," Kimmie says, turning away slightly so I can't see her face—how emotional she's getting just talking about all of this. "You're my best friend."

I reach out to touch her shoulder, but she pulls away. "You're my best friend, too," I tell her.

"Then let's keep it that way."

"What do you mean?"

"I mean, don't you think you've been through enough? Your aunt wasn't able to handle all this psychometric stuff. What makes you think that you can?"

I want to assure her that everything will be fine, but I end up remaining silent, because I honestly don't know if it will.

Dear Jill,

It was only five minutes past the hour, and already you were pacing in front of the window of the coffee shop, worried that I might not show up.

Does it please you to know that I'd been sitting outside your shop for more than an hour, with the engine cut and the lights turned off?

But you had no idea I was even there. No idea that I'd been watching you check your reflection in the handheld mirror you kept stashed beneath the counter. That I'd seen you braid and unbraid your hair at least five times, and reapply that silly lip gloss.

If only you'd known that it wasn't solely your looks that I found attractive, but also your solitude, your uniqueness, your earnest efforts, and your desire to be understood.

I wanted to understand you. I was pretty sure I already did. I couldn't wait to find out.

. . .

Dear Jack:

I remember the stabbing sensation that pressed into my gut because you still hadn't shown up, and it was already twelve past nine. I watched the clock, unable to stop thinking about the perfect timing of things: not only had you known that I had to work that night, but you'd picked nine o'clock for a meeting time. My shift ended at 8:30, and it normally took me thirty minutes to cash out and clean up.

You obviously had known that somehow— obviously had taken note of my work schedule, when my shifts started, and when I got out. I have to admit: the thought of someone like you taking so much interest in someone like me was beyond exciting.

Still, I remember holding my breath as the seconds ticked away, doing my best to focus on how much happier I'd been since you started coming around. As cliché as it may sound, you gave me a purpose for getting out of bed in the morning, when only weeks before it'd seemed pointless.

When Carl noticed I was still lingering, he asked if I needed a ride home, saying he was giving Dee a ride anyway. But I shook my head, unwilling to give up on you just yet. And so I went to touch the piece of sea glass around my neck in an effort to reassure myself.

But all I felt was panic, because I didn't feel the stone right away. Was it still there? Had it caught on something? Why did it seem that the cord of the necklace was so much longer than I remembered?

That's how wrapped around your finger I already was.

Finally, I found the stone, dangling right over my heart. At the same moment, I found you. You were sitting on the bench in front of Muster's Bakery, just as you'd said you would be.

. . .

20

*A*FTER KIMMIE LEAVES, I spot Ben. He's standing by a group of pine trees—what the Tree Huggers Society planted this past fall in an attempt to create a sanctuary of sorts (even though it's located just to the right of the parking lot, where it's privy to stuff like car fumes, screeching tires, and cigarette smoke).

Ben waves when he sees that I've noticed him, and I make my way over, feeling like I've just been punched.

"Hey," he says, smiling at first. But his smile fades when he sees me up close—when he notices how troubled I must look.

He leads me into the circle of trees and gestures for me to sit on one of the five granite-slab benches that together make a pentagon. "Sip?" he asks, offering me some of his iced black coffee.

"No, thanks," I say, wondering when he got it. The

cup is nearly full, from the Press & Grind.

"I had a free last block," he says, as though reading my mind.

"And you came back here because . . . ?"

"Because I really wanted to talk to you." He sits down beside me, and his thigh accidentally bumps against my knee. He notices and scoots away on the bench. "Care to tell me about what's going on?"

"Not really," I say, staring at the ground, trying to appear aloof.

"Do you honestly expect me to believe that?"

I shrug and peer over my shoulder, through the trees, wondering where Kimmie has gone off to, and if I should stop by her house on the way home.

Ben ventures to touch my forearm, forcing me back into the moment. "Just because we're not seeing each other doesn't mean we're not friends, right? We can still talk about stuff."

"It's too hard," I tell him, feeling more friendless than ever before. I mean, being his friend, opening up, having him be one of the only people who can somewhat understand what I'm going through, and then seeing him with Alejandra . . . "I should go."

"You've been having more visions, haven't you?"

I pull my arm away from his touch, wondering if that's how he knows, or if he sensed it near my locker the other day.

"Talk to me, Camelia. You're not alone."

I press my eyes shut, remembering what Kimmie

said—how this probably isn't the best time to stop all communication with Ben. "I've also been hearing voices," I say, finally. "And so I've tried to avoid sculpting—like how you tried to avoid touch—but that doesn't seem to work."

"No," he says, looking down at his hands, just a finger's length now from my knee. "It definitely doesn't."

"And so, what's a psychometric girl to do?" I fake a smile and meet his eyes, choosing to keep things light.

But Ben's face remains serious. "How can I help you?"

I shake my head, knowing he can't—that what's going on inside my head has nothing to do with him. "Don't worry about it. I think I'm just feeling really stressed right now."

"So, then let me feel it, too," he says.

"What do you mean?" I ask, completely confused.

Ben extends his hands to me, as if silently asking me to weave my fingers through his. "I mean, let me feel whatever it is you're going through."

I gaze into his dark gray eyes, almost forgetting that we're no longer together. My chest tightens until I can barely breathe, and a tiny gasp escapes my throat.

"Will you let me?" he asks, his hands still extended. There's a pleading look in his eyes, as if he truly wants me to touch him.

I bite my lip, wondering if what he's proposing is remotely possible—or if I even want it to be. Do I want to open up to him? Wouldn't it be a whole lot smarter to keep all personal business under wraps in an effort to protect my heart?

I rack my brain for something rational to say—some explanation as to why this isn't a good idea. But before I can, Ben reaches out to touch the side of my face. I open my mouth to tell him to stop, but no words come out.

Because deep down, I want him to feel what I'm feeling, too.

His eyes locked on mine, he slides his fingers down my cheek.

"Ben," I whisper, knowing that I should go.

But his touch compels me to stay.

Still looking into my eyes, he peels off my jacket and moves his hands up the length of my arms, beneath the sleeves, causing my insides to tremble and whir.

"Do you sense anything?" I ask him. My whole body feels suddenly swollen.

Instead of answering, Ben moves his fingers along my neck, sending tingles straight down my spine. I tilt my head back, imagining him drawing out all of my secrets, until I'm completely exposed.

After a few moments, I look at him again. His eyes are closed, and his forehead is slightly furrowed, as if he can indeed read my thoughts.

"Ben?" I ask, noticing that his neck is splotched. I start to pull away, but he tightens his grip. His fingers press into my throat, and I let out a splutter.

Ben jumps and drops his hands.

"I'm fine," I tell him. "You didn't hurt me." I rub the spot on my neck, feeling a slight sting.

Ben gets up from the bench, taking a couple of deep

breaths to regain his composure. "I'm sorry," he tells me, over and over again.

He seems almost as disappointed as I am.

"It's just that I thought I could handle this." He looks at me, his lips parted. His eyes look tired and red.

"What did you sense?" I ask, eager for the answer.

"What's your connection to Danica Pete?"

"Nothing," I say, wondering if he knows it's a lie—if he can sense the guilt I still carry, four years later. "And what's *your* connection to her?"

"No connection," he says, a little too quickly—like he's not being honest either.

"I saw her approach your lunch table today," I tell him. "Why are you still keeping secrets from me?"

"I'm just trying to protect you."

"Like the last time . . . when I was trying to help Adam?" I look away, thinking about how secretive he'd been—and how that secrecy helped drive us apart.

Still, he doesn't comment.

"Are you and Alejandra seeing each other?" I ask, before I can think better of it.

Ben's eyes search my face, landing on my lips. "Are you and Adam seeing each other?"

"Is there a reason why we shouldn't be?"

He swallows hard. I watch the motion in his neck. And for five amazing seconds I think he's going to give me a big long list of reasons, the top of which would include the fact that he wants me all to himself. But instead he simply shakes his head and tells me there's no reason at all.

21

I LEAVE BEN IN THE Tree Huggers' sanctuary, feeling even worse than I did before. Ben feels worse, too; it's obvious from his posture—his elbows resting on his knees, his hands combing through his hair, and his eyes focused on the ground—making me think that maybe we're just not good for one another.

I head out to the parking lot in search of Wes's car, in the hope that he might still be around, but it seems he's already left. On a whim, I catch the Number 42 bus across the street, feeling somewhat brave after opening up to Ben. Brave because the Number 42 bus takes me to Mill House Park, which is right near Danica's house.

I haven't actually been to her house before—not to visit her, anyway. But four years ago, in junior high, a bunch of people went down to Mill House Park to hang out. Surprisingly, I was included in the group, but it was pretty much by default. I'd had soccer practice that afternoon with Rhiannon (a.k.a. Randy) Lester, one of the original Candy girls. Our coach had to bolt early for an unexpected emergency, and though most of the other teammates got picked up soon after, Randy and I were left to wait.

But we weren't alone.

Randy's entourage of Candies were there (most of whom had already graduated), not to mention her boyfriend, Finn Mulligan. As horrible as it is to admit now, it felt kind of good to be included in their group. But as I watched Finn climb the steps of the swirly slide, with an evil grin on his face, and a box of some sort in his arms, I knew that trouble was imminent.

It took me a moment to realize that he was carrying a crate of avocados, straight from the store.

Once he got to the platform at the top, he took one of the avocados out to show us, and squeezed it so we could see the overripe green guts ooze.

Randy and the Candies were laughing and cheering, all of them in the know as to what he was up to. Meanwhile, I remained somewhat oblivious, merely reveling in the fact that they were allowing me to be there with them.

Finn turned toward the house directly behind the slide, just beyond a chain-link fence. "Hey, Pete," he called out at least a dozen times, until Danica finally appeared at the sliding glass doors. Finn waved when he spotted her, acting excited to see her there.

I almost didn't recognize her at first. She was wearing a towel-turban that covered her hair, a thick terry cloth robe that made her look much bigger than she actually was, and her face was red from the shower. She waved back, but it wasn't with the same excitement Finn had shown. There was a confused expression on her face, especially when Finn motioned for her to open the door.

I shook my head, hoping that she wouldn't, wishing that she would just look at me and see that I was silently telling her no.

But instead she did just as Finn said, most likely swept up in all the attention, and took a step out onto the balcony.

"Are you feeling a little green?" he shouted out.

She took another step, apparently unable to hear him. A second later, Finn chucked one of the rotten avocados at her. It exploded against the door ledge, and green ooze pelted her in the face.

"I'll bet you're feeling green now!" he shouted.

Still she didn't move. And so three more avocados came flying at her—hitting one of her ears, splattering against her shoulder, and then dripping down the side of the house.

Finn was laughing, the Candies were begging to have a turn at it, and I was left feeling guilty for just standing there. And watching it all.

Finally, Danica went back inside the house. She tried to close the door, but it seemed to be stuck. Meanwhile, more avocados hit her—one of them smack against the top of her head.

After a few moments, she vanished from the door, but

Finn and the others persisted in throwing the remaining avocados—what had to have been a good twenty or so. Only now, they went soaring into what I guessed was her bedroom (I could see part of a bed and dresser in the background).

I wonder whether Finn and the Candies truly felt good about it all, or whether the image of her crying, with avocado splattered over her face, still haunts them today—the way that the memory of just standing there and doing nothing still haunts me.

I move around to the front of Danica's house, feeling my pulse race. Standing at the end of the walkway, I can tell that her house used to be nice: three stories, windows galore, and an entryway with columns. But on closer look, you can see that the paint is peeling, the shrubs are overgrown, and the shutters are broken and falling off.

I take a couple of steps toward the door with the sudden sensation that I'm being watched. I search the windows, wondering if Danica might be spying on me as I procrastinate here. But I don't see her anywhere. Nor do I spot her parents or any siblings. I look out at the street, noticing a man carrying groceries into his house, as well as a car parked about halfway down the block.

I focus hard on the car: a black four-door sedan. The motor's running and the windows are tinted, but I can't quite tell if there's anyone inside. I move back toward the sidewalk, pretending to have dropped something, in an effort to get a better look.

I can almost see the silhouette of someone at the steering wheel. At the same moment, the car backs up. The driver puts the car in reverse, backs into a driveway to change direction, and then speeds away.

"Um, hello," a voice says, coming from just behind me. "Care to tell me what you're doing here?" I turn to look, startled to find Danica there. She's standing on her doorstep with a backpack slung over her shoulder, seeming to be on her way out.

"Hi," I say, trying my best smile.

Danica's changed into a pair of pair of sweats, no longer in her spaghetti-stained clothes.

"How did you know where I live?" she asks.

I open my mouth, ready to make something up, surprised that she doesn't automatically flash back to the image of me from her balcony four years ago, just standing there, doing nothing.

But at the same moment, I spot it.

Around her neck, fastened with a black leather string: a piece of sea glass.

Pale blue and diamond-shaped, it's just like the one my aunt painted. "Where did you get that?" I ask, without even thinking.

It takes her a moment to figure out that I'm referring to the necklace. She touches the thick glass piece, about the size of a silver dollar. "Why do you care?"

I move closer to look, but she's covering the piece with her hand now, loosening the clasp so that it hangs further down on her chest.

"It's just that I've seen it before," I explain. "Or at least one that looks a lot like it."

"You've *never* seen it. It was found on the beach."

"Found by whom?" I ask.

"What are you even doing here?" she asks again; her tone is both irritated and defensive.

"I'm worried about you," I say, deciding to be honest. "I didn't like what happened in the cafeteria today. And I definitely didn't like what the Candies wrote in the locker room."

"Since when does that sort of thing bother you?" she asks, folding her arms.

"Look, I'm just trying to do the right thing here."

"Yes, but *why?*"

I look away, remembering how in the seventh grade, Chelsea Maloff dropped a pocketful of crabgrass onto Danica's lunch tray and dubbed her Horse Face. The following year, Jazz Minkum drew a picture of a monster in art class. When Ms. DiPietro asked him what his inspiration was, he said, "Danica," and everybody laughed.

In neither of those incidents was I one of the people cheering, or laughing, or egging the instigator on. But, as in the incident in the park with Finn, I didn't do anything to stop what was happening, either.

And so Danica has no real reason to trust me.

"I think you might be in trouble," I tell her, feeling my insides shake.

"What are you talking about?" She takes a step closer. "And why do you care?"

"Because I'm trying to be a friend," I say, knowing how awkward the answer sounds; but it's precisely how I feel.

"I know who my real friends are," she scoffs. "And obviously you're not one of them." She turns on her heel and takes off down the street, as if I'm no longer a second thought, and maybe I never was.

22

IMMIE DOESN'T CALL me all weekend, so I know she's still upset. The last time we went this long without talking, it was over summer vacation and she and her family had gone into the hills of East Bum Suck, Vermont, where her cell phone didn't get any reception.

By Sunday night, I try giving her a call. When she doesn't pick up even after my third attempt, I text her that I want to talk.

Unfortunately, she doesn't text back.

Monday morning, as usual, I wait for her by my locker, where we always meet before homeroom. As expected, she doesn't come by.

Somehow, I manage to get through my next four classes. Somehow, I manage to beat Wes to the cafeteria (so I'll have some time alone with Kimmie), even though my last class takes place on the opposite side of the building.

Kimmie is sitting at our usual table in the cafeteria. I hurry over, taking a seat across from her. "We need to talk," I tell her, all out of breath.

"About what?" she asks, as if she couldn't possibly have a clue. Still, her demeanor says otherwise: shoulders stiff, body angled away from me, and no eye contact.

"Did you get my text last night?"

Instead of answering, she waves Wes over, lighting up at the sight of him—at the fact, perhaps, that she no longer has to be alone at the table with me.

While Wes quizzes her for a Spanish test, I swallow what's left of my chick-un sandwich and do my best not to cry.

After school, Mom picks me up, and there's a brief exchange of nothingness.

"How was school?"

"Fine. How was work?"

"Not bad. Did you enjoy the chick-un sandwich?"

"It was okay."

Mom pushes the play button on her CD player to resume listening to her daily inspirations. Dr. Wayne Dyer's voice comes out of the speakers, telling her how to change her life.

If only I could change mine.

Finally we arrive at Dr. Tylyn's office for my much-needed appointment, and Mom pushes the pause button. "How do you like this Tylyn woman? Do you feel like she's helping you?"

"I feel like she *can* help me," I say, hoping it's the truth.

"That's good," she says, relaxing in her seat, failing to ask me anything else, even when I wait a full five seconds. It's as if she's finally resigned to letting go—to letting someone else ask all the tough questions. But not even Kimmie is asking them anymore.

"I'll be back in two hours," she says.

Two hours: the length of time that Dr. Tylyn recommended we'd meet.

I hurry inside the main campus building and up the stairs, two at a time. Dr. Tylyn is already in her office when I arrive.

"How are you doing today?" she asks, turning away from her computer. The voodoo doll has graduated from her chair to the top of her desk. Without waiting for my answer, she gets up to light a stick of incense, then joins me on the sofa with her tea. "I'd like to start this session by talking about the real reason you've come to see me."

The *real reason*? "I'm here because Ms. Beady said I needed a therapist."

"Well, I think there's more to it," she says, staring straight at me.

I wriggle in my seat, unsure of how to respond.

"I'm a firm believer that people create their own reality," she continues. "You *wanted* to come see me. It was a conscious choice that you made."

"Meaning I made all of this happen?" I ask. "The hallucinations? The voices? The instances when I've felt like I'm literally coming apart at the seams?"

"No, but I *do* believe that some part of you—subconsciously—chose to bring those voices to a head at a specifically opportune time, so that you'd require some sort of intervention."

"Except I wouldn't exactly call freaking out in the middle of art class an opportune time," I tell her.

"Why not? It got you here, didn't it?" she says. "Let's face it; our brain protects us in so many ways. Perhaps yours was leading you to help."

"Maybe." I shrug, wondering if she might be right.

"So, what's the real reason you're here?" she asks again.

I sit on my hands to keep from fidgeting, surprised at how good she is at getting to the truth. We spend the next several minutes talking about my aunt—how I found her diary, how she's been in and out of mental hospitals, and how I know she has the power of psychometry.

"Is that what you think you have, too?" she asks, not showing even a hint of alarm.

I nod and tell her about Ben, about how he used his power to save my life, and about how I've been able to predict the future, too. "But through my pottery," I explain. "Through sculpting, or even just dreaming about sculpting . . . sort of like how my aunt is able to predict stuff with her paintings."

"But unlike you, Ben has never questioned his own sanity," she points out. "Why do you think that is?"

"Maybe because he doesn't hear voices? Because he doesn't have an aunt who's tried to kill herself a bunch of times?"

"Your aunt isn't you," she says.

"Yes, but sometimes history repeats itself."

"It doesn't always have to—at least, not in your case. Sometimes history repeats itself because people follow patterns that they didn't create."

"I didn't choose to hear these voices," I assure her.

"No, you didn't," she agrees. "But how you deal with the voices *is* your choice—at least, it is for now."

"Meaning . . . ?"

"Meaning, you need to create your own patterns. You need to give yourself a chance."

"Isn't that why I'm here?"

"I hope so," she says, leaning forward over her notes. "You chose to find me, after all . . . and that's a big step in the right direction."

I take a deep breath, focusing on the idea of choice. I know that it was Ben's choice to stop punishing himself for his past, to try and start anew, which is why he moved to Freetown.

"What will *you* choose?" Dr. Tylyn asks me.

If only I had the answer.

23

*B*Y THE TIME I LEAVE Dr. Tylyn's office, my head is absolutely spinning. I start down the hallway toward the exit, noticing that Hayden's night classes are already in full swing; most of the classrooms are packed with students. I'm just about to head down the stairs when I hear a male voice call out my name.

I turn to look, thinking it's Ben, feeling my heart start to beat at quadruple its normal speed.

But it's Adam.

"What are you doing here?" I ask him.

He's sitting on a chair outside the dean's office, partly blocked by a cleaning cart. "Well, last I checked, I was kind of a student here." He smiles, standing up to greet me.

"Are you taking night classes?" I look toward the chair for a bag or some books, but it appears he's empty-handed. "You're posing tonight?" I guess.

He shakes his head, suddenly appearing nervous. He tucks the tips of his fingers into the pockets of his jeans, but then ends up folding his arms. "I was actually waiting for you," he explains.

"You were?" I ask, completely confused. I gaze back toward Dr. Tylyn's office, wondering how he could possibly have known that I had an appointment.

"I was picking up my check from Dwayne when I saw you go in," he explains.

"Two *hours* ago." I look at my watch.

"I didn't know how long you were going to be, so I decided to wait. After about an hour or so, I told myself to leave, but then I'd already been waiting so long it would've been stupid to give up. Anyway, here I am." He smiles again. "But, fear not, I had company." He pulls his cell phone from his pocket and shows me the screen, where he's got a game of solitaire in progress. "I also raided the candy machine a couple of times." He reaches into his jacket for a box of Jujyfruits. "Your favorite, right?" He hands me the box.

"How did you know?" I ask, dumbfounded that he would've waited so long, that he *did* wait so long.

Just for me.

"I'm cool that way." He winks. "So, what do you say? Can I give you a ride home? Can I buy you a late-night dinner? A walk to your car? A coffee to fulfill your all-night cramming needs? An ice cream at the nearest dairy establishment?"

"That's quite a list of choices."

"I'll take whatever I can get."

"Well, in that case," I say, reaching for my phone to dial my mom, "I'll see what I can do."

Unfortunately, Mom doesn't pick up; she probably still has her cell phone set to silent mode because of yoga class (a fairly regular occurrence). Adam and I exit Hayden's main campus building, and I spot her, already parked and waiting by the curb.

She rolls the passenger-side window down when she sees Adam and me approach. "It's good to see you," she tells him.

Adam returns the sentiment, saying that he's missed chatting about soccer with my dad, and that he was recently telling someone about my mom's Elvis-inspired rawkin' raw-sagna.

But, before they can continue to bond, I interrupt this program to mention that Adam's offered to take me out for a quick bite.

"*Now?*" Mom asks.

"If it wouldn't be a problem," Adam says. "And I'd be happy to bring Camelia home afterward."

"It'll only be an hour or so," I assure them both.

Mom doesn't argue, perhaps glad to see me doing something "normal." Instead, she reminds me that it's a school night, and that I need to be home by ten. I hop into Adam's Bronco, and he takes us to a 1950s-type diner. There's nothing rawkin' about this place. It's my mother's worst nightmare come true, complete with cheddar fries, strawberry milkshakes, and old-fashioned burgers—all of which is served right to your car window by a server on roller skates.

I take a sip of my shake. "You're just like my dad, you know that?"

"Just what every guy wants to hear."

"I mean that you always know the best places to eat. It's a compliment." I smile.

"Are you sure?" He smiles back. "Because I kind of thought that telling a guy he has a really nice butt, or saying how jacked his arms are, was far more complimentary . . . especially after seeing him naked."

"Fishing for compliments, are we?"

"More like begging for them."

"Well, in that case, you never fail to make me laugh."

"The kiss of death." He lets out an exaggerated sigh. "And now for the burning question."

"I'm almost afraid to know."

"What's with you and a two-hour meeting with Tylyn?"

"Oh, that," I say, chewing the question down with a fry.

"I hope it's not because of me," he continues, "because of all the torment I put you through."

"It's actually because of me," I confess. "I'm going through some pretty tough stuff right now."

"Anything I can help you with?"

I shake my head, at first assuming that I shouldn't tell him. But on second thought, I change my mind, because Adam and I have been through a lot together these past few months. He might actually be able to understand.

"I have reason to believe that a girl in my school is in danger," I say.

"You have reason to believe?"

"I'm sure of it." I take a nervous bite of my burger.

"Sort of like the way you knew that I was in danger?"

I hurry to finish what's left in my mouth, ready to object—to make up yet another excuse as to why I suspected something was going wrong with him two months ago—but instead I decide to be honest. "Can you keep a secret?" I ask him.

"Sure." He sets his milkshake down, sensing how serious this is.

"Okay, well, this is going to sound a little nuts," I begin. "But I've been having premonitions."

"Premonitions . . . as in, crystal-ball, tarot-card, scrying-mirror stuff?" he asks, surprisingly up on his New Age lingo.

"Right, but without the cards, the ball, or the mirror."

"Commando," he says, once again getting me to laugh.

"Not exactly," I say, still feeling a smile on my face. "Images about the future come to me when I'm doing my art . . . when I'm sculpting, I mean."

"And have those images ever included a certain tall, dark, and incredibly good-looking college guy whose name just happens to rhyme with *madam*, being victimized by a fellow classmate who is sending him creepy crossword puzzles that spell out clues?"

"How come you don't sound so surprised?" I ask.

155

"Because I'm not," he confesses, looking down at his shake. "I always knew there was something very different about you."

"Definitely different," I say, feeling like a virtual alien.

I spend the next several minutes giving him the CliffsNotes version of what happens whenever I sculpt something—minus the voices, the instances of zoning out, and any info about Ben or my aunt.

"Seriously?" he asks, looking at me like maybe I *am* from out of this world.

"I know," I say, feeling completely self-conscious. "Which is why I've become a Tylyn Project. Hence the two-hour appointment. I've been working on a sculpture of a figure skater, and all this stuff's been happening ever since."

"That must be pretty intense," he says. "I mean, to be able to know what's going to happen before it actually does. . . . That's obviously why you contacted me after everything I'd put you through," he says.

I nod, unable to deny the fact that I had an ulterior motive when I first called him this past winter, and that it wasn't of the love-stricken kind.

Adam sits back in his seat looking off into the night. The light from the moon illuminates the tension in his jaw. "And all along I thought it was because you were missing me."

"I did miss you."

"But you were scared for me. You were doing the right thing. That's the real reason you reached out to me."

"Does it even matter?" I ask, wondering if maybe I should've kept my secret.

But Adam finally turns to me again and tells me that it doesn't at all. "What matters is that you cared enough to want to help me despite what an absolute tool I'd been."

"Well, you've come a long way since then."

"I'm glad you think so," he says, glancing at my salty lips. "But now *I* want to help *you*."

"What do you mean?"

"How can I help you with this girl who's in trouble?"

"Danica."

"Is she a friend of yours?"

"Not really."

"Then why are you having premonitions about her? You realize how sci-fi that sounds, don't you?" He smirks.

"I guess I'm a sci-fi kind of girl."

"You're a magical kind of girl," he says; his face gets serious again. "At the risk of sounding cheesy, that is."

"I like cheese," I say, feeling my cheeks go pink. I look down at the mound of cheddar fries, trying to find a distraction.

Adam reaches out to take my hand, clearly sensing the heat between us. His fingers weave through mine, which makes me think of Ben.

I do my best to block out my Ben-thoughts by focusing on how thoughtful Adam is, and how he's always so willing to tell me how he feels.

"Do you want to talk about Danica?" he asks me.

I shake my head, but not because I want to keep anything from him. "I'm just feeling really exhausted," I say. "Another time?"

"Definitely."

We spend several minutes just holding hands, snuggled together in his Bronco, not quite ready for the moment to be over. I gaze out of the fog-covered window, reminding myself of what Ben said the other day—that there's no reason I shouldn't be seeing Adam.

"I'd better get you home," Adam says, checking the dashboard clock. It's quarter to ten, and he promised to have me home by the hour. "I want to keep on your parents' good side. I have a feeling that we'll be seeing each other a whole lot more often. Can I call you tomorrow?"

I nod, wishing that we had more time. Still, Adam hurries to clean up our snacks and then puts the car in drive, leaving me hungry for more.

Dear Jill,

You were so nervous—even more than I was
used to—and it was making me nervous, too.
You may not believe this, but after only about
five minutes on the bench with you, I actually
considered calling the whole thing off. But
then I asked if you'd told your boss about us
meeting, and you shook your head and mumbled
that he thought a friend was picking you up.

There it was: already you were lying for
the sake of our relationship. And so who was
I to cave under pressure?

I needed to fight for our relationship too.

I tried to boost your confidence with
compliments. I even bumped my knee against
yours as a way to soften you up. But you kept
fidgeting in your seat, looking over your
shoulder, and clenching your jaw

Do you remember how concerned I was, how I
kept asking you what was wrong? I wondered if
part of your anxiety might've had something to
do with the girl who'd been scoping you out.
I'd spotted her a couple times: at your house
and at your work. I hadn't liked the looks of
her, and I suspected the feeling was mutual.

"Well?" I asked.

You may not want to hear this, but my
distaste for your parents was growing stronger
by the moment. I blamed them for your
inability to see what was truly best for you.
And I vowed to make them pay.

. . .

Dear Jack:

You looked so nice, sitting on the bench in front of Muster's Bakery. The streetlamp shined right over you, making you look like one of those artful ads for designer jeans or musk cologne.

"I'm so glad you came," you said, standing as I approached. You saw that I was shivering, and took off your sweatshirt, wrapped it around my shoulders, and motioned for me to sit. The sweatshirt smelled sickly sweet, like rotted fruit, making my stomach churn. But still I didn't want to take it off.

You sat beside me, and your leg bumped against mine. "Sorry," you said. A smile crept across your lips, like maybe you weren't that sorry at all.

You looked older up close—at least 25, with wrinkles in the corners of your eyes, and a bit of stubble on your chin. I wondered if you knew I was only in high school and that being with me probably violated at least ten different laws. It was exciting to imagine that you did indeed know, but that you still didn't care, as if your desire to be with me trumped any risk.

"You're so pretty, you know that?" you said, catching me off guard. "I'm sorry, did I just say that out loud?"

I clenched my jaw, suddenly fearing the worst:

that someone would jump out from behind a bush, put an end to the moment by exposing the joke that it was.

"What's wrong?" you asked.

It was so much easier to talk to you on the computer, to fantasize about you at my leisure, and to watch you doing homework at the back of the coffee shop.

"Well?" you asked, still waiting for me to speak.

"It's just that no one's ever talked to me the way you do," I said. Before my mother had left, and before my sister had turned into a virtual stranger in our home, we'd had a running joke in my family that I'd been abandoned on my parents' doorstep at birth, because I was nothing like them—not half as confident and nowhere near as talented.

"Nobody ever talks to you like what?" You reached out to stroke the side of my face. Your fingers were warm but rough.

A stray tear trickled down my cheek. You wiped it with your thumb, saying that you couldn't possibly imagine what I was talking about. "I'd love to get to spend more time with you," you said.

I wanted to ask you why, but I couldn't, because more tears dripped down my face. "I'm sorry," I whispered, feeling like such a freak, disappointed to be letting you down.

"Don't be. Just let me be here for you." You

slipped an arm around my shoulders. The embrace was awkward and stiff. Like me.

"Just let me be your friend," you said.

I continued to let you hold me, even though my gut told me to pull away.

. . .

24

$\mathcal{J}$N MY ROOM, I change into a pair of sweats and then lie back on my bed. My bedroom window is open a crack, and the cool March air filters into the room, making me feel more alive than I have in a long time, despite all the drama in my life.

I draw the covers up, still able to feel Adam's arms around me. I close my eyes, imagining him here beside me, and thinking how comforting it is to always know exactly what's on his mind.

A second later, my cell phone rings. I pick it up, hoping it's Kimmie and that she's feeling every bit as horrible as I am that we haven't talked.

But it's actually Ben.

"Is everything okay?" he asks as soon as I say hello.

I sit up in bed, suspicious of his seemingly perfect timing. "Why wouldn't it be?" I ask him.

"Just making sure. We kind of left things weird the other day," he says.

"Is that the only reason?"

"Should there be another?"

I look out my window, remembering the nights when he used to linger outside, waiting for me to come home. "You aren't outside my house, are you?" I ask, almost feeling paranoid. But the street looks fairly empty tonight. I don't see his motorcycle parked anywhere.

"Ben?" I say, when he doesn't answer. There's a tense silence on both ends of the line.

"I'm still here," he says. "And I still want to discuss the whole Danica issue."

"Yes, but that doesn't answer my question."

"First try answering mine: have you talked to Danica?"

I clutch my pillow, wondering if he might've followed me to her house the other day. "Yes, but we didn't really get too far."

"Will you call me after you've spoken to her again?"

"What do you know about her?" I ask him.

"Not so much more than you."

"Is there something that I should know?" I ask, fairly confident that he's lying, but still giving him one more chance to open up.

"Only that I'm trying to help you, so I'd appreciate it if you could keep me in the loop."

"Is that all?" I ask, tired of talking in circles and still suspecting that he might have some other reason for calling me.

"Isn't that enough, Chameleon?"

I continue to gaze out the window, surprised to hear him call me that, and curious to know if he might be trying to tell me something. I close my eyes again, picturing the chameleon tattoo on his upper thigh. He got it before he came to Freetown, before he ever met me. He'd recently touched his mother's wedding band—something that reminded him of soul mates—and then couldn't get the image of a chameleon out of his mind. And so he had it tattooed on his thigh, hoping its permanence might help him understand it more—might help him understand his own future soul mate more.

"Were you waiting for me to come home tonight?" I ask him.

"Would that be such a bad thing?"

"I'll take that as a yes," I say, my heart beating fast. I search the street for shadows, eager to find any trace of him.

"I'm just looking out for you," he explains.

"What for?" I ask. "I mean, you said it yourself: there's no reason why I shouldn't be seeing Adam."

"Yes, but there's no reason you *should* be seeing him, either."

"How about the fact that he's straight with me, that he doesn't play mind games, and that he tells me how he truly feels?"

"And how do *you* feel?" he asks. "How do you really feel spending time with him?"

"I should go," I say, unwilling to indulge his probing

165

for another second. I tell him good night and snap the phone shut.

At the same moment, there's a knock at my bedroom door. "Camelia?" Dad asks, stepping inside before I invite him in. He comes and sits at the foot of my bed. "How did things go today with the therapist?"

"They went well," I say, curious as to whether he heard any of my conversation with Ben.

"Are you sure? Because just say the word and we'll switch you to somebody more helpful."

"Dr. Tylyn *is* helpful. We've talked a lot about choices. And, I don't know, as obvious as it may sound, the idea of having choices over what could possibly happen in my future feels really empowering." More than any super-power could.

He glances at my night table, where I keep Aunt Alexia's journal tucked inside. "Do you feel like you can tell her things?"

"Yes," I say, surprised when I think about how much I've already told her. "She seems really knowledgeable about stuff."

"Well, that's good," Dad says. A smile crosses his lips, but I can tell there's something still on his mind. He keeps looking around my room, as though trying to find the answer to a question he has yet to ask.

"I think Dr. Tylyn might be a good fit for Aunt Alexia as well," I venture.

"Funny you should say that, because I did some asking around about the doctor. It seems she has an interest in the supernatural and metaphysical." He studies my face, seemingly eager for some sort of reaction.

"And?" I ask, eager for his reaction, too.

"And I'm almost surprised that Ms. Beady would recommend someone like that."

"Do you believe in supernatural powers?" I venture, feeling my lip shake.

Dad's eyes remain locked on mine. "I'm starting to," he says, in a voice much softer than usual.

The next thing I know, Mom barges into my room, breaking the moment to ask me about my time spent with Adam (rather than my time spent with Dr. Tylyn).

"It was fine," I tell her.

"Just *fine*?" she asks, fishing for more details.

I bite my lip, disappointed that only minutes ago I was so excited about him, but that now, between her and Ben's probing, things are starting to feel a bit lackluster. "He's nice," I say, suddenly desperate to be alone.

"*Nice?*" Dad asks, getting up from my bed. "That's the kiss of death."

I feel myself smirk, knowing that Adam would've said the same—that he did in fact say the same when I told him how funny he was.

Finally, my parents wish me good night, perhaps sensing my longing for alone time. But they fail to even make eye contact with one another as they exit the room.

I click off my lamp and lie back in bed. The cool night air continues to filter in through the window, over my face.

But instead of enlivening me as it did before, it makes me ever more on edge.

I sit back up, wondering if I should pull the storm window closed. And that's when I hear it: the familiar rumble of Ben's motorcycle as it starts up, and then drives away in the distance.

25

*J*SPEND THE NEXT FEW DAYS trying to talk to Danica: before school, when she gets off the bus, in the library during my free blocks, and between classes whenever I spot her by her locker.

But not once during any of those times does she even breathe in my direction, let alone engage me in any conversation that involves more than a grunt in passing to acknowledge my existence.

Not so different from Kimmie.

Though Kimmie and I still sit together at lunch and in sculpture class, our conversations have been mostly superficial, centered around safe topics (those that don't include Danica, touch, or anything extrasensory).

I've continued to try to talk to her about the rift in our relationship, asking if we can get together, if I can come over to chat, if we can go split a peanut-butter barrel at Brain Freeze like we used to. "I'm sorry," I told her voice mail last night, devastated by the idea that she no longer cared—that she could so easily cut me out of her life. I slept with my phone clenched in my grip, hoping she'd call me back.

But, sadly, she never did.

And so I've decided to give her some space and focus my attention on Danica. By Thursday after school, I finally get Danica to talk.

She's sitting on one of the benches in front of the main building. I cross the lawn and stand right in front of her, waiting until she acknowledges me.

"You of all people should know there's a law against stalking," she says, barely looking up from her notebook.

"Are you planning to report me?" I ask.

"I'm thinking about it."

"Okay, but can you please just give me five minutes of your time first? I promise I won't bother you any longer than that."

"Five minutes," she says, glancing at her watch. "Then I have to go to work."

I sit down beside her and gaze out over the lawn, where the first signs of spring are breaking through the soil in the Tree Huggers' flower bed. Danica props her backpack between us, to block what she's writing, perhaps, and I notice an ad for vaginal itch cream stuck to the front pocket.

"So, what's all the fuss?" she asks.

"Like I said before, I'm trying to be a friend here."

"Yes, but why?"

"Look, I know I was there that day . . . at the park . . . with the Candies and the avocados . . ."

"Excuse me?" she asks, pretending to be confused. She looks away, and I rip the itch cream ad from her bag. "Am I really that much of a charity case?" she asks.

"Danica—no."

"It was actually a rhetorical question." She slams her notebook shut. "I've known the real answer for years now, but it's not like I even care."

"I need to ask you something," I tell her.

"Hence the reason you've been stalking me?"

"Do you have any enemies?"

"Another rhetorical question?" She nods toward the pack of Candies standing in front of the auditorium doors. All are wearing matching puffy pink jackets; they stare at us, making the *L*-for-Loser sign by holding their fingers up to their foreheads.

"I mean, *significant* enemies," I say to clarify. "Is there anyone you think might want to cause you harm?"

"I repeat: is that a rhetorical—"

"I'm being serious," I say, cutting her off.

"And so am I. I can't even remember the last time anyone's paid this much attention to me. And if you haven't already noticed, I sort of like it that way."

"Your parents must pay attention to you."

"Try to even find my parents." She stuffs her notebook into her bag.

"What do you mean?" I ask, wishing she'd take me back to her house, thinking that I may be able to find out more there. "Are they away? Are you staying by yourself?"

She zips her backpack, readying herself to leave. "Who wants to know?"

"Whose car was that in front of your house yesterday?"

"What car?" she asks, seemingly confused.

"When I came by your house, there was a car parked a few houses down the street. A black sedan with tinted windows . . ."

Danica stands up, clearly frustrated by all my questions. "I have to go," she says, tugging at her skirt; it drags on the ground, nearly catching under her shoes.

"There's something you're not telling me," I persist. "Are you seeing someone? Do you know whose car that was?"

"What is all this about?"

"I have reason to believe that you might be in danger." My pulse is absolutely racing.

But Danica seems less than startled. She looks back at the Candies, perhaps suspecting an ugly prank.

"Have you been getting any weird phone calls or texts lately? Is there anyone new in your life that you don't fully trust?"

"What is all this about?" she repeats.

"Let's just say that I heard something," I tell her, referring to the voices.

"From whom?"

I close my eyes, completely frustrated by how ridiculous the answer sounds inside my head, never mind how it will sound out loud. "I don't know," I tell her finally.

"And you know what *I* heard?" she asks, her tone much braver than before. "That Camelia Hammond is crazy—that she had some sort of maniacal attack in sculpture class."

"I'm trying to help you."

"Help yourself," she says, raising her voice. "Because, for the first time in a long time, I'm doing just fine on my own."

26

*A*T SCHOOL THE NEXT DAY, I see Danica bolt out the front exit, clearly on a mission. Just before homeroom, I made yet another attempt to talk with her, but she simply slammed her locker door and walked away while I was midsentence.

"Do I smell a scandal?" Wes asks, sneaking up behind me at the front of the building.

"You smell something, all right," I say, catching a whiff of his cologne, the scent of which reminds me of burnt apple pie.

"Details, please."

"Where's Kimmie?" I ask.

Wes shrugs. "I think she has some online design thing she's working on."

"Whatever. I know she's avoiding me."

"Funny, but she says that *you're* avoiding *her*. . . .

Something about you skipping out on sketching naked people together."

"Life drawing," I say, smacking the side of my head, having completely forgotten Dwayne's class last night. "Is she pissed?"

"About you blowing off class? I doubt it."

"And about my desire to help Danica?"

"Not pissed, just scared. There's a difference. It's all about psychology," he explains. "If she puts some space between the two of you, your relationship will weaken on its own, before it has the chance to change as a result of a) your untimely death (by either your own or someone else's doing), or b) your ending up in a padded room because of all the voices inside your head."

"She actually told you all this?"

"I have eyes," he says, crossing his own to be funny. "And the way I see it: you two need to talk. Haven't you noticed that the poor girl is desperately trying to stay in the Land of Denial with respect to your touch stuff?"

"I have," I say, remembering how she questioned whether the premonition I had in my basement studio was even significant, and how she also insisted that I stop doing pottery altogether.

"Bottom line," he says, "the girl loves you more than Lycra, but she needs to know you're not going to be sporting a straitjacket anytime soon."

"I miss her," I tell him, looking away, feeling my heart ache.

"I'll see what I can do, okay?"

I nod and let out a breath, trying to hold it together. A moment later, Danica crosses the front lawn, passing Tess Moon, the new transfer at school, who's rumored to be Debbie Marcus's cousin.

Debbie is the girl who told everyone she was being stalked, though nobody believed her. Instead, they blamed her "stalking" on practical jokes played by friends. But Debbie was convinced otherwise, thinking that Ben was the one who was after her. One night, on a walk home from a friend's house, paranoid that he might've been following her, she wasn't paying attention to where she was going and was struck by a car. The accident almost killed her.

When she came out of her coma two months later, even though Ben wasn't to blame, she made it her mission to see that he paid for her lost time. And so she tried to frame him for stalking me, in the hope that he would be forced to leave our school once and for all. Only, in the end, she was the one who was forced to leave.

"New blood," Wes says, nodding toward Tess. "Interested?"

"Maybe I should be. My dad said that if I don't start coming home with something soft and curvy, he's going to take away my car."

"Will a blow-up doll do? Or a really juicy pear?"

"Been there, tried that. I'm going to have to get serious."

"As in, finding a real girlfriend?"

"Or better yet, hire another one." He's talking about

last fall, when he hired Wendy, a struggling college student who worked part-time at the Pump & Munch, to pose as his main squeeze. "Less drama, much less complicated. Plus, believe it or not, it's actually a whole lot cheaper."

"Fewer rose bouquets to buy for screwing up?"

Wes doesn't answer. Instead he follows my gaze toward Danica. She's just crossed the street, headed for the bus stop. "So, I hear Danica Pete's the new VIQ?" he says.

"What's that?" I ask, scrunching up my face.

He rolls his eyes, frustrated at my failure to be fluent in Wes-speak. "Victim in Question."

"Oh, right," I say, finally noticing the red and black Where's Waldo scarf wrapped around his neck. "I think she's the one I've been having premonitions about."

"Fascinating," he says, tapping his teeth in thought. "How so?"

"Because I may have spotted Benny Boy studying with her in the library today. Coincidence? I think not." He reaches into his pocket for some licorice; only the licorice no longer has its packaging, so there's a bunch of lint stuck to the sides. "Something sweet?" he asks, offering me a stick.

"What do you mean by 'studying'?" I ask, forgoing his sickly sweet offer.

"I mean, they were doing that thing, you know, with books. . . ."

"Were they talking?"

"I don't know. Maybe a little. I wasn't exactly stalking." He winks.

I bite my lip, suspecting that Ben knows a whole lot more about Danica than he's actually letting on. "Danica's definitely in trouble," I whisper, thinking aloud.

"Then what are we waiting for?" Wes crams two licorice sticks into his mouth and grabs the keys to his car.

27

*D*ANICA IS JUST BOARDING the T-bus as Wes pulls out of the school parking lot, turning onto the main road to follow.

"You know where she's probably going, don't you?" Wes asks in a tone that tells me he does.

"How would I?" I ask, surprised at how sure of himself he seems.

He tsk-tsks at my obvious ignorance. "Still living under that rock, I take it?"

"So then, excavate me, will you? But don't take too long." I check the time on his dashboard clock. "I have to be to work in an hour."

"The excavation will have to wait," he says, switching lanes. "I have a bus to pursue and more licorice to eat. Plus, I like to see you suffer." He pulls a few more lint-covered sticks from his pocket and shoves them into his mouth.

A few minutes later, the bus pulls over in front of Landry's strip mall. Wes follows, finding a parallel spot with a fully fed meter.

"She works here," Wes says, nodding toward the Press & Grind.

"No way," I say, completely dumbfounded to think that in all the time I've been coming here I've never once noticed her.

"It's true. I was a wee bit shocked myself when I saw her carrying a tray full of brownies from the back room."

"So, it's a new job?"

"One would assume. I mean, let's face it, this place is practically my second home. I even noticed when they changed their brand of t-paper—to the sandpaper stuff, FYI—but you also never know. Maybe she only works in the back, prepping all the bakery stuff. Maybe that's why we've never seen her."

"Maybe," I say, more than eager to ask her about it.

"Hey, check it out," Wes says, pointing toward Ben's motorcycle, parked in the corner of the lot. "It looks like we're not the only fans of this fine establishment."

"What's he doing here?" I ask, knowing it must have something to do with Danica.

A couple of seconds later, the bus doors thwack open and Danica gets out, pausing a moment to tie her hair into a tiny pigtail and pull an apron from her bag. She fastens the apron around her waist and then makes her way inside the shop.

"Should we go in?" Wes asks.

I'm about to get out of the car when I notice a black sedan parked in front of Muster's Bakery—the same car that was parked a few houses away from Danica's on the day I paid her a visit.

"What's wrong?" Wes asks, turning to look.

"That car," I say, squinting hard, trying to see if I can make out anyone inside, though the tinted windows make it nearly impossible.

"Ford Taurus, late nineties. Not really my taste," Wes says, trying to be funny. "I prefer the kind of German engineering that only rich parents whose goal it is to try and make their dorky kids look cool would purchase." He grabs a rag to polish the Audi logo on his steering wheel.

"You know you're not a dork," I say, rolling my window down.

"Are you kidding? My dad reminds me of it at least once a day."

"Whoever's in that car has been following Danica," I say.

"And you know this because . . ."

"Because the car was parked outside her house the other day."

"Are you sure it's the same one?" he asks, ever the devil's advocate. "Because shitboxes like that are a dime a dozen around here."

"It's the same," I say, pretty positive that I'm right.

"And so maybe the driver lives in her neighborhood and happens to love coffee."

I stick my head out the window to get a better look.

The car's license plate is tilted forward, making it hard to read. "Any chance you could drive by so I can get a closer view?"

"Sure thing," Wes says, but just as he does, the Taurus moves away from the curb, out onto the street.

I tuck my head back inside Wes's car and scramble to close the window.

"So, if this guy's supposedly stalking the Stick—my code name for Danica, FYI—why does he take off just as soon as she arrives?" Wes puts his car in drive, makes a U-turn, and starts to follow the Taurus, four cars behind.

"I don't know." I shrug. "Maybe he wanted to see that she arrived at work safely. Maybe he forgot something at home and plans to come back here later."

"That's my vote," he says. "If it was purely about safety, he would've followed her right from school."

"Do you think this is a good idea?" I ask. We're only two cars behind the Taurus now. "Maybe we'd be better off talking to Danica inside the shop, or finding out what Ben's doing there."

"You can't be serious," Wes says, eating more licorice.

I shake my head, knowing he's right, but nervous just the same.

We follow the car for several miles, finally entering the town of Hayden, not far from the community college.

"What'd the odds be of this cretin living in the same apartment building as Adam?" Wes asks.

I feel my stomach churn, imagining that the driver may have noticed us behind him. There's only one measly street sweeper vehicle between our car and his now, and it seems we're heading into a seedier part of town. The streets are less congested. There's trash on the sidewalks, spilling out from Dumpsters and garbage cans. And a lot of the houses—aside from a string of brownstones and a curiously placed piano store—have been boarded up or fallen victim to tagging.

"Maybe we should turn around," I tell Wes.

"No way," he says. "I haven't had this much excitement since the season finale of *CSI*, 2009. . . . You know, when Grissom was still on the show . . ."

The street sweeper takes a turn down a dead-end road, and now we're directly behind the Taurus. I try to read the license plate. But not only is the plate tilted forward, there's a shadow box covering it, making the numbers even harder to decipher.

A moment later, my cell phone rings in my pocket. I check the ID, seeing that it's my mom. I switch the phone to silent mode, just as Wes takes a detour down a dark alley.

"What are you doing? We're going to lose him!" I shout.

"That's what you think." Wes turns down another alley, surprisingly confident in our surroundings. He gets about halfway through, then pulls over to the side. A moment later, the car in question drives past our street.

"How did you do that?" I ask, impressed by his maneuvering.

Wes hesitates before driving to the end of the alleyway.

He takes a turn to resume following him again. The Taurus is a good ten houses in front of us now, crossing over a set of train tracks.

The next thing I know, the road begins to close behind the Taurus, signaling that the train is on its way. Wes steps on the accelerator, hoping to cross the tracks before the train comes, but a barricade drops down in front of his windshield, stopping him. A few moments later, a train whistle sounds.

"We've lost him," I whisper as the train comes speeding by, passing right in front of us. At least ten train cars later—I eventually stop counting—the crossing sign lifts and the Taurus is nowhere in sight.

Wes brings his fist down hard against the steering wheel. "Crap!" he shouts.

"Because we lost him?"

"Because he knows," he says, shaking his head, his voice barely above a whisper.

Dear Jill,

I asked if you wanted to ride around for a while, telling you about the beautiful view of the moon over Breakneck Pond. But you weren't fully checked in. Sitting on the bench, you kept fumbling with your necklace and fishing inside your backpack. Were you searching for your cell phone? Did you have some sort of weapon in there?

Still, you got into my car, which told me that deep down you truly wanted this. I suppose my stories about growing up near Breakneck Pond—how my parents used to take me there every summer—made things a little easier.

I'm sure that by now you know the real truth about my childhood. Needless to say, it doesn't paint nearly as pretty a picture as swimming and picnics at a pond. I hated having to lie to you, but you have to admit, there's something comforting about picturing people engaging in familial pastimes. And you deserved to be put at ease, regardless of the consequence.

We pulled off down a narrow dirt road, where it was quiet and secluded—again, I picked a tranquil place, keeping you in mind. I remember looking into your face, suddenly reminded of the girl just before you. But not really lookswise: she'd been a lot shorter than you, with curly hair rather than a long braid. Her face was a bit chubbier, too:

rounder, with double the freckles. But she'd been awkward like you, so unsure of herself in her circle of friends.

I hate to bring her up, but at this point you must've heard some stuff about her—about what happened to her. For the record, it isn't true. I'd barely just picked her out, barely had even started to watch her, when fate intervened. Please know I'd never let anything like that happen to you.

You were getting all teary again, so I pulled a couple spiked lemonades from my cooler, still trying to get you to let down your guard. I led the conversation while you drank, explaining that I knew how it was to feel like a misfit all the time.

"I can help take your pain away," I said, assuming you'd be happy about the offer, but you were still looking a bit shaken. You'd almost completely torn the label off your bottle; the glue and paper remnants were stuck beneath your fingernails.

I truly felt sorry for you.

About halfway through the bottle, you asked me how I could take your pain away. Finally, you were getting it.

"Just watch," I said, putting my car in reverse.

You got startled when I accidentally steered the car into some tree branches.

"Relax," I said, complaining that there weren't nearly enough lights out there. "Not even the moon can help us," I joked.

You asked me where we were going, and I
told you to have another drink. "The cooler's
in the back," I said. "Now, hang on tight and
enjoy the ride."

. . .

Dear Jack:

It's strange the way fate works. I'd been working behind the scenes at the coffee shop for over a year—in the back room, opening boxes full of frozen pastries, lining the sweets up on big metal cookie sheets, and heating them in the ovens.

Barely coming into contact with anyone.

And then one day, Olivia called in sick, and I was forced to work the front counter. Carl said he liked me at the cash register. Apparently it hadn't cashed out as accurately in months. And so he asked me to work there permanently, which is how I met you.

I have no idea why I'm telling you any of this, except maybe to give you some insight as to who I am. Or who I was. Not the most experienced type of girl. Someone who believed that you were the person she wanted—the type of person that people are supposed to want all along. But sitting in your car that night—in the dark, in the middle of nowhere, with the smell of rotted fruit thick in the air (was there an apple you'd forgotten about in your glove box? An old banana peel left under the seat? Or maybe it was just the heat inside your car)—I had a feeling I'd made a big mistake.

If there was a pond, like you said, I couldn't spot it anywhere. There were tall, sprawling trees surrounding us. Their branches dangled onto your car, shrouding us even more. You'd said you wanted to show me the moon, but for all the time you'd spent describing how pretty it was when it reflected off the water, you didn't mention it once when we got there.

I stared out the window, avoiding eye contact. Looking at you only made everything more real. I thought about opening the car door and fleeing, but I knew I wouldn't get very far. The brush was so thick; I wouldn't be able to run very fast. Plus, I doubted anyone would hear me if I screamed.

"I know what it's like for you," you said. "To feel like a misfit all the time. To feel like you don't belong. Even at home."

"How do you know the way I feel at home?" I looked at you again. The overhead light enabled me to see that your face was sweaty. Mine was, too. It had to have been at least ninety degrees in your car, with the heat pumping through the vents and the windows fogging over.

You moved in a little closer and touched my neck, making a spiral shape on my collarbone with the tip of your finger. Over and over and over again. I dug my fingernails into the lemonade bottle in my lap, clawing away at the label, trying my best to stay calm.

Your fingertips felt coarse, and I wondered if they were leaving a mark. You told me that you were very observant. I wasn't sure if it was in response to my question, or if you were just trying to inform me. But your words made everything feel darker than normal, boxing me in, making me feel confined.

You told me how pretty you thought I was, and then you asked if you could show me that it was true.

"How?" I asked, wishing I'd stayed quiet. Because the next thing I knew, there was a weird grin across your face. It exposed the hole in your smile: a small gap right beside your incisor where the flesh of your tongue poked through. I hadn't noticed that about your smile before, and now it gave me the chills.

You put the car in reverse and began to back out through the tunnel of trees.

I looked away again, out the fog-covered window, telling myself to relax. But then you started whistling a tune. "Yankee Doodle Dandy." Eventually you added words, but they were the wrong words: "Jack and Jill ran up the hill to fetch a pail of water," you sang. "Jack fell down and broke his crown, and Jill came tumbling after."

"It's a nursery rhyme, not a song," I said, correcting you, without thinking better of it.

You told me how much you loved nursery rhymes, saying that they had a soothing quality, bringing one back to the simplicity of childhood. "'Jack and Jill' just happens to be my favorite," you told me. "I like how in sync the two of them are, working together. They're partners forever."

Somehow I nodded, trying to play it cool. Meanwhile, bile coated the inside of my mouth. I swallowed it down, just as you told me to have another drink. You motioned to the cooler in the backseat.

I know it may sound naive, but I'd been so nervous when you handed me that first bottle of lemonade that I didn't even notice it'd been spiked. There's a reason that people become victims. And by that point, I knew I had become one of them.

. . .

WES SMACKS HIS HAND down against the steering wheel several more times on our drive back to Freetown.

"You definitely think he knew that we were following him?" I ask.

He pulls up in front of Knead. "At first I didn't, but then it seemed kind of obvious, like he was trying to get away."

"So, why didn't you stop? Why didn't we turn around?"

"I'm sorry," he says, putting the car in park. "I got a little carried away. I tend to do that sometimes." He nods toward the backseat, where he's got a pair of binoculars, his camera bag, and a fresh box of latex gloves.

"So, what now?" I ask.

"I don't know, but it might be a good idea to discuss all of this with Ben . . . just in case."

"In case what? What does Ben have to with any of this?"

"Why don't you ask *him*? He *was* at the Press & Grind, after all. So maybe he's more involved than you think."

"Not just *maybe*," I say, in light of the most recent Ben-and-Danica sightings (in the library and the cafeteria, and now, allegedly, at the Press & Grind). *"Probably."*

"So, he can *probably* help you. I mean, you have to admit, the guy's saved your life four times now."

"Since when are you Team Ben?"

"Correction: I'm Team Camelia." Wes lets out a sigh and looks away, more flustered than I've ever seen him before.

"The danger is directed at Danica," I remind him. "Not at me. I'm just trying to help her—the way I helped Adam."

"You had your whole head sticking out the window at one point, Camelia."

"So?" I swallow hard.

"So, if he saw you, and if he saw that we were following him, you can bet he's going to find out who you are."

"You don't know that."

"I do," he says, looking back at me. His dark brown eyes are sullen and serious.

"And how are you so sure?" I ask, remembering how this isn't the first time that the guy saw me—how he peeled out down the street when he spotted me in front of Danica's house.

"I'm just looking out for your best interests."

"And what's *in* my best interest?" I ask him. "To end things right now? To ignore the fact that Danica's in trouble?"

To my surprise, Wes shakes his head. "It's too late. You're already involved. Maybe that's what the *'there are two'* clue is all about. Maybe there are two potential victims here: Danica and someone else."

"Someone else . . . meaning me?" I ask, trying to catch on.

"I don't know." He shrugs. "But if I were the psycho in question, and I found out that some girl was having premonitions about what I was up to and then started following me—"

"How's he going to find out I'm having premonitions?"

"Have you told anyone else about them?"

I clench my teeth, thinking about Adam.

"I have to assume that I'm involved, too," Wes says, thinking out loud. "For all I know, he saw my license plate."

I want to reassure him that everything will be okay, but I have no idea if it will—if either of us should feel reassured about anything. "I have to go," I say, suddenly feeling sick.

"Yeah," he says. "Me, too."

I get out of his car, forgetting to thank him for all his help. I turn back to flag him down, but he has already pulled away from the curb and turned onto another street.

29

As soon as I walk into Knead, Svetlana practically pounces on me. It seems several of the adults want to try the wheel and Svetlana can barely get them past the centering stage. I spend several minutes explaining the steps of throwing a bowl, but a couple of the women want to see me do it for real.

"Please," Svetlana insists, proceeding to tell me that one of the women asked to get her money back when she found out that Spencer wasn't going to be teaching tonight.

I take a seat at the wheel, anxious about what may happen once I start to sculpt. And so I re-explain the steps, adding more details about posture, pressure, and moisture. By the time I finally touch fingertips to clay, the moment feels so completely clinical that I'm almost sure nothing weird will happen.

As soon as I get the students going on their bowls, I

move over to my work in progress, eager to have another look. I remove the tarp and focus hard on my vaselike bowl, reminded once again of Ben, and of that moment when he was in the hospital—when I held his hand and he woke up, and then when he asked me never to let go.

"Would you mind giving me a little help?" a woman asks, jolting me out of my reverie.

The woman—one of the older students—stands at my table holding a ball of clay. "I have arthritis," she explains. "Would you mind lending me a hand with wedging?" She sets the clay down in front of me, complaining that she signed up for this class to paint, not to sculpt.

"Why not paint this?" I ask, turning away to grab one of the already-fired humping bunnies from a shelf. I place it on a tray along with a few jars of paint.

"Thank you, but I'd like it wedged out anyway," she insists. "Maybe I'll poke a finger into the center and call it abstract art."

"Sure." I smile, proceeding to smack her clay ball against my board, trying not to think about anything in particular.

"And what are *you* working on?" She takes a seat, swipes my spatula, and uses it to point at my bowl.

I gaze at some other students two tables over, wondering why she doesn't join them instead.

"Cat got your tongue?" She makes a sucking sound with her own tongue.

Eventually I cave, and end up rambling on about my project—how I'm not really sure where I'm going with it, but how I'm determined to get it to where it needs to be.

The woman listens, using my spatula to scratch behind her ear. Finally, it seems I've bored her, and she resumes her work, sponging the clay dust off the humping bunny figurine as if I'm no longer even there.

I continue to wedge out her clay, working all the air bubbles out, until she interrupts me again. She leans across the table in my direction and whispers something about "following her."

"Excuse me?" I ask, feeling my face scrunching up.

Her lips peel open, exposing a gap in her teeth where her tongue pokes through. "Stop following me," she snaps.

Before I can say anything else, she spins her tray around to show me her work. Instead of a face on her bunny figurine, she's painted the letters *DM*.

"*DM*?" I ask.

"Die much?" she says, with a menacing grin. She lets out a giggle, and her tongue waggles out through the hole in her teeth, as if this is all part of one big joke.

I shake my head, completely confused. But no one else in the studio seems to notice her.

I get up and move away from the table, toward the others, as the woman continues to laugh at me.

I glance at Svetlana, who's dumped an entire tray full of bunnies onto the floor. Only, I don't hear the crash, just the old woman's laughter. Her voice plugs up my ears and fills my head with more whispering. The letters *DM* repeat inside my brain and knock me to the floor.

30

*L*YING ON MY BACK, with my eyes closed, I feel
someone take my hand.

"Ben?" I whisper. My eyes are still closed,
but I'd know his touch anywhere.

People are speaking in hushed tones, evidently wondering what just happened. I'm relieved to be able to hear
them—that the laughter has finally stopped, and that
there are no longer any voices inside my head.

I open my eyes and try to sit up. The fluorescent
studio lights overhead nearly blind me, reminding me of
the camera flashes from my premonitions.

A moment later, I see Ben's face. It's hovering right
above mine now.

"What are you doing here?" I ask him.

Ben takes off his coat and pulls his sweatshirt off over
his head. He drapes the sweatshirt over my shoulders and
then helps me to sit up.

"Thanks," I say, noticing the people standing around me. I try to assure them I'm fine, making excuses about how the heat from the kiln room, coupled with an empty stomach, no doubt did me in.

But then I spot the older woman, using my spatula to scratch behind her ear again.

"We were having such a pleasant time," she says. "You told me about your vase . . . and you were helping me wedge my clay. The next thing I knew . . ."

"What?" I ask, anxious to hear how things happened.

"You don't remember?" Her lips fall open, and I see her teeth—there's no gap to speak of, no tongue sticking out.

The woman looks away when I don't answer, pretending to resume her work in progress. I get to my feet and rotate her tray, desperate to see the bunny's face.

But it's blank. The letters *DM* are no longer there. They were probably part of a hallucination.

"Camelia?" Ben asks, taking my hand again.

Meanwhile, Svetlana comes and gives me a paper towel for my sweaty face.

"*DM,*" I whisper, still focused on the woman.

"What does it mean?" the woman asks. She gazes at my work station, and it suddenly dawns on me that I'd been working on something, too, wedging out a mound of clay. Only now it's no longer a mound at all.

The letters *DM*, carved into the clay, stare up at me from my work board.

"We should probably go," Ben says, clasping my hand harder.

I pull on his sweatshirt and grab my coat, not even asking where he's taking me. Because I honestly don't even care. As long as it's far, far away from here.

31

I HOP ON THE BACK of Ben's motorcycle and he takes off right away. I wrap my arms around his waist as he drives along the beach, straight toward the setting sun. The salty air rushes against my skin and helps me feel a little less unhinged.

After several minutes, he slows down a bit, making me think that we're going to turn around and head back. But instead he takes an on-ramp, to go onto the highway, and I feel a giant sense of relief.

Because we're not going home just yet.

We drive for a good twenty minutes before he finally takes an exit and then drives down one street after another till we pull into what seems to be a retreat center of some sort. A long brick driveway leads us to a giant stucco house with bright blue shutters and a clay roof.

"What is this place?" I ask, noticing a tulip-shaped water fountain and a large koi pond.

"You'll see," he says, driving us around to the back, where there appear to be acres of land. A tennis court separates a picnic area and a place for outdoor concerts. Ben proceeds along a dirt path, taking us to the edge of a forest. Tall trees—pine, maple, and oak—line a woodsy trail that leads to a sanctuary of sorts.

"Where are we going?" I ask, once he cuts the ignition.

"Follow me," he says, taking my hand to help me off his bike. His sweatshirt smells like bike fumes.

Ben leads me farther inside the wooded area, where leaves are just starting to bud. Iron lamps help illuminate the area, and so does the sun; its orangey glow seems to follow us, penetrating the tree branches and making everything look all aglow.

"Are you sure we're allowed to be here?" I ask.

"Relax," he says, giving my hand a squeeze.

"Meaning, we don't have to worry about getting arrested tonight?"

"Meaning, we don't have to worry about anything."

He leads me past a tall Buddha statue, which reminds me that I should probably touch base with my mom. I grab my cell and text her that all is well and I'll be home soon. Meanwhile, Ben moves to stand a few paces in front of me. He gazes up at the sky, and the sun shines right over him, highlighting the sharp angles of his face, the scruff on his chin, and his rumpled dark hair. He looks too beautiful to be real.

He notices me staring, and grins subtly. "Is everything okay?" He motions toward my cell phone.

"It's fine," I say, managing a nod, trying to keep my cool. "Do you come here a lot?"

"Enough," he says, staring at *me* now. His eyes roam across my face, my hair, the motion in my neck as I swallow. "It's part of my meditation." He smiles.

But I know he's not being funny. Ben's been practicing meditation, tai chi, and other mindful disciplines in an effort to control his touch powers.

"Come on," he says, extending his hand to me once more.

I take it, feeling my insides warm like toast. We walk for several moments before arriving at a partial clearing. Logs, boulders, and heaps of rocks are strategically placed to form a maze of sorts, about the size of a basketball court, and no taller than knee-high.

"It's a labyrinth," he explains.

"I can see that," I say, remembering having seen one on the Cape last summer. Only it was nowhere near as enchanting as this.

"I used to go to one regularly back home," he tells me. "I felt like it really helped me, so I did some research to find one around here."

"It's beautiful," I tell him, amazed that a place like this even exists so close to home.

"Do you want to give it a try?" He gives my hand an extra squeeze, sending tingles all over my skin.

"What do we do?" I ask. The smell of a campfire is somewhere in the distance.

"There are no tricks and no dead ends," he says. "So

there aren't really any rules. All you have to do is walk it. The toughest part is deciding where you want to enter the maze and which way you want to go."

As Ben continues to explain the nonrules of labyrinths—how you can go at your own pace, find your own rhythm, and walk for as long as you wish—I do my best to focus on his words and not lose myself in the magic of the moment.

"Some people like to go in with a specific question in mind," he says, still holding my hand. "Others use the maze as a means of letting go . . . stepping into a sacred space and shedding the cares and stresses of the day."

"How do you like to go in?" I ask him.

"I find that walking here helps to quiet my mind. Times when I'm feeling stressed or sorry for myself, or when I just feel like life is getting too big to handle . . . I come here to center myself."

I nod, trying not to look surprised, because I *shouldn't* be surprised, because, as fearless as Ben often seems, he definitely has issues, too.

"Some people use labyrinths as a way to pay respect to the gifts they have," he says. "I guess I'm still trying to work on that one."

"Maybe I should be, too," I say, knowing that this touch power is indeed a gift of sorts—that it helped save Adam's life.

"It *is* a gift," Ben says, as if reading my mind. He lets go of my hand to stroke the side of my face. His thumb grazes my mouth, and I feel my lips part.

"It took me a long time to figure that out," he continues, catching himself. He takes a step back and withdraws his hand.

Meanwhile, my heart hammers inside my chest.

"I can't stop sensing things," he continues. "But I *can* try to adjust what happens when I do."

"What do you mean?" I ask, wondering if he's talking about me.

"I mean that maybe you can't quiet the voices, but there's no reason why you can't quiet your mind."

"I don't know," I say, remembering how Wes suggested something similar.

"Come on," Ben says. "At least give it a try." He moves to the edge of the labyrinth, stepping onto the outer path and moving slowly in a clockwise direction.

I watch him for several seconds as he takes turns and alternate routes, before beginning on my own path. It feels sort of silly at first, until I find my stride. I close my eyes, concentrating on my breath, and on the crunching sound of dirt beneath my feet. I stumble a couple of times along the way, bumping into a rock or a log, but trying not to rely on sight—to focus instead on what I can hear: the rush of water from a nearby fountain; the wind as it combs through the branches; and the sound of Ben walking somewhere behind me.

After several moments, I come to a stop. My eyes still closed, I can tell that the sun has set. The darkness blankets me, providing a comforting sensation. And yet there's a nervous sensation, too, because I can no longer hear Ben's footsteps. I open my eyes to make sure that the lampposts are still lit.

Ben is standing right in front of me now. His expression is both needy and full of questions.

"Are you cold?" he asks.

"Not really," I say, even though the temperature's dropped.

"Do you want to keep walking?"

I shake my head, wishing that things between us could be different.

"So, we should probably talk about what happened at the studio," he says.

"Probably," I say, taking a step closer. My forehead grazes the material of his jacket, and I can't stop myself from touching him—from sliding my hands around his waist and resting my cheek against his chest. "I've missed you," I say, without thinking first.

He nods, like he's missed *us*, too, like he can feel the same hollowness inside him. Still, he averts his eyes, perhaps trying to stay in control.

But I insist on making things messy.

I place my palms against his face, forcing him to look at me again.

"We need to talk." His eyes are fixed on mine, fighting to stay open. But I brush the skin of my lips against his mouth, and finally he caves and kisses me. His lips fold over mine, and I can taste the salty sweetness of his mouth.

I tuck the tips of my fingers into the back pockets of his jeans and draw him closer.

"Wait," he says, pulling away, breaking the kiss. His breath is labored and quick. "We can't do this."

"You're right," I say, knowing we can't. But still, something inside me really wants to.

"I'm sorry if I led you on, just now, during our phone call the other day, at school—but trust me when I say that this isn't what you want."

"How do *you* know what I want?" I press my cheek against his chest once more, able to hear his heart race. "What do *you* want?"

"It doesn't matter. What matters is that I'm trying to do the right thing."

A cool breeze rushes down my back, urging me even closer—until his lips are just a hair's breadth away from mine again. "And this isn't the right thing," I say—more a statement than a question.

"It isn't the responsible thing."

Still, I kiss him again, unable to hold back. And soon we find ourselves on the ground, atop a pile of silkweed and soil. Lying on top of me, he searches my eyes, maybe trying to spot even a blink of hesitation. When he doesn't find any, he kisses me, pinning me with his weight. The back of my shirt rides up, and the cool, lush soil feels like velvet against my skin.

"Wait," he says, pulling away after several moments. He gets up and extends his hand to help me up as well.

But I choose to get up on my own.

"I'm sorry," he says, completely flustered. His hands fly up to his head. "That shouldn't have happened."

"Because of Alejandra?"

"Because you deserve better—much better than what I can offer you."

"You're right," I say, feeling my heart wrench. "I *do* deserve better."

"Look, I still want to help you. But I can't give you what you need."

"I'm a big girl," I tell him, assuming he's still afraid of hurting me. "And I know what I need."

"Do you?" He focuses hard on me. "Do you need someone who's going to continue keeping secrets because he's afraid to let anyone get too close? Do you need someone who'll never fully open up because he suffers from serious trust issues?"

"I'm willing to wait," I say, my eyes filling up. "In time I can regain your trust."

"This isn't about what happened in Adam's car," he says, clearly referring to the kiss.

"Then what *is* it about?"

"I have to go away for a bit," he says. "It'll only be for a few days, but we should talk more when I get back."

Only a few days. "Then why bother telling me at all?"

"Because I know there's something going on with you, and I don't want you to feel like I'm leaving you on your own."

"Where are you going?" I ask, feeling stupid for having thought that his stopping by Knead happened simply because he'd wanted to see me.

"Back home."

"To see your parents?"

"Not exactly." He kicks at a mound of dirt on the ground, seemingly as uncomfortable as I am. "I've got some stuff I need to take care of."

I bite my lip, wondering if his wanting to get away has to do with more legal stuff, even though he was acquitted, or if maybe it has to do with old ghosts.

He reaches into the front pocket of his jeans for his motorcycle keys and then looks back in the direction we came from. "I talked to Adam," he says. "He promises to keep an eye on you while I'm gone."

"Adam?" I ask. It's like a blow to my gut. "Since when are you two talking again?"

"He's done some pretty stupid things in his life," he says, "but he's a really good guy. And he really does care about you."

"You're not seriously endorsing him for me, are you? Wasn't it you, on the phone the other day, who said there was no reason why Adam and I should be seeing one another? I mean, talk about mixed messages!"

"Guilty," Ben says. "My messages *have* been mixed. And, once again, I'm sorry. But here's a message that won't ever change: you deserve the best. And unfortunately, I'm not it."

"And Adam is?"

"He'll be looking out for you," he says; the words catch in his throat.

"I don't need looking out for," I say, holding back more tears. "I'll be just fine on my own." I turn on my heel, neglecting to tell him about what happened today at Knead, or about the car that Wes and I followed. Because finally he's got one thing right: I deserve someone a whole lot better than him.

32

$\mathcal{J}$ BOLT FROM THE LABYRINTH and out of the woods, grateful for the lamps that light the way. I can hear twigs snapping on the ground as Ben follows me, but I don't turn back for a second, even when he attempts to apologize—yet again.

I make it around to the front of the retreat building when it finally dawns on me that I have no idea how I'm going to get back.

"I'll give you a ride," Ben says, at my side now.

"Fine," I say, unable to look at him. "Can you take me back to Knead?"

"I'll take you wherever you want to go. And, for the record, I know I'm not your favorite person right now, but someday you'll see . . . this is only because I care about you."

If only I cared as much about myself. Maybe then I wouldn't open up to him, allowing myself to get hurt by him once again.

Ben hands me his helmet and then drives me to the pottery studio.

"Can I call you later?" he asks, once I get off his bike.

But I don't even dignify the question with an answer. Instead I peel off his sweatshirt, toss it back in his general direction, and head inside the studio.

Svetlana seems happy to see me, telling me how scared she was for me earlier, and asking if there's anything she can do. Spencer is there, too, but he seems far too preoccupied with his bronze ballerina to worry about me.

"Bad day?" he asks, adjusting the respiration mask on his face.

I assure them I'm fine and then call my mom, wishing that Kimmie were here. I tell Mom that I'm leaving Knead to go grab a bite with Adam, which is practically the truth (minus the grabbing-a-bite part)—only Adam doesn't know it yet.

Mom says it's fine if I'm home by ten, and so I call Adam and ask him to meet me at the Press & Grind, anxious to get his side of things.

I head down the street, able to see the Press & Grind from more than a block away, and wondering if Danica might still be working.

When I get there, the place is pretty quiet. There's a group of knitters sitting in a corner, a lady working on her laptop, and some guy doing homework.

The guy glances up at me. He's good-looking, probably in his late twenties, with brownish blond hair and deep blue eyes.

I give him a slight smile when he continues to stare at me, wondering if I should say hi—if maybe he's one of my mother's clients that I'm not remembering, or maybe someone from the Sanskrit reading club that she used to lead.

"Can I help you?" the girl at the counter asks me.

I turn away from him to order something, noticing how familiar the counter girl looks. Unlike the guy doing homework, this girl I've definitely seen.

"Hi," I say, racking my brain, trying to place her. "I'll take a large vanilla latte. And could you also tell me if Danica Pete is working?"

"Are you a friend of hers?" she asks, typing in my order. Before I can answer, she scrunches her freckled face and then lets out a sigh. "Carl," she calls, waving the manager over. "I think I made a mistake."

Carl voids the error on the register and asks me to repeat my order. "And will that be all?"

I shake my head. "I was wondering if Danica Pete might be working." I continue to gaze around.

The guy doing homework is looking in my general direction—but whether at me, at the girl, or at Carl, I can't really tell.

I turn back, still awaiting Carl's response, but he's no longer standing behind the counter. Did someone call him to do something? Did he go out back to get Danica for me?

I watch as the counter girl starts to make my drink. "Do I know you from someplace?" I ask her. "You look so familiar."

The girl shrugs and puts a lid on the drink, barely looking me in the eye.

"Wait, do you go to Freetown High?" I ask her.

"No," she says, turning her back like maybe I've irritated her.

At the same moment, Danica Pete comes out of the back room with Carl following close behind. "Three words," she says, coming to stand right in front of me. "Leave. Me. Alone."

"I only want to talk to you," I say, keeping my voice low.

"You've already talked. We've already been through this." Her apron is stained with cinnamon powder.

Carl points to the door. "Take it outside."

"No need," she says, getting right up in my face. Her pale blue eyes are wide. "I don't want your so-called help. I don't want you coming by my house, or trying to talk to me at school, or making up stupid stories because you supposedly want to be my friend."

"Danica, you've got me all wrong."

"Do I?" she asks.

Before I can respond, Adam touches my shoulder from behind, having apparently just come in. "Is everything okay?" he asks.

My face feels flushed. My insides shake. Meanwhile, Danica disappears into the back room, leaving me in the proverbial dust.

Yet again.

* * *

"What was all that about?" Adam asks, once we step outside.

I rub the front of my head, which has begun to ache, suddenly realizing that I left my coffee on the counter. "Do you think we could go someplace quiet to talk?"

"Sure thing," he says, nodding toward his Bronco. He opens the passenger-side door and I hop right in, grateful for the getaway ride.

Adam drives around for a while before pulling into the parking lot of a golf club. "So, what's up?" he asks, cutting the ignition.

"Ben told me that you two talked," I say, forgoing the Danica details for now.

Adam manages a nod, clearly embarrassed, as if I've suddenly caught him in a lie. "It was really no big deal."

"What did he say to you?" I ask.

He talks in circles for several seconds, mentioning some of the stuff Ben said earlier—how Ben only wants what's best for me, how he asked Adam to keep tabs on me while he was away, and how he'd "die" if anything bad happened to me. "He seemed really sincere, Camelia."

"So, does this mean that you and Ben are friends again?"

"I wouldn't go that far, but maybe he hates my guts a little less."

"Well, I guess that's a start."

"A very good start," he says, and looks away, as if maybe he's not telling me everything. "So, please tell me that the update on Project Ben wasn't the *only* reason you called me."

"Thanks for coming to meet me," I say, suddenly

215

realizing that I hadn't yet said it.

"Anytime." He smiles. "But next time, if you could wait until *after* I order a brownie to get yourself kicked out, that would be ideal."

"I'll keep that in mind." I smile, too.

"So, do you want to go get a bite and talk about Danica? Remember, I'm willing to help out however I can."

"I know," I say, grateful for his friendship.

"But . . . ?"

"But I guess I'm feeling a bit overwhelmed."

"So, let's talk about it. I mean, don't shut me out. I want to help you solve this thing."

"I know you do," I say, thinking how ironic it is that he should say this, because it wasn't so long ago that I said something similar to Ben about feeling shut out. "And I'm grateful for your help. Believe me."

"So, then, what's the deal?" he asks.

I gaze out the window at the vacant golf course, knowing that regardless of what Ben said to him today, Adam is always in my corner. But now that the former friends *have* indeed talked—now that Ben's given Adam his *permission* to spend time with me—I kind of want to be alone. "Can we talk more tomorrow?" I ask him.

Adam doesn't answer. Instead, he drives to my house in silence, perhaps feeling every bit as lost as I did months ago, when Ben was keeping secrets. I know I should probably reassure him that everything's okay between us, but he pulls up to my house, and I wish him a quick good night, relieved to finally be home.

33

I HEAD INTO THE KITCHEN, where my parents are engaged in a seemingly civil conversation, complete with eye contact and encouraging body language. Mom laughs at something Dad's just said, and Dad reaches out to touch her hand.

"Hey," I say, hating myself for interrupting them.

"Did you have a nice time with Adam?" Mom asks. "Where did you two go?"

"It was fine," I say. "But I actually have to run. I need to finish up an already overdue essay for English."

"Would you like a snack?" she asks.

I'm starving, but since I'd like to give them more alone time, and since I was supposed to have had dinner out with Adam, I lie and say that I'm stuffed, knowing I've got some emergency snacks tucked away in my backpack.

In my room, two granola bars later and three pages into my *Wuthering Heights* essay, I can't stand it anymore.

I need to call Kimmie.

I pick up the phone and dial her number, but she doesn't answer, even when I call back two more times. I leave her a message, and then I try Wes's cell. He isn't picking up, either.

The phone still clenched in my hand, I consider giving Adam a call, wishing I'd taken him up on his offer to talk more. But I already told him that I wanted to be alone.

I told Ben that I didn't need any help.

I tell everyone that everything's always fine with me.

But now that I am alone, that I have no help, that things aren't fine, I feel like I'm stuck in a deep, dark hole with no one to dig me out.

I grab my aunt's journal, desperate for some sort of a connection. I page through to the middle and read one of the entries.

February 14, 1984

Dear Diary:

It's Valentine's Day, and in school we had to make cards for someone we care about. I made one for Jilly. Using chalk pastels, I drew a great big heart man with Cupid's arrows for his arms and legs, and mini-hearts for the eyes, nose, and mouth.

I sat away from everybody else because Mrs. Trigger thinks I'm scary. It's true. Even since I did that portrait of blood running from my wrists, she moved my seat to the corner, and she barely ever comes around to check my work.

I thought the heart man would make her happy, but it wasn't long before things took a bit of a turn. Using my fingers to blend the colors, I got sucked into my work. That's when the voices started coming. They told me to make a star on my wrist.

I didn't question why. I only wanted the voices to stop. And so I grabbed a black marker and drew the star shape on the underside of my wrist, where the veins are, hoping it would do the trick.

It didn't.

The voices continued for the rest of the day: through gym class, lunch, English, and math. They kept telling me the same thing over and over: make a star, make a star, make a star, make a star, make a star, make a star, makeastar, makeastar, makeastar, makeastar, makeastarmake astarmakeastarmakeastarmakeastar makeastarmakeastar . . .

Later, when I got home, I grabbed some supplies and locked myself in the bathroom. I ran the shower water to drown out the voices and stuffed rubber erasers into my already aching ears.

Still I could hear them.

And so, unable to even think straight, I grabbed a marker and drew X's over my ears as a last resort.

I don't remember what happened after that. But Jilly found me some time later, naked on the bathroom floor, the shower water still running (I have no idea if I ever actually got in), and with those huge X's over my ears.

Love,
Alexia

I close the journal, wondering if it's normal for me to understand just how she feels.

If my shortness of breath is because I'm coming down with a cold.

If this dizzy sensation will subside in an instant.

Or if this is the beginning of crazy.

I count to ten, trying to get a grip, wondering if the star could purely have been a coincidence, or if I had this power even back then—when I was six, when I drew a star on Miss Dream Baby's back.

A moment later, the scratching sound returns at my wall. I move out of bed and cross the room. Aunt Alexia is obviously awake. Has she somehow sensed that I was reading her journal? Is it possible that she wants to talk?

My hands trembling, I press them against the wall, tempted to scratch back. But then I gaze over at my cell phone, and decide to try Kimmie again.

She still isn't picking up. I leave another message and then dial Wes's number. He's still not answering, either.

Sitting on the edge of my bed, I bury my head between my knees, feeling more alone than I ever thought possible. Meanwhile, the scratching sound gets louder, tearing across the length of my wall, practically speaking to me on its own.

I slip the phone into my pocket and move out into the hallway, hoping that Mom and Dad might still be up. But it seems they've already gone off to bed.

Not knowing where else to go or what else to do, I go down to the basement, eager to lose myself in my skating sculpture. I spend several seconds moistening the clay, trying to get myself into the moment, even though I feel like I'm jumping right out of my skin.

I add texture to the skater's skirt, definition to her calves, and more detail to her hands. I grab an X-Acto knife from my jar of tools, feeling confident that the skater's nearly done. I'm just about to carve my initials into the base when I notice a smudge of red by the skater's foot.

I check my sponge, in search of the source. It's clean. The table's clean, too. I start to wipe the smudge away when I notice more of the color. On my hands; all over my palms.

Deep red.

Like blood.

With *DM* written right through it.

34

*J*STARE AT MY TREMBLING PALMS, at the letters written through the redness, wondering what the initials mean. *Die much? Danica M-something?*

My pulse racing, I look around my pottery studio. Aside from my hands, everything appears normal. So, then, where did this redness come from? And who scribbled the letters across it?

A moment later, my cell phone rings in my pocket. I want to answer, but my brain is no longer in sync with my body.

It's several seconds before I'm able to reach for the phone. Before I'm finally able to snap back to reality.

Before I see that my palms are no longer red. They probably never were.

"Hello," I answer, hoping it's Kimmie at last.

"Come upstairs," a voice whispers from the receiver.

I pinch the gooseflesh on my arm to make sure this

isn't a dream. "Aunt Alexia?" I ask, wondering if she's okay.

"Come see," she says; her high-pitched voice is followed by a giggle. And then she hangs up.

I hang up, too. And hurry upstairs. Through the kitchen. The light over the sink illuminates the area just enough for me to find my way.

I stand at the end of the hallway. Her bedroom door faces me, makes me dizzy, and steals my breath.

I recheck my palms—still clean—and then I start down the hallway. The floorboards creak beneath my feet. A shadow moves on the floor and plays in the crack below her door.

She's waiting for me.

Standing directly in front of her door now, I raise my fist to knock. But then a light flashes in my bedroom, just to the right of me. I take a step inside. My lamp is off, but a light shines in from the street. I move to the window over my bed and peer out from behind the drapes.

Someone's out there, in a car, blocking the street. Headlights shine toward my window. Bright, then dull, then bright again.

I double-check my window to make sure it's locked. And draw the drapes. My first thought is that it's Wes, just being his obnoxious self, especially since I called him earlier. But it quickly dawns on me that Wes would never be that insensitive. Nor would he ever risk the chance that my parents might catch him.

The headlights remain shining through the four-inch gap of my drapes, illuminating my entire room. I'm pretty sure it isn't Adam either. I can normally hear the roar of his Bronco's engine from at least a couple of streets away, even with the window closed. I sneak another peek, trying to tell if it might be the Ford Taurus that Wes and I followed. But before I can, the car's lights move away from my window as the driver backs up, turns, and finally speeds off down the road.

With the headlights gone, the room is dark. I close my eyes, trying to remain calm. Meanwhile, a gnawing sensation eats at my gut.

I open my eyes, able to sense something more.

And there it is: on my wall, directly in front of me. The letters *DM* glow in the darkness. And send shivers down my spine.

35

*T*HE INITIALS ARE LARGE, taking up half the wall in front of my bed. It looks like someone painted them quickly. You can see where drips of paint ran down the wall and bled into a puddle on the floor.

I click on my night-table light, and the letters disappear—just like that. Whoever painted them must have used glow-in-the-dark paint, intending the clue for my eyes only.

I look toward the wall that separates Aunt Alexia's room from mine, wondering if she's still waiting for me. Slowly, I move out into the hallway, knowing I should tell my parents about the car.

The house is quiet and dark, and the hum of the dishwasher is the only sound I hear. Keeping my bedroom door open for light, I raise my hand to rap gently on their door.

But then I turn to look.

225

Aunt Alexia is there, standing in her doorway. Staring straight at me.

"What took you so long?" she asks.

I open my mouth, but I can't find the words. Meanwhile, I feel dizzy again.

Aunt Alexia turns her back, leaving her door wide open, perhaps eager for me to follow.

And so I do.

I venture into her room. My eyes zoom in on her bed first. The blankets have been tossed to the floor. The sheets sit in a heap at the headboard, and the pillows are stacked up at the foot. I gaze around the rest of the room, suddenly realizing that I don't see Aunt Alexia anywhere.

Is she hiding from me? Am I having another hallucination?

"Aunt Alexia?" I call, noticing a giant tarp covering the floor, protecting the wood. Sketch pads, canvases, and tubes of acrylic paint sit in piles.

I look toward our shared wall, curious again about the scratching sounds. And that's when I see it: a giant mural of a baby grand piano. Painted atop the piano is a vase of flowers—*red* flowers—which explains the red paint I've seen on Alexia's hands.

There's another tarp, half attached to the wall—what Aunt Alexia must've been using to protect the mural and keep it hidden. I take a step closer, noticing how several of the piano's keys are depressed, as if someone's playing music, and yet no one's sitting on the bench.

My initial thought is that maybe she hasn't finished

the painting yet; maybe she still needs to add the image of a person. But the bench looks fully painted. There's even a ray of light across the seat. And she's already signed her name in the corner.

"Aunt Alexia?" I call again, about to leave the room. But then I finally spot her, crouched down against the far wall, sending chills all over my skin.

Wearing a paint-spattered dress and half-concealed by a canvas, she almost completely blends in with her surroundings.

"Alexia?"

Her eyes appear wide and alert, focused on the mural. She whispers something, but I can't quite hear it.

"Excuse me?" I ask, moving closer.

"The piano plays by itself," she says, just a wee bit louder.

"You mean it's a player piano?"

Sitting hunched over with her knees drawn up to her chest and Miss Dream Baby clenched against her stomach, she remains looking off to the side, failing to answer my question.

"Aunt Alexia?" I scoot down in front of her.

"He's following me," she whispers.

"Who is?"

"He followed me here."

"Is he someone you know?" I ask, assuming she's talking about the car outside—the one that shined its headlights into my room. "Someone from Ledgewood, maybe?" I look back toward the mural for a clue, but I can't see much detail from this angle.

"He's someone *you* know," she says, looking directly at me finally. Her eyelids are swollen and red.

"I don't know anyone with a piano like that."

"Well, he knows you," she insists, still whispering. "And if you're not careful, he'll take you captive, too."

"Meaning he's going to take someone else captive?" My mind flashes to Danica.

"He'll lock you both up and throw away the key." She nibbles at the skin on her kneecap.

"Are his initials D.M.?" I venture.

Shaking her head, she digs her teeth in deeper.

"Did you paint those letters on my wall?"

"Don't be fooled," she says, avoiding the question. But still, she doesn't deny it.

"Fooled by what?" I ask; my heart beats fast.

"There are two," she reminds me. "But you're only looking at one."

"One, meaning Danica? Or meaning the person I think might be following her? Or the person who's following you?"

Alexia extends her hand toward mine, wanting to touch palms. I focus a moment on the star-shaped scar on her wrist, reminded of her diary entry.

I reluctantly place my palm against hers, even though my hand is shaking.

"Just about the same size," she says, marveling at how similar our hands are. "Like sisters."

"That's what Dad thinks. That we're connected

somehow. He told my mom that he thinks we're kindred spirits."

"Your dad's a smart man." She focuses harder on me. Her emerald green eyes, flecked with gold, are almost a mirror image of my own, nearly making me forget that we *aren't* long-lost sisters. That she isn't twenty years older than me. And that her stay here isn't permanent.

"There's a girl who might be in trouble," I tell her, segueing back to the initials on my wall. "So, if you know what those letters stand for . . ."

She drops her hand, leaving a thick black smear of paint on my palm. "Those girls didn't want her to skate. She was better than they were, and they knew it."

"What girls?" I ask. "Who are you talking about?"

"When they played that trick, locked her up, it put her over the edge. She got taken out of public school and put in a private place."

"Who?" I ask again.

She gives the doll a kiss. "You know, I was there the day you got this doll. It was around the time when I wasn't doing so great, when the voices had started to seep into my dreams." She straightens out the front of Miss Dream Baby's dress and then makes the legs kick back and forth.

"For my birthday," I say, remembering the star-themed party. Star streamers, star-shaped cake, glow-in-the-dark stars on the ceilings and walls.

Was all of that a coincidence, too?

"I'd started to have dreams about painting," she continues, "since I'd tried giving it up altogether. Those dreams haunted me, so much that I'd started setting my alarm clock to go off every half hour. *Anything* to avoid sinking into a deep and dreamful slumber."

"And did it work?" I ask.

"What do *you* think?" She smirks. "That wasn't the first time I'd tried giving up my art—like a bad habit that you keep going back to. But it *was* the first time that my dreams got hijacked. Anyway, you were so happy when you opened the box with the doll in it. I asked what you were going to name her."

"Miss Dream Baby," I say, watching as Alexia attempts to clean the doll's face with a fingertip moistened with spit.

"Yes, but it was the *way* you named her. The way you looked at me, with wide eyes and a knowing grin—like you could see through me, into my soul—as if you knew about my power even back then. And as if you had it, too. That's when you told me that her name was Miss Dream Baby, and that she'd help keep nightmares away."

"I remember," I say, feeling a smile form on my face.

"I thought that by giving her that name, it was your way of telling me I could keep her."

"It was," I say, not quite sure if that's the truth.

"There are two," she reminds me, switching gears again. "And now I've told you all I know." She resumes biting the skin on her knee.

I try to push her with more questions, asking if the *D* stands for Danica, if the person she claims is following her might really be looking for me, and if she has any details about what this person looks like. But with each question, her teeth sink in deeper.

Until she draws a trickle of blood.

I hurry out of the room to get my parents. Both shoot out of bed, perhaps fearing the worst. Mom bandages the cut. Dad makes an emergency call to Alexia's doctor.

Mom makes the bed.

Dad helps Alexia into it.

They both ask her if she'd like something to drink, a bite to eat, a warm compress for her flushed face.

Meanwhile, horrified at the idea that I'm the one who got Aunt Alexia so upset, I slip back into my room and try calling Kimmie a couple more times, desperate to hear her voice. But when for the umpteenth time she doesn't pick up, I pull the covers over my head and cry myself to sleep.

Dear Jill,

I remember pulling onto the main road,
wishing you'd known how much I'd sacrificed
for you: all the time I'd spent watching, and
learning, and planning.

But all you wanted was to leave me. To
give up on us. I could hear the desperation
in your voice as you lied and told me you'd
accidentally left your cell phone behind.

Your face was sweaty, but I turned the heat
up higher, hoping you'd finally be honest.
With suffering comes honesty, and you needed
to tell me the truth if we were going to have
trust.

"Please," you just kept begging, like a
disobedient dog who wants to be let out.

Meanwhile, I hummed a favorite tune,
silently telling myself that in time you'd
see that this was truly for the best.

. . .

Dear Jack:

I couldn't find my cell phone. It wasn't in my bag or in any of my pockets. And so I asked you to take me back to the coffee shop to see if I'd left it there, but instead you just kept singing your Jack and Jill song, making my skin crawl.

Still, I tried to tell myself that everything would be fine. Tried to picture you as a little boy swimming with your dad at the pond. Tried to imagine you showing your artwork at a gallery, or sitting in a college lecture hall discussing romanticism in literature.

We drove for several minutes down a long, dark road, where there wasn't a lot of traffic. I looked out the window, scanning for shops or businesses, but they were few and far between. "Where are we going?" I asked you.

"Surprise, surprise, will meet your eyes. Be a good little girl, and get a great big prize."

I swallowed down a mouthful of bile with more lemonade.

"Relax," you said once again. "I'm going to take away your pain, remember?"

"But I'm not _in_ pain."

"No need to pretend, my little friend. Just tell the truth again and again."

I clenched my teeth and held back tears, still trying to convince myself that everything would be okay, that we'd eventually stop somewhere, that I'd excuse myself to go to the bathroom and would be able to escape.

A few moments later, you pulled down a side street and into a back parking lot. We were partially concealed by a long row of trees. I peeked through them, spotting a couple of ivy-covered brick houses sandwiched together. There was a sign outside one of them. I squinted hard, trying to make out what it said, but all I could see was a picture of a piano sitting beneath a string of blurry words.

Still trying to be hopeful, I asked, "Is this where you live? Are we here to look at your photographs?" I knew that we had to have been at least a town or two from home.

You put the car in park and cut the ignition. Without turning to face me, you told me to be a good girl and to do as I was told.

"Why are we here?" Hearing the tone of my own voice scared me even more.

"Be a good girl," you repeated; your voice was smooth and even.

Shaking all over, I glanced toward the door handle, wondering if I could get out now and run away. But to my complete and utter horror, the handle had been removed.

. . .

36

*T*HE FOLLOWING MORNING, my parents are already gone by the time I wake up. Aunt Alexia is gone, too. Her bedroom door is open a crack, and when I peek in, I see that her bed's been made, and her room's been cleaned up—aside from the mural, that is.

In the kitchen, Dad's left a note for me, saying that he, Mom, and Alexia have gone to meet with Aunt Alexia's doctor—no doubt in response to what happened last night. I grab a rag and make an attempt to wash the glow-in-the-dark paint from my wall, but my phone rings, interrupting me.

"Hey," Kimmie says when I pick up. Her tone is oddly cheerful.

Whereas mine is completely spent. "Hi," I manage to utter.

"What's wrong?" she asks, as if there were any doubt.

Anger bubbles up inside me as I think about how desperate I was to talk with her last night and how she refused to answer my calls.

My thumb hovers over the off button, wondering if I should let her go. It's what she's been wanting for a while now anyway.

"Okay, so you're obviously mad about how completely standoffish I've been. Am I right?"

I don't answer.

"And I totally get that," she continues. "I'm sorry I wasn't around for you last night—for the last couple of days, actually."

I think it's been longer than that. It feels like she's been pulling away for weeks—like there's been less and less I can share with her.

"I'm sorry," she says again. "But I want to make it up to you."

"Why?" I ask; I'm suddenly feeling as guarded as Danica—as if there may be some secret joke being played on me.

"What do you mean, *why*? Because I'm your friend."

The word makes my lip tremble. In some way I feel relief, because I seriously thought that I'd lost her. But I also can't help feeling furious, because I needed her friendship last night.

"So, what do you say?" Kimmie asks. "Shall we go get ourselves some answers?"

"Answers to what?"

"To all this Danica drama, of course. What do you say?

You and me, at Danica's house, in one hour. I'll come pick you up."

"What's with the sudden change of heart?" *Did something happen? Does she know something I should?* "I thought you said I shouldn't get involved."

"Yes, but you kind of already *are* involved. And if you are, then so am I. So, what do you say? Are you game, or what?"

"Game," I say before hanging up.

I forgo washing the wall and instead leave a note for my parents (tacked up on the fridge, right below theirs), telling them I'll be home around lunchtime.

Kimmie pulls up about twenty minutes later in her mom's car. "Feeling bold?" she asks, giggling at my bright yellow sweater.

"Feeling like crap?" I joke, nodding toward her brown one. She's got it paired with a matching checked skirt.

"Okay, so, I already know that Danica's not at work," she begins. "I called the Press & Grind earlier and asked if I could speak with her. Whoever answered said that she was off until tomorrow."

"Well, you've certainly done your homework."

"You honestly have no idea."

"Meaning?"

"I found a skater, or at least a *former* skater," she says, clarifying matters. "Mandy Candy."

"Excuse me?" I ask, feeling a bit lost.

"Let's just say a friend of a friend of my mom's hair-stylist of a friend got talking to me about sports and stuff.

237

I brought up skating, because, let's face it, you never know who's in the know. Not to mention the fact that hairstylists know just about everything. And, anyway, yes, it's true: Mandy used to skate. Apparently pretty well, but then she ended up sucking ass during an all-important competition. Not literally ass-sucking," she says, as if I needed the clarification. "And so she up and quit."

"When?" I ask, wondering if Danica used to skate as well—if that might explain some of the animosity between her and the Candies.

"Unfortunately, the friend of a friend couldn't remember," Kimmie says, "but she said that it had to have been at least five years ago."

"Interesting," I say, gazing out the window, at a sudden loss for words. There's so much I haven't told her, but I'm not quite sure I should.

"Look," she says, forcing me to face her by yanking the sleeve of my coat. "I *am* your friend. Whether you like it or not, you're stuck with me."

"Is this because I called you a kajillion times last night? Because now you're feeling guilty about not picking up?"

"I'm sorry I didn't pick up. But *you* have to understand, too: this hasn't been easy for me. So much has changed between us."

"You're right," I say, thinking how it wasn't so long ago that the height of our adventures involved afternoons spent making double-fudge fajitas behind my mom's vegan back. "But I've given things a lot of thought. And, well, it was stupid of me to try and take away my friendship when I was accusing you of potentially doing the same one day."

"That's awfully deep for a Saturday morning, don't you think?"

"It's Wes's psychoanalysis, not mine. Don't tell him I said this, but that boy is freaking brilliant, and his dad's an absolute tool for not seeing it."

"His dad's an absolute tool—period."

"Brilliant Boy also told me that he recommended you talk with Ben." She bats her gold-coated eyelashes at me.

I nod, and then tell her about our time together at the labyrinth. "I honestly don't know why I let myself open up to him, because he clearly isn't interested."

"Are we both talking about the same touch boy here?"

"Well, he has a funny way of showing his interest."

"Because coming to your work, whisking you away to an enchanted labyrinth, and sticking his tongue down your throat are such unclear signs."

"You know what I mean."

"Not really," she says, looking at me the way the kids at school do—like I'm some freak science experiment that they don't quite understand. "I haven't even mentioned the fact that Ben gobbled his pride by contacting his ex–best friend just to make sure that you're okay while he isn't around. I mean, it's obvious the boy's in love with you."

"I'm not so sure," I say, thinking how it isn't obvious at all.

"Where's he going, by the way?"

"He said he had to head home for a bit, but he wouldn't tell me why. Translation: more secrets."

"And speaking of . . . you've yet to tell me why you called last night. I mean, I know you don't need a reason, but it seemed kind of urgent."

"It was Aunt Alexia," I say, proceeding to explain what happened. "I feel partly to blame—like maybe I pushed her too far, which got her upset."

"She's mentally *ill*, Camelia. They do things like that: biting body parts, painting walls, talking all gibberish . . . But still, you have to admit, it's pretty impressive that she was able to predict the camera clue and some of the stuff that happened in the locker room."

"Not to mention the sea glass clue," I tell her. "I saw Danica wearing it around her neck on the day I stopped by her house."

"See, there's no denying it." Kimmie wraps her faux ponytail around her finger. "You and your aunt are clearly connected. I mean, it's almost eerie how much."

I nod, remembering how Dr. Tylyn said that life was about making choices, and that I shouldn't choose to become overwhelmed by how similar Aunt Alexia and I seem.

"So, we need a plan," Kimmie says, taking a sip of soda (even though it's barely ten a.m.). "Should we tell Danica that we were just in the area and thought we'd stop by? Or should we go for brutal honesty and say that we have reason to believe that her days are numbered?"

"I'd go with option number two," I tell her. "But I don't think we need to be that brutal."

"Agreed. Now, what do you say we go get ourselves some answers?" She gives me a high five, and we set out for Danica's.

37

WE ARRIVE ABOUT FIVE MINUTES LATER. Kimmie is already halfway up Danica's walkway before I even step out of the car. I look around, checking to see if the Taurus is parked anywhere, but luckily it doesn't appear that it is.

"Are you coming?" Kimmie asks, just before ringing the doorbell.

I join her at the door, and Danica answers almost immediately. "Shall I call the police to report you for harassment *now*?" she asks, glaring at me. "Or wait until Monday, when I'll be sure to find a dead rodent with your fingerprints all over it stuffed inside my locker?"

"Calling the police is actually a good idea," Kimmie says. "Word is, your life could very well be at stake."

"I was referring to Camelia's apparent need to stalk me," Danica says.

"FYI: stalkers don't ring doorbells," Kimmie tells her.

"They follow you around when you least expect it, prank you with harassing phone calls, and then tie you up in the back of trailers."

"Well, the two of you should know," she says, folding her arms.

Kimmie peers past Danica into the house. "Can we come in to talk? I promise it'll just be a couple minutes."

"And then *she'll* be out of my hair for good?" Danica asks.

Kimmie doesn't answer this, but Danica lets us inside anyway. She leads us to a family room at the back of the house. Like the outside of the house, the interior has definitely deteriorated with age. Similar to a fraternity house, minus the beer-guzzling college students, there isn't much in terms of decor. A portable fridge in the family room doubles as a coffee table, and there's even the requisite stack of old pizza boxes collected near a recycling bin.

"Are your parents at home?" I ask, remembering how she mentioned that she barely ever saw them.

Danica shakes her head, but once again she doesn't elaborate. Instead, she takes a seat on the arm of a chair (because the chair itself is loaded with old newspapers and take-out menus) and demands to know what all of this is about.

"I know I told you this before," I begin, finding a vacant spot on the couch beside Kimmie, "but I think you might be in trouble."

Danica lets out an obnoxious yawn.

"Camelia doesn't make this stuff up," Kimmie insists.

"No, she just has full-on convulsions in her sculpture classes, shouts out random phrases, and claws at people's eyes."

"That only happened one time," I say, knowing how stupid the excuse sounds. "And it wasn't exactly like that."

"Bottom line: we think someone might be out to hurt you," Kimmie tells her.

"Who?" Danica asks, checking her watch like we're wasting her time.

"There's a guy who's been following you," I tell her. "In a black Ford Taurus, with tinted windows . . ."

"Do the letters *DM* mean anything to you?" Kimmie asks.

To my surprise, Danica actually entertains the question, staring off into space, as if trying to think of any names or abbreviations she may know. But a couple of seconds later, she shakes her head.

"Well, have you noticed if anyone's been following you?" I ask. "Or have you been getting any weird phone calls lately?"

"No one's been following me, but I *have* gotten a few weird calls. Hang-ups, mostly. My dad's gotten them, too."

"And do you check the caller ID?" I ask.

She nods. "But it always comes up blocked. We figure it must be telemarketing." She pulls the elastic from her pigtail so that the hair falls in a bob, framing her face. The golden-brown color complements the natural glow of her skin, and if it weren't for the constant scowl on her face, I'd say she could be really pretty.

"How long have you been working at the Press & Grind?" Kimmie asks, gesturing toward the paper cup that sits on the portable fridge–turned table. It has the shop's logo printed on the side (a picture of an old-fashioned coffee press "holding hands" with a grinder).

"Not long. It's a fairly new gig. I usually work in the back. Now, will that be all?" She fakes a smile.

"You wouldn't happen to figure-skate, would you?" I ask, totally taking her off guard.

Danica's eyes narrow into tight, angry slits. "Is this some kind of a joke?"

"Did some girls ever play a trick on you while you were skating?" Kimmie persists. "Were you sent to a special school because of it?"

"You need to go," Danica says, getting up from her chair. She storms out of the room, moving toward the front of the house.

"Why?" I ask, following right behind her. "Was it something we said? Something we asked?"

"Go!" Danica says, standing at the front door now, clearly unwilling to explain.

Kimmie and I make an attempt to apologize as we exit her house. But Danica isn't having any of it, nor is she acknowledging our concern for her safety.

"We're on your side," I say, standing at her doorstep. "You've got it all wrong about me."

"Do I?" she asks. "Because, the way I see things, *you're* the only one harassing me—coming by my house uninvited, bothering me at school, prying into my business, and showing up where I work."

"Danica, you don't understand—"

"No, I understand perfectly," she says, cutting me off. "Come here again and I *will* call the police."

And with that, she slams the door.

38

"*W*HAT THE HELL JUST happened?" Kimmie asks, once we get back inside her mom's car.

"We pissed her off, that's what." I look out at the street again, but I still don't see the Taurus anywhere.

"Yes, but *how?*"

"Do I seriously need to start a list?" I ask. "Number one, we showed up at her house. Number two, we told her once again that her life might be in danger."

"And number three, we brought up the topic of skating and switching schools," Kimmie says.

"Agreed. It did seem like she went a little ballistic when we started probing her about skating."

"So, there's definitely some shred of truth in there," Kimmie says. "Except, Freetown High is hardly considered a 'special school.'" She makes air quotes around the words.

"Unless all of this is connected to something that

happened in her past—meaning that she *was* a skater but isn't any longer because of that one big and traumatic event?"

"That's my vote," Kimmie says. "But then, what special school did she go to in the past?"

"I don't know," I say, remembering my conversation with Aunt Alexia—when she said that whoever was in danger had been driven over the edge after being tormented by a group of girls. "A school for students with emotional problems, maybe?"

"Does one like that even exist around here?"

"Yes, but that's the puzzling part," I say. "Because Humphrey School is for grades seven through twelve. Danica's been in Freetown Public with us since then."

"Which brings us to the next question: are you sure Danica's the one in trouble?"

"She has to be," I say, thinking about all the clues so far. "Plus, why else would she have gotten so upset when we asked her about ice-skating?"

"Maybe because she's talentless. Isn't that what the voices keep repeating inside your head?"

"Yes, but then, why would my aunt say that the person in trouble was *more* talented than the other girls? *So* talented that they played a trick on her—one that ended in her getting locked up or confined in some way?"

"Unless, of course, maybe Danica was one of the bullying girls . . . one who helped play the trick on another girl—i.e., Mandy Candy—because that girl was the better skater."

"Good point," I say, thinking how that almost makes sense, considering Danica's prickly side. Is it possible that Danica was one of the bullies in this case? "You do realize how much I envy your corrupt and suspicious mind, don't you?" I ask, ever awed by Kimmie's ability to ask all the right questions.

"Honey, there's a whole lot enviable about me." She starts the car, but then pauses a moment and turns to me.

"What's wrong?" I ask her.

"Okay, so, there's just one more thing that I have to ask." Her face gets serious. "What did you mean before, when you said that you *owed* it to Danica to help her?"

I bite my lip, reminded of how well Kimmie knows me, even when I do keep stuff to myself. And so I fill her in on the whole humiliating story of what happened in junior high.

"And now you're trying to make things up to her?" she asks.

"Yes, but that's not the only reason I'm helping her. This isn't just about me. It's not about how guilty I'm feeling, or how much better I'll feel once Danica's safe. I mean, when I really stop to think about it, I couldn't *not* help someone if I knew they were truly in trouble."

"Which is why I'm proud to be your friend."

"No prouder than I am to be yours. And, by the way, I owe you an apology, too. You aren't the only one to blame for the weirdness between us. It takes two to make tension, after all."

"Apology accepted." She smiles.

We hug—a long-overdue-squeeze-until-your-eyes-turn-runny hug. "Don't ever be afraid to tell me anything," Kimmie says. "You've seen me in period panties, after all."

"And with your finger lodged up your nose," I add.

"Right." She grimaces, breaking the embrace. She pulls away from the curb and takes me home.

To my surprise, Adam's Bronco is parked in my driveway.

"Scandalous plans that you neglected to tell me about?" she asks.

"Not that I can recall," I say, spotting Adam standing at the front door. It looks like my parents aren't home yet; Dad's car is still missing from the driveway.

Adam waves when he sees us pull up in front of the house.

"I wonder what he wants," I say.

"Okay, so maybe it's *my* turn to start a list," Kimmie says, "the top of which would include the fact that Adam's hot for you and can't stay away. The bottom of which would be that he's here to spy on you for Ben's sake."

"Be serious," I tell her.

"Slightly gelled hair, dark-washed jeans, and an Abercrombie-inspired sweatshirt . . . I'd vote for option number one, but I'll leave that verdict up to you."

"And where do you think you're going?" I ask her, signaling to Adam that I'll only be a minute.

"Date with Dad," she says. "He's got some major making up to do after blowing me off for that hoagie the other night."

"Is Tammy really all that bad?"

"She's *nineteen*," Kimmie reminds me. "I mean, think about it: my future stepmom and I could theoretically hang out in the same clubs, and no one would think anything of it."

"Is it Tammy you're really mad at, or your dad?"

"Getting all shrinkified on me, are you?"

"Not shrinkified, just curious."

"Well, trust me when I say that I have ample reason to hate my father."

"Hate?"

"Okay, I'm pissed." She lets out a sigh.

"But still you persist in wanting to spend time with him?"

"Because, my dear Chameleon, there's a very small but self-torturous part of me that still pines for his approval."

"Wait, does being pissed have anything to do with the Big D?" I motion to the henna tattoo on her hand. "Any chance it might stand for 'anti-divorce'?"

"I'm impressed," Kimmie says with a smirk. "It seems that my corrupt and suspicious mind is rubbing off on you."

"But that doesn't exactly answer my question."

"And I don't exactly want to get into it right now, especially since there's a hunky male literally knocking at your door. Call me later?"

"Definitely," I say, giving her another hug and thanking her once again for being the amazing friend that she is.

39

ONCE KIMMIE PULLS AWAY, Adam greets me with a bag from the Press & Grind. "Triple fudge brownie?" he asks. "I've had a craving since last night, and luckily they allowed me back in," he jokes. "I half expected to find our pictures nailed up on the door with giant X's marked over our faces."

"Very funny." I fake a laugh.

"So, anyway, I figured that since I was in your area . . ."

"Is that the only reason for your visit?" I ask, giving him a suspicious grin.

"Am I that obvious?"

"In a good way," I say, taking a seat on the front step.

Adam joins me. "Okay, so maybe I was feeling a little confused after last night . . . after you kicked my butt to the curb." He rubs the alleged bruise on his butt.

"It was only because I thought I needed some alone time. For the record, I thought wrong."

"You could've called me." He bumps his shoulder against mine.

"I wish I had," I say, feeling partly responsible for the insecurity he feels. "But I guess that after all that butt-to-the-curb-kicking, I didn't feel I had any right to call."

"You can always call me. No matter what."

"Well, thanks," I say, feeling a smile cross my lips.

Adam smiles, too, taking an extra moment to push a strand of my hair back from my face. "And not only have I come bearing treats, but I've also come fully loaded with highly valuable info."

"What kind of valuable info?"

"I've been asking around about Danica," he explains. "More incentive to get you to talk to me."

"I *want* to talk to you."

"Good," he says, "because I really want to help you, for no other reason than because I care about you and want you to be safe."

"Well, thanks," I say, feeling my face heat up, and thinking how while Ben's away, having other people look out for me *for* him, Adam's here, trying to help me out on his own. "Do you want to come in?"

"Is that a rhetorical question?"

I smile and get up to unlock the door. In the kitchen, I fetch us a couple of plates for our brownies, and then we sit down at the kitchen island. "So, what did you find out?" I ask, recalling that the only thing I told him about Danica was that she was someone I went to school with and someone I thought might be in trouble.

"You mentioned that she might be a skater, or might be connected to a skater," he begins. "And so I asked a friend who's well connected in the whole sporting circuit in this area—"

"Do you mean Janet?"

"Right," he says, lighting up, having apparently forgotten that I met his gymnast friend a couple of months ago at his apartment. "Janet's dad, who's also her coach, works at the Flint Arena in town, as does Janet, from time to time. I guess that's where most of the local skating competitions take place."

"And?" I ask, anticipating the news.

"And both Janet and her dad know a bunch of the skating coaches. So, I asked Janet if she'd mind calling a few of them to see if they'd worked with someone by the name of Danica."

"Had they?"

Adam shakes his head, seemingly even more disappointed than I am. "And one of the coaches has been working there, teaching all levels of skating, for over twenty years."

"Well, thanks for trying," I say, taking a defeated bite of brownie. "Thank Janet for me, too."

"Sure thing," he says, "but don't think I quit there. I started asking around campus—people who are from Freetown—if anyone might know a Danica. I mean, you have to admit, it's not exactly a name you'd forget."

"Seriously?" I ask, flattered by his efforts.

"Deadly." He gives me a mock-menacing grin, suddenly reminding me of Wes. "Anyway, there was this one girl—Marcie something—who said she knew a girl named Danica from her church. I guess Danica's family was super into it: they'd attend the weekly services, help out on Bake Sale day, clean up after the Christmas bazaar, et cetera, et cetera. Then, one day, the mom left, and the family sort of fell apart."

"Fell apart?" I ask, thinking how Danica had mentioned barely ever seeing her parents.

"Marcie said there were at least two kids in the family, including Danica, but she couldn't remember how old the other one was, or if it was a girl or boy. Marcie also thought the dad worked in construction, because he helped rebuild the church's holy center."

"Wow," I say, utterly impressed.

"Now, tell me, was all of that worth me busting in on you?"

"Are you kidding? These brownies alone were worth it," I say, taking another bite.

"Using me for my chocolate, are you?"

"I'm really glad you busted in," I say, feeling bad for pushing him away before, when it's so obvious that he belongs right by my side.

"Well, I'm probably going to regret telling you this," he begins, "but Ben called me to check in last night . . . to see how you were doing."

"And what's so regrettable about telling me that?"

"What do you think?" His dark brown eyes grow wide.

I reach out to touch his hand, hoping to reassure him— but of what I'm not quite sure.

A moment later, I hear the front door swing open.

"Camelia?" Mom calls.

I tell her I'm in the kitchen, and in the time it takes for Adam and me to gobble up the remainder of our butter-and-eggs-laden brownies, Mom and Dad come in and assume their positions at opposing ends of the kitchen island.

"Camelia, your father and I really need to talk to you," Mom says, acknowledging Adam with a polite nod.

Dad's acting no-nonsense as well. He gives Adam a terse hello, rather than taking him hostage in the living room as he usually does so the two of them can discuss soccer.

"What happened?" I ask, suspecting that it must have something to do with Aunt Alexia.

"Maybe you can call Adam later," Mom suggests, ignoring the question.

"No," I say, taking Adam's hand again. "Adam can hear whatever it is you have to tell me."

Mom turns her back, clearly frustrated, but she doesn't argue. Instead, she gets herself a shiny green pill and chases it down with a full glass of iced dandelion tea. She sits beside me at the island, somehow already a little less lucid. "So, we spoke with Alexia's doctor about what happened last night," she begins. "He kept her overnight at the hospital for some tests, and then we met with him again this morning."

"And?" I ask.

"And he thinks it best if she stays there for now."

"Meaning, she's locked up again?" I can hear the alarm in my voice.

"Not locked up. It's only temporary, until we decide our next steps."

"No," I say, feeling my blood run cold.

"Look, it's important for me that you don't blame yourself," Mom continues, as if reading my mind. "This was ultimately my decision. I just didn't think it was the healthiest thing for her to be here—not healthy for me, not healthy for you, not healthy for things between your dad and me, and especially not healthy for her."

"It was fine," I say, nearly coughing up my brownie. "She was doing well here, talking to me, starting to really come around. . . ."

"What *were* you two talking about last night?" Dad folds his arms, slightly confrontational.

"What do *you* think?" I ask, challenging him to come clean.

He looks at Mom and then turns away, backing right down.

"It's only temporary," Mom says again.

"Prison's only temporary for some people, too."

"This isn't prison, Camelia. It's the local hospital. They have a mental health unit with qualified staff. Alexia's even allowed to walk around outside." Mom gets up from the kitchen island and fills her glass with more tea.

I shake my head, thinking about how much Aunt Alexia's helped me. Not just with her power, but also simply with herself—with how much she's opened up to me. "You've got it all wrong about her," I snap, feeling a lump forming in my throat. "This wasn't the way things were supposed to happen."

Still holding my hand, Adam gives it another squeeze, trying his best to make me feel at ease. But I can't help feeling that this is my fault. If I hadn't gone into her room last night, she'd never have gotten so upset.

"You can visit her," Mom says. "I'll even take you there myself. Now, how about something to eat?"

"Does she have her doll with her, at least?" I ask, ignoring her offer.

"What doll?" Mom turns to me, reliably clueless. Dad's face scrunches up in confusion as well.

"Forget it," I say, getting up from the island. I tell Adam it's time for both of us to go, and then I lead him out the door.

*A*DAM DRIVES US AROUND for a while, working feverishly to cheer me up. He asks if I'm hungry; offers to take me to the movie of my choice; and tells me that as hard as it is to accept or understand, my parents did what they thought was best for everyone.

"Did my dad slip you a twenty to say that?" I ask.

"A fifty." He grins.

"My aunt doesn't belong in there," I say, getting emotional all over again. "People don't understand her the way I do."

"Care to try to make *me* understand?" He pulls over to the side of the road.

"What do you mean?" I ask, noticing how warm it is in his car. I try to angle the heat vent away from me, but it doesn't seem to move.

"I mean, tell me about your aunt," he says. "What is it about her? What makes her so misunderstood?"

I feel a smile cross my lips, never ceasing to be amazed by him. "You're very sweet, you know that?"

"Except, 'sweet' wasn't exactly what I was going for."

I wait for him to make a joke, but his face stays completely serious, showing me how much he truly cares.

"I'd love to be able to tell you everything," I say. "And I *will*. In time. It's just that right now I need to talk to Dr. Tylyn."

"I seriously can't win." Adam leans back against his seat, running his fingers through his hair in frustration.

"Don't be upset," I tell him.

"Then, how should I be? Because I feel like you keep pushing me away."

I bite my lip, thinking how "pushed away" is exactly how I feel most of the time with Ben. "I'm so grateful to have you in my life, but there's some major stuff going on in my life right now—stuff that Dr. Tylyn already knows about. Believe me when I say that it isn't personal." I lean over to kiss his cheek.

Adam forces a tiny smile, but then starts driving again.

"I'm sorry," I whisper, but Adam doesn't respond.

And so I call Dr. Tylyn on her cell and tell her that I need an emergency appointment. "Can you drop me off at her office?" I ask Adam, once I hang up.

"Sure thing," he says; they're the last words I hear from him before he pulls up in front of her building.

"I'll call you later, okay?"

"Sure thing," he repeats, and he drives away as soon as I shut the car door.

*　*　*

I wait a few minutes outside Dr. Tylyn's office until she finally arrives. "I'm sorry to bother you," I tell her.

"Don't be," she says, unlocking her door. "I gave you my emergency number for a reason. I'm glad that you actually used it."

"Well, thanks," I say, noticing that she's dressed in her weekend wear (a T-shirt and jeans), rather than her usual skirt and blouse, reminding me that I've interrupted her weekend—as if I couldn't possibly feel worse.

I enter her office; it smells like day-old vanilla incense.

Dr. Tylyn switches on some lights and takes a seat across from me on the talk sofa. Her expression is as neutral as Switzerland.

"My aunt's back in the hospital," I say, before she can ask me anything.

"I see," she says, studying my face. "And that makes you feel . . ."

"Scared, sad, guilty."

"Why guilty?"

"Because I was supposed to help her," I say. There's a crumbling sensation inside my heart.

"Were you good to her? Did you talk to her? Did you make her feel that she was welcome in your home?"

"I think so."

"Did you treat her any differently than you would someone else? Someone who wasn't undergoing psychological care, I mean?"

I shake my head, thinking about the conversation Aunt

Alexia and I had in my room—when we talked about my star-themed birthday party. "I felt like we were getting closer than ever."

"Then you probably helped a lot more than you know."

"So, then, why do I feel like I failed her?" I ask, hearing the dryness in my voice.

Tylyn must hear it, too, because she gets up to fetch me a bottle of water from her minifridge.

"Thank you." I take a sip. The rush of coldness down my throat is almost sweet to the taste. "I just wish I could've done more."

"Like what, specifically?"

I shrug, reluctant to get into it—to get into the fact that I'd hoped to save my aunt from psychosis by bonding with her over psychometry. As if I were suddenly some expert.

"Camelia?"

I'm eager to change the subject, and so I proceed to tell her about all the clues that Aunt Alexia predicted.

"Were they clues? Or might they just have been random premonitions? Like with what happened in the locker room with those girls . . . with the lipstick and the broken mirror? I guess what I should *really* be asking is: how are you so sure there's something bigger going on?"

"Because I feel it," I say, fully aware of how weak the answer sounds.

"Just a feeling? There's no concrete reason?"

My jaw tenses and I take another sip, wondering if maybe I'm wasting my time.

"I'm just playing devil's advocate here, Camelia . . . just making sure that your actions are in line with your thoughts. I'm not denying anything. It's important for you to know that."

"Okay," I say, feeling a tinge better.

"So then, tell me why you think your aunt is giving you clues to something bigger," she says, "to some grand puzzle that needs a solution."

"It's hard to explain, but in that moment, when I zone out—when the voices tell me how worthless I am, and that I'd be better off dead—I almost believe it. I almost believe what the voices are saying."

"Have you ever thought about hurting yourself, Camelia?"

I shake my head, surprised that she'd think so. "As soon as I snap out of it, everything goes back to normal."

"As soon as you wake up or come out of the hallucination, you mean."

I nod and take a deep breath, suddenly feeling as if there's a lack of air in the room and in my lungs.

"So, then I'll ask you again: what makes you think there's a bigger picture here?"

"Because there have been bigger pictures before. In the past, I mean." When Adam was in trouble and I helped save him. When I was in trouble and what I sensed and sculpted turned out to be clues that helped save me.

"Have you talked to the girl you think might be in trouble?"

"A few times."

"And has she given you any reason to believe that her life's in any sort of danger?"

"No." I sigh, feeling more self-conscious by the moment. "But I don't believe her. She's hiding something."

"Do you know that for a fact?"

"I think that the voices in my head telling me I'm worthless and that I'd be better off dead are a pretty good tip-off, don't you?"

"They *could* be," she says, ever the devil's advocate. "But we shouldn't ignore other possibilities, either, especially when the writing on the locker-room mirror had more to do with harassment than with actual death."

I shift uneasily in my seat, suddenly wishing that I'd stayed with Adam.

"What do you think?" she asks, when I don't say anything. "Again, I'm merely raising questions. It may take a bit of work to find the answers. I've worked with people whose premonitions add up to one all-encompassing event, and others whose premonitions are more about predicting unrelated incidents. Let's be open to both possibilities until we have reason to believe otherwise. Sound okay?"

I take another sip, feeling the bottle shake, thinking about some of the unanswered clues so far: the camera, the initials *DM*, the player piano, and the thing my aunt said about a skating competition. Is it possible that those things don't have anything to do with Danica?

But then what about Aunt Alexia's sketch? Or the fact that Danica got so upset when Kimmie and I mentioned skating?

"Well?" Dr. Tylyn asks.

But by now I've forgotten the question. "I think that my aunt and I are truly connected," I say.

"And you two share the same power," she agrees. "But that doesn't mean that you have to share the same destiny."

I look away, but out of the corner of my eye, I can see Dr. Tylyn staring at me, studying my every blink, swallow, and twitch.

"That's what this is really about, isn't it?" she asks. "If your aunt is out of the hospital, it means that she isn't mentally ill. And if *she* isn't mentally ill, it means that you won't one day become mentally ill, either. Well, guess what? I can't promise you a life of sanity. I can't promise it to you, or for anyone else."

"How do you know that I'm not already crazy?" I ask, staring right at her now, feeling tears course down my face.

"Simple," she says, handing me a tissue. "Because what you predict comes true. Don't ever lose sight of that. And don't ever forget that you have choices here, Camelia. What is it that *you* want?"

"To not end up like my aunt," I say, looking down at my wrists.

"Be more specific."

"To not handle my power the way she handled hers." I wipe my tears, feeling guilty for passing judgment on Alexia.

"Better," she says, finally showing a hint of emotion; a subtle smile sits on her lips. "Don't become a victim of someone else's choices."

"What if I don't have a choice?" I ask, hearing a quaver in my voice.

"There's always a choice. Even in the face of tragedy, you can choose to overcome, to gain wisdom, to practice compassion."

"But my aunt doesn't have those choices," I say.

"Maybe she doesn't anymore, but I'd be willing to bet that at one point she did. She tried to suppress her powers, and in the end they overcame her."

"So, what does that mean for me?"

"What do *you* think it means?" She narrows her eyes.

"That I shouldn't be afraid of my power?" I ask, feeling a grin form on my face, knowing that I've gotten the answer right.

"It's a part of who you are," she says. "So, why not embrace it?"

I nod, feeling the proverbial hairs standing up on the back of my neck. Because at last, I finally get it.

Dear Jill,

We arrived at my apartment, and you were
still acting resistant. I knew you didn't like
it, but I had no choice other than to tell
you how to act. Imagine if someone saw how
troubled you looked and thought that something
was wrong?

"You can trust me, remember?" I reminded
you, taking hold of your arm despite all your
squirming to be let go.

You started to cry harder, stumbling as you
walked, making things so much more difficult
than they needed to be.

We entered through the back of the
building, behind the surveillance cameras, to
give us more privacy. I thought that'd make
you more comfortable, but you screamed once we
got inside, like something serious was wrong.
Luckily my father's music drowned out your
voice. We didn't need any extra attention. In
time you'd understand that.

I'm sorry that I accidentally pushed you—
and that you fell down hard on your back. But
you really gave me no other choice.

"What do you want with me?" you asked,
still on the ground, scooting away as I
approached. Tears rolled down your cheeks. You
were the most beautiful thing I'd ever seen.

"I'm your friend, remember?" I knelt down
beside you and wiped your tears with my thumb.
"And if you let me, I'll take all your pain
away."

"What pain?"

"All of it, Jill. From grade school until now. You'll feel like a brand-new person."

"But my name isn't Jill."

"It is now," I said, taking your hand and leading you inside my apartment.

. . .

Dear Jack:

Why did you keep calling me Jill and insisting
that I call you Jack? Why did you sing me
nursery rhymes and ask that I join in? When I
didn't, you set the tune to "Yankee Doodle Dandy"
on your player piano, so that it played over and
over again while you filled in your own lyrics. I
hadn't known that Jack and Jill had more than
one stanza, but you knew at least four by heart.

Your apartment was huge, with high ceilings,
almost like a city loft. You had the entire floor to
yourself.

"I've got a surprise for you," you said, crossing
the living room like it was Christmas morning;
there was an extra skip in your step.

It looked like you really were a photographer.
There was a tripod set up and some overhead
spotlights with a white backdrop. From behind an
L-shaped sofa, you pulled out a large box with a
red ribbon.

"I've been counting the days till I could give
this to you." You seemed so happy, but then you
forced the box into my hands, shoving me back,
showing me who was boss.

I knelt down on the floor. With jittery fingers, I
untied the bow and removed the lid, surprised to
see what was inside: a short white dress with
gold trim.

"For skating," you said, squatting down beside me. "You used to love to skate. You said so yourself."

I nodded, remembering having told you that during our chat.

"Go try it on," you insisted. "The bathroom's over there."

"It's too small," I said, checking the size on the dress label.

"Try it," you demanded. "Don't be ungrateful."

Do you remember how I clutched the uniform against my stomach? How more tears rolled down my face?

"I also got you some skates," you continued, wiping my tears with your thumb again. "Eventually I'd like to take some photos of you skating. I want to show you the way I see you: beautiful." You got up and removed your camera from the tripod. You took one, two . . . nine, ten . . . twenty-seven, twenty-eight photos of me.

From different angles.

From various points of the room.

Close-ups and long shots.

As more tears ran down my face. And the skating uniform still balled up against my stomach.

"It might be hard now," you said; click, click, click. "But soon you'll see how beautiful you really are."

"And you'll take my pain away," I whispered, hearing the sobs in my voice.

"All of it," you said, finally pausing from snapping photos, relieved to see that I was finally coming to my senses.

. . .

41

*B*EFORE I LEAVE DR. TYLYN'S OFFICE, I ask her if she'd be willing to visit my aunt at the hospital—to see if she might be able to help her. Thankfully, she agrees.

I exit the main campus building and try giving Kimmie a call, as promised, but the phone goes straight to voice mail. I leave her a message and then head for the bus stop. To my complete and utter shock, Wes is there. I spot his Where's Waldo scarf from a block away.

"What are you doing here?" I ask, once he's within earshot. "At a bus stop in the next town over, when you have your own car?"

He looks startled to see me as well, but as I get closer, his expression morphs into defensiveness: his lip twitches and his nostrils flare. "I could ask you the same," he says, standing right in front of me now.

"I was at Hayden, talking to my therapist. What's your excuse?"

He tugs nervously at his scarf. "I was trying to get away."

"Away from what? Does this have something to do with why I couldn't reach you last night?"

He swallows hard, then lets out a breath. His eyes are runny from the cold; at least, I think it's the chill that's making them tear up.

"My dad's pissed. Someone keyed my car, so he took it away."

"And that's your fault?" I reach into my pocket for a tissue, suddenly realizing how distraught he is.

"Everything's my fault."

"You know that's not true."

"Well, it feels like it is."

I look toward the billboard poster that hangs over the bus stop—an ad for some dance club in the next town over—still wondering what he's doing *here*, of all places, and not stewing over cappuccino at the Press & Grind, or taking photographs in the middle of nowhere (his new favorite pastime). "Was the keying really bad?"

"Kind of. My dad's having the entire car stripped and repainted as a result. Pink," he adds. "That's what color he thinks I should be driving."

"Wes, that's crazy."

"I haven't even told you the *real* crazy part: the keying was an actual message, rather than just scratch marks."

"And what did it say?" I ask, already sensing the worst.

"It said, *You're out of your league*." His chin quivers, but he clears his throat, still trying to be strong.

"Who would *do* that?" I ask, feeling my heart plummet. "Do you think it was that guy we followed?"

I peer down the main boulevard, remembering having gone in that direction on our chase, and how Wes seemed to know the area well. "Maybe he got your license plate. Where was your car parked when the keying occurred?"

"At home." He shrugs. "But I'm not even sure if that's the guy who did it."

"Who else could it have been?"

He checks his watch, just as the Number 12 bus turns the corner, coming toward us. "This is my ride."

"You're not going home?" I ask, feeling my face crumple up in confusion. The 12 goes in the opposite direction of Freetown.

"Honestly, if you were me, would *you* want to go home?"

"Come to my house, then," I suggest. "Or better yet, let's go grab a bite to eat. We need to talk about this, don't you think?"

"Can't," he says, looking toward the bus, now at the curb. "I'm actually going to see a friend."

"What friend?"

Instead of answering, he gives my cheek a tiny smooch and turns toward the bus. The doors snap open and he climbs the steps, leaving me even further in the dark.

42

*S*TILL AT THE BUS STOP, I try calling Kimmie again, to see if she might have more insight into the whole keying incident with Wes's car, but she's not picking up. And so I decide to go to Knead, eager to sink my hands into a piece of clay.

As soon as I get there, I see that Spencer is hard at work on his life-size ballerina, which reminds me of my work in progress as well. I remove the tarp from my vaselike bowl, and immediately my mind goes to Ben. I cover the bowl back up and then fetch myself a thick hunk of clay, ready to start something new.

There's a tiny piece of me that still feels intimidated by the process, but with each smack, plunk, and slam of clay against the board, I can't help feeling empowered, because I'm facing my fears head-on.

I close my eyes and press my fingers into the mound; the texture is soft and slick. After several seconds spent flattening the clay with both my palms, images of all sorts start fleeting through my brain. I concentrate hard, trying to focus on the strongest one, and then I start to sculpt.

I move my fingers over the clay mound, picturing an ivy-covered building. I start to sculpt it, expecting the voices to come at any moment, but, surprisingly, they don't. I continue to work for what must be at least another hour, forming double doors and shuttered windows.

The image of a door knocker pops into my mind, and I want to sculpt it, too. I grab another hunk of clay and begin to replicate its shape; the knocker looks like an acorn. Smooth on the bottom and with a narrow tip, the cap has diamond-shaped grooves, formed in rows, for the necessary texture. I spend at least forty minutes working on the acorn knocker, about the size of my palm, getting all the details just right, and wondering about its significance.

And then I feel someone tap my shoulder from behind.

I turn to look, but no one's there. And the studio lights have been dimmed. It appears that Spencer's cleared out the aisles of greenware and replaced them with an L-shaped sofa and a wooden floor. How is it possible that I didn't notice these changes on the way in?

I open my mouth to try to call Spencer, but to my horror I discover there's an object wedged inside my mouth, pressing against the back of my tongue, making it impossible to talk. I go to take a step—to see if Spencer's still in his office—but I end up lurching forward and falling down hard on the floor.

Someone's bound my feet. And put a thick chain around my wrists.

"What are you going to do *now?*" a male voice asks, clearly making fun of me; I can hear the sarcasm in his voice.

I let out a muted cry, wondering where the voice is coming from—if maybe it's coming from downstairs, from one of the heat vents in the floor.

"You should've done what you were told," he says.

"Spencer?" I try again, harder this time, choking on his name. A trickle of wetness runs down my face—whether it's sweat or tears, I'm not quite sure. I look to the right and left, but the sofa is all I can see—all that's illuminated. I do my best to wriggle forward as best I can. My cheek scrapes against something sharp, and I feel my skin tear open—a burning, stinging sensation. Out of the corner of my eye, I see a door that's slightly ajar. It's not the main entrance to the studio, but a different one, mahogany with brass fixtures.

On the ground, using my elbows and knees, I struggle toward the door, unable to hear the voice now. Maybe it's finally leaving me alone.

My cheek feels seared. Blood drips onto my lip—I can tell it's blood by the metallic taste—and my body is steeped in sweat.

But still I can see the door; it's just inches away now. I scrunch my knees up under me to sit up, and make an effort to raise my arms, but my fingers can't quite reach the handle.

Using all the strength in my legs, I try to stand without losing my balance.

At the same moment, someone yanks my hair from behind, grabs my ear, and pulls me across the room. "You should've done what you were told," he says, over and over again. "You should've listened, but you're just so ungrateful."

He starts humming a familiar tune: "Yankee Doodle Dandy." But instead of singing the words that go along with it, he uses the words to the "Jack and Jill" nursery rhyme, even adding in a few lines he's made up himself— lines that include the words *love*, *intervene*, and *die*.

He brings me to where it's dark, drags me down so I'm on the floor again, and then closes the door.

I pretend to be unconscious, as I have no idea on which side of the door he stands—if we're in the same room, or if he's locked me up on my own.

And I'm terrified to find out.

43

$\mathcal{H}$E ROLLS ME OVER, slaps my face, checks my pulse.

All the while, I hold my breath, still pretending to have passed out.

When it seems he's given up, I still remain there, hoping to hear him leave through the main door.

Instead, his breath is at my ear again. "Just relax," he says, as if trying to soothe me, hoping maybe that I'll cooperate more. He dislodges whatever's wedged inside my mouth.

And I hear myself scream. A ripping, searing, gouging wail. One that I don't even recognize.

I scream for him to leave me alone, to unchain my wrists, to unbind my feet. I scream until my throat burns and I let out a gasp.

"Take it easy," he insists. "Breathe."

Finally, he frees my legs. I know, because I can move

them again. My eyes still closed, I thrust my hips from side to side, trying to gain leverage with my feet.

"You're going to hurt yourself," he says. "Please, just try to relax."

He unchains my wrists next and can finally move my hands again. I strike out, pounding the air with my fists, suddenly realizing that I'm still screaming, still writhing around, still trying to get up, to get out.

"Camelia, open your eyes!" he shouts.

I don't. Because I don't want to see him. Because I don't want to be here. Because I don't want to acknowledge this. Because salty droplets of sweat sting my eyes.

"No other choice," the voice says. At least I think that's what he says. I'm screaming too hard to hear.

The next thing I know, something sharp jabs into my thigh. And everything gets heavier. And everything gets lighter. And I'm able to open my eyes.

And see.

That the lights are all on.

And a couple of uniformed men are squatting on either side of me. Spencer's there, too. He paces back and forth in the background, chewing his fingernails, explaining to the men that he tried to rouse me—even though he could tell I wasn't really asleep—but that I refused to respond.

"It was like she couldn't even hear me," he says.

I'm still in the studio.

A sea sponge sits beside my head. It's wet and stained with clay. Is that what was wedged inside my mouth? Did I cram it in there myself?

"Camelia?" one of the uniformed men asks. An EMT guy. "Can you tell me where you are?"

My lips move to form words, but everything feels foggy now. Foggy and clear at the same time. The fog moves in behind my eyes, and I allow myself to melt into it.

44

"IT LOOKS LIKE SHE'S DREAMING," I hear Mom whisper. "Her eyes . . . They're moving beneath the lids."

Is this a dream? Should I wake up?

My mother's voice rises over other voices: pieces of the past swirl together forming a giant mosaic that I'm unable to interpret:

You have choices, Dr. Tylyn says. *Even in the face of tragedy, you can choose to overcome, to gain wisdom, to practice compassion. Don't become a victim of someone* else's *choices.*

"What happened here?" the EMT asks.

Your aunt wasn't able to handle all this psychometric stuff, Kimmie snaps at me. *What makes you think that you can?*

"She was just doing her sculpture," Spencer tries to explain. "I was out back, working on my own stuff, when I heard something hard hit the floor."

Soft, then hard, then soft again.

My aunt is crouching down against the wall of her room, clutching Miss Dream Baby.

My aunt rocks back and forth in the art therapy studio, telling me that I deserve to die.

My aunt places her bloodstained palm against mine and tells me how alike we are. *Like sisters*, she whispers. Her wide green eyes stare back at me through a camera lens. Her star-shaped scar presses against my wrist.

What will you choose? Dr. Tylyn asks.

My mind tells my body to roll over, but my body isn't listening. Ben reminds me how much he cares about me. Meanwhile, Adam tells me not to shut him out. *I want to help you solve this thing*, he reminds me.

Men hold me down against my will, jab my thigh with a needle, and then carry me away.

Exactly like what happened to my aunt. When I visited her at that mental hospital in Detroit.

"Unfortunately, this isn't the first time something like this has happened with Camelia," Spencer tells them. "I wasn't around that first time, but one of my employees was, and she saw the whole episode."

"I think she's coming around," Mom says. "See, there . . . her eyes. They're moving again."

Only I don't want to come around.

I want to remain asleep.

For how long, I've yet to decide.

45

I WAKE UP. My head still feels fuzzy—fuzzy and thick, heavy and slow—as if someone had extracted all the blood from my veins and replaced it with cold maple syrup.

"Hey, there, Pumpkin," Dad says, just like he used to when I was five. "How are you feeling?"

It takes me a moment to realize that I'm in a hospital, that Dad's sitting beside me on the bed, that Mom's standing in a faraway corner. And that this definitely isn't normal.

"Are you hungry?" Dad asks.

I look down at myself, noticing that my clothes have been replaced with a hospital gown. "What's happening?"

"Just relax," he says.

"Who brought me here?" I sit up. "How long have I been sleeping?"

Mom stares at the wall, her back toward me, apparently

unwilling to answer. Meanwhile, Dad takes my hand and looks deeply into my eyes, perhaps hoping that I'll put the pieces together.

And I do.

They come back to me like a bolt of lightning. I touch my cheek where it's bandaged up, feeling a rush of heat charge across my face. "We've got to help her," I say. "Someone's taken her captive. They've put a chain around her wrists. Her feet are all bound up, and she can barely breathe."

"Relax," Dad says again, as if my words have no relevance.

"You don't understand," I insist. "If we don't help her, she'll be gone for good. He won't let her get away."

"Who'll be gone for good?" he asks. "Who are we talking about here?"

"Danica."

"And how do you know her?"

"She goes to my school," I blurt out. "She used to be a skater, and I've been sensing stuff about her . . . whenever I do my pottery."

Mom remains with her back toward me. Her shoulders are shaking from crying, as if I'd suddenly died.

"Mom?" I ask, wishing she'd look at me.

But she shakes her head, blocking me out, all but covering her ears. "There's going to be an evaluation," she says; the words are muddled by tears.

I have no idea if she's talking to me, or trying to reassure herself, or if she's just saying the words out of fear. "What kind of evaluation?" I ask.

"Nothing to worry about." Dad's voice is like snow: soft and powdery. "One of the psychiatrists is going to ask you some questions. They have a really great mental health ward here. That's where Aunt Alexia is."

"You think I'm just like her, don't you?" I ask Mom. Still refusing to look at me, she moves to sit in the corner chair, curling up into a ball, her head resting on her knees.

I try to edge myself off the side of the bed, but Dad forces me back on. "Your mother doesn't think that at all," he whispers purposely, so she can't hear. I know he's lying, that for Mom this is a fate far worse than death. "I'm not like Aunt Alexia!" I shout.

"No one ever said you were," he says, still trying to restrain me—to hold me in place on the bed.

"I sense things," I blurt out. "I hear voices. I have this gift that I never asked for, and I can't return it, or exchange it, or throw it in the trash, or pretend it doesn't exist."

"No!" Mom wails, covering her ears for real now.

"But it's not going to make me crazy." Tears course down the sides of my face, but Mom's crying even harder. She looks so fragile, tucked up on the chair, like a little girl who needs her doll. I almost don't even recognize her.

At first, her behavior surprises me, but then I remind myself that I shouldn't be surprised—that Mom's behavior, ever since my aunt's most recent suicide attempt, has foreshadowed this very moment.

"Mom?" I ask. My throat is sore from screaming.

A second later, a nurse comes in. Her badge reads EMERGENCY, so I know I haven't been transferred anywhere yet. "Is everything okay in here?" she asks.

No one speaks.

"Well, I'm glad to see you're awake," she says, breaking the tension as she focuses on me. "You'll be here for a little while longer, until we can secure you a bed in the other ward."

"What other ward?" I ask, assuming she's talking about the psych unit.

"It's only for questioning," Dad tells me. "Right?" he asks the nurse.

She peeks inside the folder she's carrying, but then closes it up just as soon as she has her answer. "I'll have the doctor come down and explain things fully," she says. "Now, Camelia, would you like me to get you something to drink?"

"I would like you to get me Dr. Tylyn Oglesby," I tell her, "as well as the police."

The nurse nods reluctantly, before leaving us alone again.

"I want to talk to the police," I tell Dad, in case he wasn't listening.

"Don't do this!" Mom shrieks, still hysterical with tears. Finally, she lifts her head to look at me. Her eyes are red. Her complexion is raw.

"You just don't get it," I say, frustrated that she's already made her decision about me, and that she isn't trying to understand. "Haven't you been listening to anything I've been saying? Someone's in trouble."

"I know," she says, between clenched teeth, as if the someone in question is definitely me. "Now, calm down, or they'll come in here again. Do you want them to give you another one of those injections?"

"Let them try," I say, moving out of the bed. This time, Dad lets me. I grab my clothes off the end of a chair.

"Where is she going?" Mom asks. A fresh batch of tears works its way down her face.

"To talk to the police," Dad says, finally taking a stand. "And I'm more than willing to let her."

46

*D*AD ASKS MOM TO STEP OUTSIDE for some fresh air, and then he calls the police in himself. Officer Len Thompkins, probably a little bit older than my parents, has his partner cover for him in the lobby (apparently the emergency room here always has police on duty) while he comes into my room to talk.

"What can I help you with?" he asks; his voice is much deeper than I expected it to be, based on his looks. Standing about five feet five inches tall, he has pale blond hair and a tiny frame.

"I think someone might be in trouble," I say, fearing that timing may be an issue. Back on the bed now, I pull a blanket over my legs, wishing I'd changed into my clothes.

Officer Thompkins takes a notebook and pen from his pocket and begins to write down what I say. He has me go over the details at least three different times, as he twists, turns, and contorts the same questions. I tell him how I've been having premonitions—how I've been sensing for some time now that Danica's life is in danger. "I think someone's been following her, pretending to be her friend, and giving her gifts," I say.

"Has this kind of thing happened to you before?" Officer Thompkins asks.

I nod and look at Dad. "It's been happening for a while now."

"And do any of your premonitions come true?" There's a slight smirk on the officer's face, making me think that these questions about my powers are merely for his own amusement.

"A couple months ago I helped save a good friend from being killed."

"*Really?*" The smirk widens into a smile. "Care to elaborate on that one?"

"Care to go check on Danica Pete before she ends up on the front page of tomorrow's newspaper?" I ask him.

The officer flips his notebook shut and raises his eyebrows at my dad, perhaps wondering why he doesn't scold me. But I don't even care, because a huge weight's been lifted from my shoulders now that I've finally chosen to ask for help and told my dad the truth.

The officer assures me that he'll check on Danica right away. After he leaves, Dad comes and sits beside me on the bed. His eyes are as red as mine feel. "I'm sorry," he says, wrapping his arms around me.

"Sorry that I have to deal with all this stuff?"

"Sorry that I never asked you about it." His voice is much weaker than normal.

"Because you knew what was going on with me?"

"I'm sorry," he says again, which I take to be a yes. He breaks the embrace to look into my eyes—to wipe my tears away with his hand and to ask me if I'll ever forgive him. "I just didn't want to believe it was true. I wanted there to be some logical explanation."

"You read her journal, didn't you?" I ask.

He nods. "But I wasn't prepared to talk about it, wasn't ready to make that connection . . . because I didn't want the same fate for you."

"It won't be the same fate," I say, wiping away his tears now. I grab a tissue from the box by my bed, unable to remember a time when I saw him look so broken. "I have a much better support system around me." Not to mention that I'm no longer ignoring my art or obsessing over the fact that Aunt Alexia and I have so much in common. Instead, I'm trying to think of my power as a gift. "And I'm choosing to handle things differently."

47

*E*N ROUTE TO—OR IN LIEU OF—getting some fresh air, Mom must have taken a detour to the cafeteria. She returns to the room with a peanut-butter-and-jelly sandwich. "It was the only vegan choice on the menu," she says, setting it down on my bed table.

"Thanks," I say. Even though I'm not a vegan.

I scarf it down, suddenly realizing that I'm absolutely starving. I stuff two huge bites into my mouth, fully aware of the silence in the room—of the fact that Dad has yet to say anything to my mom about the police or my power. But before he can broach the topic, she gets emotional all over again, like she can't even stand the sight of me. Dad goes over to comfort her—to help her into the chair, to give her some tissues, to kiss the top of her head. But nothing seems to help.

And then, a second later, there's a knock on the door.

Adam is there, with a bouquet of daisies in his hand.

"Hey, stranger," he says, lingering in the doorway, silently asking permission to come in. "All this fuss just to get my attention? You shouldn't have."

"Hey," I say, happy to see him despite the situation.

"How are you feeling?"

"How did you even know I was here?"

"Spencer," he says, setting the bouquet down beside me. "I stopped by the studio to see how you made out with Dr. Tylyn, and he told me what happened. He seemed really worried about you."

"Well, I'm fine," I say, aware of how ridiculous the statement sounds. "At least, I will be."

"He said you had an attack of some sort?"

Before I can answer, Mom gets up and leaves the room, her hand cupping her mouth, as if only moments from barf city.

"Maybe I should go," Adam says.

"No," I tell him. "I'm glad you're here."

Dad's the one who leaves. He excuses himself to go check on Mom.

"Is she okay?" Adam asks, once we're alone.

"She will be; at least, I hope so. But right now, I have more pressing issues to worry about." I get up from the bed, grab my clothes, and change in the adjoining bathroom.

"The whole pillowcase look not working for you, I take it?" He raises his voice so I can hear him. "Care to tell me what's going on? What kind of attack you had?"

"I had another premonition," I say, joining him back in the room. "And it kind of got out of hand."

"Is there anything I can do?"

I shake my head and explain that I talked to the police. "I also told my dad about the premonitions. And, long story short, he wasn't surprised. I probably should've said something a long time ago."

"And what about your mom?" he asks.

"I don't know," I whisper, unable to put it into words—how guilty I feel, how frustrated I am, how it tears me up knowing that I've done this to her.

Adam comes and wraps his arms around my shoulders. "It's going to be okay," he says, kissing the top of my head.

"Is it?" I ask, thinking how much my relationship with Mom has changed over the past several months. She used to be so superinvolved in all aspects of my life, but ever since things got more difficult (ever since I became more like her sister than she probably ever expected), our relationship has slowly but steadily deteriorated.

Into this.

A few moments later, Dad comes back into the room.

"Where's Mom?" I ask, breaking my embrace with Adam.

"She isn't feeling too well," Dad says. "But she's in good hands. I called her a cab. She's going to meet with Amy."

Her therapist.

I nod, feeling my heart sink. But even as guilty as I feel, I'm relieved that she's gone.

48

*D*AD ASKS ADAM if he wouldn't mind staying with me for a few more minutes while he checks on the status of my impending evaluation. "But I also want you to try and get some rest," Dad says to me. "You're going to need your strength."

"No problem," Adam chirps. "I'm happy to stay." He grabs the TV remote and pulls up a chair. "Camelia won't even know I'm here."

Dad leaves, and Adam flicks on the television, muting the sound to avoid disturbing me.

"It's not like I can actually sleep," I tell him.

"Close your eyes," he orders, trying to sound intimidating despite the smile on his face. "I gave your father my word."

I lie back on the bed while Adam watches a silent rerun of *The Simpsons*. He laughs out loud and then peeks at me as if apologizing for the noise.

"Don't worry about it," I say, closing my eyes, knowing that there's no way I could ever possibly nod off.

But somehow I do.

I wake up about an hour later, all out of breath. I sit up in bed, the image of the ivy-covered building that I'd been sculpting at Knead alive in my head.

I neglected to tell the officer about it.

"Is everything okay?" Dad asks, having returned with what I hope to be the news that I'll soon be out of here.

He and Adam have been watching a rerun of *Friends* with the sound off.

Before I can answer, there's a knock on the door, and I feel my heart pound. At first, I think it's a psychiatrist, here to evaluate me. But instead, Officer Thompkins pokes his head into the room.

"Can I talk to you for a second?" he asks.

"Sure," I say, eager to hear what he's found out about Danica.

But almost as soon as he starts talking, I squeeze my eyes shut, completely jarred by all he's saying: that he went to Danica's house, that Danica was safe and sound, doing her homework and watching TV. And that Danica filled him in about me.

She told him that I've been harassing her, that I won't leave her alone, and that she's really starting to get freaked out.

"She asked me about filing a restraining order," he adds.

"Are you sure you had the right house?" I ask, grasping

at straws, knowing that what he's saying about Danica's annoyance makes sense, but that her life is also at stake.

"Right house, right girl. I spent more than thirty minutes asking her all sorts of questions. Her father was there, and I asked him, too."

"Well, can you at least have someone watch her?"

"She insisted that *you've* been watching her," the officer says.

"There's an ivy-covered brick building," I tell him, feeling my face flash hot. "I think she might end up trapped inside it."

The officer looks at my dad, shaking his head slightly, as if embarrassed for him. Meanwhile, Adam comes and sits beside me on the bed. "Danica is safe," he reminds me. "That's *good* news."

But then, why don't I feel relieved?

"The nurses tell me your daughter's being evaluated today," the officer says to my dad. "I hear there's already a bed waiting for her, so it shouldn't be too much longer here."

Dad thanks him, keeping his focus on me. His expression remains fairly neutral, but then I catch him winking in my direction, and I know he's on my side.

"Do you think you could check on Danica later?" I ask Adam, after the officer leaves. "Or maybe you could just watch her house to make sure she doesn't go anywhere? I could give you her address."

"Anybody home?" someone calls, rapping lightly on the door.

Even better than a fairy godmother, Dr. Tylyn joins us inside the room. "A little bird told me that this is where I could find you," she says, smiling at my dad. She asks both him and Adam to step out of the room as she takes a seat by my side.

"Thank you so much for coming," I tell her, once Dad and Adam have left.

"I was actually here anyway."

"You were?" I ask, though I already suspect the reason why.

Dr. Tylyn tells me that she spent some time talking to Aunt Alexia. "I agree with you," she says. "She does have a remarkable gift."

"But . . . ?" I ask, sensing her hesitation.

"But she doesn't have the resources to handle it."

I swallow hard, feeling a giant pit in my throat. "Can you help her?" I ask.

Dr. Tylyn gives me a subtle smile. "I'm going to try. But first, I need to help you."

I spend a good half hour telling her about what happened at Knead, how I told both the officer and my dad everything, and how my mom is on the brink of a nervous breakdown because of me.

"Probably not a smart idea to add the weight of your mother's breakdown to your already overloaded shoulders, okay? Right now, I'd like you to have a look at this." She hands me a napkin. On it, someone's drawn a brick building, covered with ivy. A baby grand piano sits below it, as a separate doodle, and there's a picture of a grandfather clock in the corner. The face of the clock doesn't have any hands, but the pendulum itself—the way it's drawn—gives the illusion of motion.

As if time is definitely ticking.

"Aunt Alexia gave this to you, didn't she?"

Dr. Tylyn nods. "Do you know what it means?"

I shake my head, wishing I did, explaining that the brick building has been on my mind, too.

"Well, maybe it'll come to you," she says.

"Meaning, you don't think I should try to forget about everything? You don't think it might be just a random premonition?" I ask, referring to our last therapy session, when she was trying so hard to play devil's advocate.

"You have a gift," she reminds me. "Better start thinking of it that way."

"Or else?"

"I have to get back to your aunt," she says, leaving me to read between the lines. "I'll be back in an hour or so; sound good?"

I hold the napkin-note tightly in my grip, about to ask if she wants it back. But then I reconsider, wondering if Aunt Alexia asked her to give it to me—if maybe my aunt is trying to tell me something, and if maybe she knows that I'm here.

49

FTER DR. TYLYN LEAVES, I concentrate hard on the image of the brick building, trying to remember where I've seen a building like this before, or if I know anyone with a baby grand piano. After only a few minutes, my head is spinning with questions. And so I count to ten, imagining the stress inside me like a ball of clay that gets smaller with each breath.

Just as I start to unwind, I hear music: the sound of someone playing the piano. The napkin still clenched in my grip, I assume the music's coming from the lobby. I try to identify the tune, but someone's screaming now—a high-pitched wail that sends shivers all over my skin. A moment later, Adam comes into the room. "You're awake," he says, a wide smile crossing his face. He starts to say something else, but I can barely hear him over the screaming.

"What's going on?" I ask, sitting up in bed, figuring

there's been some horrible accident.

But Adam appears confused. He furrows his brow and asks me something. His lips are moving, but I can't hear the words.

"That screaming," I say, covering over my ears. "The music."

Adam's confused expression morphs into a look of concern.

"You don't hear anything?" I ask him.

Still shaking his head, he gazes at my hands, noticing the napkin. "What's this?" he asks, taking it from me and holding it up to the light.

Suddenly, the noises stop—perhaps because I'm no longer holding the napkin.

"I need to check on Danica," I tell him, sitting up more in bed. "What if those are her screams? What if she needs me right now?"

"Camelia, you really should rest."

"She's in an ivy-covered brick building somewhere," I say.

"No, she's at home," Adam says, setting the napkin on the pillow beside me. "The police checked on her, remember?"

I bite my lip and glance down at the napkin again, sure that there must be something I'm not seeing. I move my head from side to side, trying to look at the drawings from different angles. I even try humming along with the piano tune. *"Moonlight Sonata,"* I say, thinking out loud.

"Excuse me?" Adam asks.

I close my eyes. The image of the baby grand is alive inside my mind.

And that's when it finally hits me.

The baby grand piano and the ivy-covered brick building—and where I've seen both of them before.

"Nothing," I say, knowing I'm not getting anywhere with him. "I'm probably just overreacting. Where's my dad?"

"Out in the lobby. Why?"

"Can you have him get me something to eat?"

"Sure thing."

"And then would *you* mind going to the gift shop to get me something unhealthy to read?"

"*Unhealthy?*" He raises an eyebrow.

"Tabloid magazines," I tell him. "Anything that looks trashy and lacking in any real substance."

"I'll see what I can find." He gives me a kiss on the forehead before exiting.

My cue to get the hell out of here.

Dear Jill,

Please know that it wasn't supposed to
happen like that, but when you refused to
do as you were told, refused to see all the
sacrifices I'd made for you, you left me no
other choice.

. . .

Dear Jack:

I told you I'd try on the uniform, but instead of going to the bathroom to change, I grabbed your camera by the canvas strap and tried to thwack you over the head with the lens.

As if by reflex, you snagged the camera, tossed it to the sofa, and wrapped your hand around my neck. "What are you going to do <u>now</u>?" you hissed.

"Please," I begged, promising to try the uniform on for real.

You brought me to a hallway closet, where you kept your supplies. How often had you actually done this? You seemed so well prepared.

The gag came first. You stuffed a rag inside my mouth—all the way in, until I choked. And then you locked a chain around my wrists.

"You should've done what you were told," you said. "You should've listened, but you're just so ungrateful." Your face was red, including your ears, as you wrapped duct tape around my ankles and made me listen to more of your singing, again to the tune of "Yankee Doodle Dandy": "Jack and Jill ran up the hill 'cause they were meant to <u>be-eeee</u>. Jack said forever, but Jill said never, and now she can't be <u>free-eeee</u>. La-da-da, let's lock her up. La-da-da, we have to. La-da-da, she won't obey. And now she has to pay. . . ."

I tried to speak—to tell you no—but the rag tasted like gasoline, burning my throat.

You dragged me to the bathroom, pushed me inside, and I fell to the floor. Then you threw the skating uniform at my face.

. . .

50

M Y HEART IS ABSOLUTELY RACING. I hike my hair up into a high ponytail and pinch my cheeks for color. A voice on the hospital intercom makes me jump. I reach for the door, but then pause to search for my coat, almost positive that my cell phone is inside it.

I check the bathroom, the bedcovers, beneath the sparse furnishings, and even under Adam's bouquet. But I can't find it anywhere. Unable to waste another moment, I open the door and slip out into the hallway, trying to psych myself up—to tell myself that I'm just here visiting, and that now it's time to for me to go.

Being Saturday night, things are bustling in the ER. A man is whisked in on a stretcher, and a hoard of medics swarm. A woman, hunched over in pain, is busy talking to the admitting nurse. And two officers (neither of whom is Thompkins) question a fifty-year-old guy who looks like he's had too much to drink as he wavers back and forth, stumbling over his feet.

I accidentally make eye contact with one of the medics, fearing that he might recognize me from my episode at Knead—that he might be one of the guys who brought me in. A stabbing sensation pierces my chest. But the medic just looks away, not giving me a second thought.

And so I scoot right out the door.

Once outside, I'm startled by the darkness. My pace quickens, until I break into a full sprint. I pass the closest bus stop, afraid it'd be the first place that Adam or my dad might look. I search my pockets for some change to use a pay phone, hoping that either Wes or Kimmie will come get me. But my pockets are absolutely empty.

I hurry into the supermarket on the corner, remembering that they have a free phone service for calling cabs. I tell the dispatcher where the cabdriver should pick me up, neglecting to mention the fact that I won't be able to pay. The driver arrives about five minutes later, and I tell him to take me to the piano studio in the next town over, remembering having seen an ivy-covered brick building with a piano sign outside. Wes passed it while we were following the Taurus.

"Piano studio?" he asks.

"Yeah," I say, proceeding to describe the place, including the sign in the shape of a baby grand.

"You mean Acorn?" he says.

I nod, feeling a chill run down my spine, still able to picture the acorn-shaped door knocker that I sculpted at

Knead just minutes before I started to hallucinate.

The driver takes me down a bunch of streets, finally crossing over into the town of Hayden and driving through the less-populated part of town. Sitting in the backseat, I pretend to search my pockets for money, knowing that I'm probably not fooling anyone. The driver, most likely in his late sixties, glares at me through his rearview mirror.

"That's my house," I lie, pointing into the darkness, recognizing the area. The piano place is about two blocks up.

"I thought you wanted to go to Acorn," he says, pulling over to the curb.

"Yes, but I need to pay you first. Maybe you could keep the meter running while I go inside for money?"

A moment later, his cell phone rings, and he shoos me away, clearly frustrated, which I decide to interpret as a yes. I exit the cab and head toward a large apartment building, pretending to go inside, but instead I sneak around to the back and hurry across a parking lot. I run the length of several houses and buildings, some of which have been boarded up, trying to figure out which one had the piano sign out front.

I stop a moment, crouching down behind a Dumpster, trying to catch my breath and gain my bearings. Most of the buildings look dark on the first floors—businesses, maybe. But the upper floors appear livelier, with lights on and curtains in the windows.

I get up and continue at a brisk pace, suddenly tripping over a plank of wood. I flop down with full force.

The undersides of my forearms break my fall, and I feel the gravel dig into my skin. I hurry to pick myself up, searching for an ivy-covered brick building, realizing that I'll probably only be able to recognize it if I move back around to the front.

I sneak down an alleyway, keeping an eye on the street, wondering if the taxi driver may still be waiting.

With the light from the streetlamps guiding my way, I pass by several three-family houses. My breath is visible in the chilly night air. I cross my arms, trying to take my mind off the fact that I'm shivering, the fact that the house I just passed has several broken windows, and the fact that I don't have my cell phone.

I blow on my palms in an effort to warm them, wondering if I should turn back around. But then I finally see it.

The tarnished piano sign is unmistakable in the moon-light. The word *acorn* is etched in small gold letters, and yet there's nothing indicating what this place really is. A piano showroom? A place where someone gives lessons? The home of a concert pianist?

A low-watt light casts a warm glow over the door. I start up the cement walkway, noting the ivy leaves crawling up both sides of the building. My fingers just shy of reaching the acorn knocker, I tell myself how crazy this is—even crazier than zoning out and hearing voices.

Because I'm totally on my own.

I consider turning away, wondering if I'd be better off going to Danica's house. But then I find myself knocking anyway, because I simply can't shake this feeling—this sensation that something horrible is going to happen if I don't go in to stop it.

I knock again when no one answers, and then finally try the door handle. It opens with a click. I take a step inside, hearing the floorboards creak beneath my feet. The place is well lit: a wide-open showroom with at least twenty pianos displayed on a red velvet carpet.

"Hello?" I call. My heart is pumping so hard that it hurts.

A baby grand piano sits in the center of the room, with a vase of red flowers on top of it. Exactly like Aunt Alexia's mural.

I take a seat on the shiny black piano bench and venture to touch one of the keys. At the same moment, music fills my ears, startling me.

It takes me a second to notice that the sound is coming from the piano itself—that it's a player piano; I must've turned it on somehow. I search for a switch to shut it off.

"Like it?"

I turn to find an older man (probably in his seventies), with thin white hair, a dark brown suit, and the palest blue eyes I've ever seen. He holds a remote control in his hand. He aims the remote at the piano, turning the music up even louder—*Moonlight Sonata*; I recognize the eerie tune.

"It's a one-of-a-kind deluxe model," he says, speaking over the music. "You won't find another like it in this part of the country."

I nod slightly, trying to keep my cool.

"We're closed," he says, when I don't respond. He looks toward the door and makes a clicking sound with his tongue, most likely cursing himself for not remembering to lock it.

I get up from the bench, accidentally catching my foot on one of the legs.

"You're not really shopping for a piano, are you?" he asks, stopping the music entirely.

"I'm looking for a friend." My voice quivers.

"I see." He takes a moment to look me up and down before reaching into the pocket of his suit and pulling out a toothpick. At first I think that something sharp equals something he's going to try to use to hurt me. But then he sticks the pick between his teeth and starts to roll it around on his tongue.

A moment later, a loud thud comes from the floor above us.

"Upstairs," I say, stifling a gasp. "My friend is upstairs. Is there an elevator or a stairway that I can use?" I peer toward the back of the store. There's an exit sign over what appears to be a heavy metal door.

"Why do you want to go up there?" he asks. More tongue-clicking, as his face goes slightly squinty.

"That's where his apartment is, right?" I ask, pretending I know what I'm talking about.

"You know Jack?" he asks.

"Yes," I manage to mutter, feeling my stomach churn.

He continues to watch me, his eyes studying every inch of my skin.

"Actually, do you think I could use your phone?"

The man gives a less-than-reassuring nod. He watches me over his shoulder as he walks away, and then turns a corner into another room. I wait a few seconds, wondering if he may just be getting the phone. But when he doesn't come back right away, and when I hear another loud thud upstairs, I decide it's time to find a way upstairs on my own.

51

*J*MOVE THROUGH THE EXIT DOOR at the back of the piano showroom, despite a sign warning that an alarm will sound.

Luckily, it doesn't.

The staircase is old and splintery. I make my way up to the second floor, hearing the wood creak with each step.

Finally, at the top, it seems there are no other floors above this one—at least, none that I can access from here. I take a deep breath, reminding myself that there are probably several other apartments in the building. I can always knock on one of their doors if I need to find help.

But, then, when I look a little closer, I see that this actually isn't the case. A long, narrow hallway faces me, and the doors that line it are all boarded up—as if maybe there once *were* other apartments, but now the only way to enter them is from the door at the very end. I start toward it, despite how dark the hallway is. Just one flickering bulb lights the way.

I search my pockets again, hoping to find a key or pen—anything to protect myself—but there's absolutely nothing.

I take a few more steps. The smell of sweet tobacco is thick in the air, almost making me choke. I cover my mouth. At the same time, a scuffling noise comes from behind me. I turn to look, but no one's there. Did it come from behind the wall? Or from the stairwell that I can no longer see?

I turn back around and continue toward the door, wondering if I should knock. My heart hammers as I press my ear up against the door, able to hear a piano playing. Did it just start? Or is it happening inside my head?

I grab the doorknob, and it turns, right away. "Hello?" I try to call, but once again no sound comes out.

The apartment is huge, as if several walls had been knocked down, leaving a wide open space. Spotlights hang over a photography setup of some sort—a white backdrop and a platform on which to stand. A baby grand piano sits in a far corner of the room, playing by itself. It's the Yankee Doodle Dandy tune, and it plays over and over and over again.

I know I've come to the right place.

The air is musty and thick; I feel a drop of sweat trickle down my face. A few feet away is an L-shaped sofa, exactly like the one I pictured when I was sculpting at Knead—when I zoned out and thought that someone had chained my wrists and bound my ankles.

I peer behind me at the door, recognizing the mahogany wood and brass fixtures. It seems that I'm alone. So then, where were those noises coming from before?

A few yards beyond the sofa, there's another door. I move toward it, again hearing the floorboards creak beneath my step. I edge the door open, relieved to find that no one's in here, either. It's a seemingly normal bedroom: a bed, dresser, and nightstand. I move in a little farther, noticing that the closet door is open a crack. I open it wider and then tug on the pull-chain light, only to discover that the closet isn't a closet at all.

It's full of photographs that are shellacked over the walls. There are faces of girls in both candid and posed shots, below a heading that reads, JACK AND JILL, made from letters cut out of magazines. And the nursery rhyme—four stanzas of it—runs down both sides of the photos, with each letter individually cut out and pasted up in the same fashion.

There's a stash of stuff—books, movies, and records (the old-fashioned kind, with the hole in the center)—on a shelf above the wall of photos. It's all varied re-creations of "Jack and Jill": *Jack and Jill*, the movie; *Jack and Jill*, the collection of poems; *Jack and Jill*, the musical . . .

I continue to look at the photos—what has to be at least a thousand of them, of at least four different girls—noting the empty section that seems to be holding a spot for more photos to come. I study the girls' faces, searching for Danica's, completely startled to find a whole corner devoted to candid photos of Debbie Marcus.

Debbie Marcus, who'd once told everyone that she was being stalked, but whom nobody had believed; who'd spent more than two months in a coma as a result of a hit-and-run accident not long after.

"DM," I whisper, knowing for sure now what those initials stand for.

My pulse racing, I back away, out of the bedroom, feeling a rush of adrenaline. In the main room again—the one with the L-shaped sofa—I hurry toward the door to get out, eager to find someone who can call the police. But then I notice a pair of ice skates sitting in front of what I presume to be the bathroom door.

My common sense tells me to ignore them. But something stronger inside of me can't. I grab the skates by the tied laces, turn the doorknob, and flick on the light.

A girl is lying there, with chained wrists and bound ankles. There's a sparkly gold garment draped over her neck, and something wadded up inside her mouth. "Danica," I whisper, unable to tell if she's awake. A few strands of hair have fallen over her face.

She moves her head to look at me.

It takes me a moment to accept what I'm seeing—that it isn't Danica at all.

It's someone who looks a lot like her—same skin tone, same hair color, same spray of freckles across her face—but this girl is taller, curvier, with much longer hair.

"Who are you?" I ask, knowing that I recognize her from somewhere.

The coffee shop. The girl who worked the front counter.

Her eyes widen, peering over my shoulder, and she tries to yell out.

A second later, someone grabs me around the neck from behind and gets me into a headlock. I do my best to take a step back—to get whoever it is to lose his or her footing—but instead I'm dragged backward and flung onto the sofa.

"*You*," he says, standing right over me.

I recognize him, too. From the coffee shop. The good-looking guy who kept staring at me.

"How did you find me?" he asks, shaking his head as if genuinely curious.

Still on the sofa, holding the skates, I make direct eye contact with him as I try to get the laces untied. But I can't quite get my fingers to work right.

"Tell me!" he demands, taking a step closer. His chest is strong and broad, and the veins in his forearms pop.

I curl my grip around both skate blades, preparing myself to fight. He notices and tries to rip the skates out of my hands, but I'm able to draw them back. I stand up from the sofa and lunge at him with the sharp, pointed edge.

It tears the hem of his T-shirt, and he lets out a laugh, amused at my attempt.

I raise the skates over my head and try to strike downward at his chest. But he pushes me back onto the sofa, snatches the skates, and throws them against the wall.

"Come on, the suspense is killing me," he says.

When I don't answer, he wraps his hands around my neck and asks me if I want to die.

"No," I sputter, keeping a close eye on his posture, trying to predict his next move.

"Are you sure?" He smiles. "Because I think you'd be far better off dead."

I try to kick out with the heels of my boots, somehow managing to knee him in the groin. He stumbles back, releasing his grip on my neck, and I'm able to get up.

"You don't belong here," he says. "This is between Jill and me."

I search the room for a phone. Instead I find a pen, tucked inside the middle of a notebook. I grab it, hoping he doesn't see.

"You've got it all wrong," he says, having rebounded from the blow. He approaches me slowly, trying to play nice. "I'm not the bad guy here. I just wanted to take some pictures—to photograph her pain away. She needs to see herself the way I see her." He turns his head, gesturing toward his photography setup.

I lunge at him with the pen, jabbing it into his collar bone. He yells in pain but grabs my arm, twisting it behind my back. The pen drops to the floor.

I kick his shin—hard. He releases my arm, but then throws me against the wall, and I slide to the ground.

The backs of my ribs ache. It's hard to breathe. But I manage to remain focused and get to my feet.

"You don't belong here," he says, even more amused.

I try to move away, inching along the wall.

But he takes a step closer, getting right up in my face: "Jack and Jill went up the hill to give love a little try," he chants. "Camelia intervened. And caused a big scene. And now she's destined to die."

"How do you know my name?" I ask, stumbling over the words. It feels as if every inch of me is sweating.

He smiles at the fear on my face. "I've done my homework," he says, watching a drop of perspiration as it runs down my forehead.

I struggle to move away once more, grinding the back of my head into the concrete wall. Meanwhile, he raises his hand, ready to strike.

"Please," I whisper, keeping an eye on his hips. I pretend to cough, hoping to distract him for just a moment. And then I knee him again in the groin.

He lets out a grunt, doubling over. I move behind him and plunge my heel down against the back of his knee. He falls forward, hitting his head against the wall and landing flat on the floor. I look around for something heavy, find an iron vase kept over the mantelpiece, and conk him over the head with it.

It works. He lies face down; his breath is shallow, and his body is still.

I look around for a phone again, but I don't see one anywhere. I head back to the bathroom and fling the door wide open.

The girl is lying facedown now. I start to help her up when I'm grabbed by the leg from behind. I go down hard; the bridge of my nose smacks down against the ceramic tiles, and I land at the girl's feet.

The man flips me onto my back and starts to drag me toward him, but I kick his face, noticing a trickle of blood running from his temple.

The sight of the blood takes me off guard. He takes advantage of the moment and grabs me by the waist. He gets back up. And drags me up with him.

"Please," I hear myself say again, on my hands and knees, truly defenseless now. Blood pours from my nose.

But he doesn't wait around to hit me this time. He smacks me in the jaw so hard that I feel the sting in my eyes.

The piano music sounds muffled.

And everything fades to black.

52

*W*HEN I WAKE UP, things are a blur. My head aches.
My nose throbs. I can barely open my eyes.

Lying on my side, with my cheek pressed
against the cold wood floor, I'm able to make out two
people fighting—men, I think. I can see their legs as they
battle back and forth.

I try to see their faces, but I can't from this angle. Plus,
the light burns my eyes. And the sockets hurt too much
for me to focus.

I start to get up, but there's a knifelike sensation
pressing into my ribs, keeping me down and making it
hard to breathe.

The fighting persists. I can hear their grunts, their
yells, their gasps for breath. "Ben?" I whisper, wondering
if one of them is him—if by some miracle he's managed to
save me once again.

My head is spinning, and I suddenly feel sick. I close

my eyes, but the spinning continues. Meanwhile, the piano still plays in the distance. It's all I can hear now. Everything else evaporates into blackness.

I wake up and notice right away that Adam is crouching down at my side.

"Camelia?" he asks, smiling when I open my eyes.

I try to sit up, but he stops me by touching my shoulder. "Don't try to move," he says. "We've called the police and an ambulance. So, the good news is that we're getting you help. But the bad news is that you have to go back to the hospital."

"*We?*" I ask. There's a sweatshirt draped over me like a blanket. It's navy blue, thick, with a zip-up front; I recognize it immediately. "Ben?" I whisper, knowing he's there. It's the same sweatshirt he lent me at the labyrinth.

Footsteps move toward me from across the room. "How's she doing?" Ben asks, squatting right beside me now. There's a pair of scissors in his hand.

He sees that I notice them and gestures to the girl from the bathroom. She's sitting only a few feet away on the L-shaped sofa, no longer gagged. The duct tape has been cut from her ankles, though the chains remain on her wrists.

"Is she okay?" I ask.

"For now," Ben says. "But she isn't talking."

"What's her name?" I ask, still dumbfounded that it isn't Danica. I start to take another look, but it hurts to move my eyes.

"Rachael Pete, according to her ID," Ben says.

"Pete," I whisper, noting the same last name. Danica's sister? Danica's cousin? "How did you know where to find me?" I ask him.

"It wasn't easy," Adam says before Ben can answer. "The ivy-covered building . . . that sort of architectural style is pretty rare around here. I forced my way into at least four brownstones tonight, but this one was the charm, especially when I picked up on the whole piano clue from the napkin drawing."

"Some charm," I say, somehow mustering a smile.

I look at Ben, wondering how he found me—if he came here with Adam, or if he sensed something on his own.

Ben's eyes meet mine, clearly sensing my question without my having to ask it. "I called Adam on my way home—just to check in and say I was coming back. He mentioned that you took off from the hospital, and then he told me about the clues on the napkin. I pretty much figured things out from there."

I run the sleeve of Ben's sweatshirt over my cheek, noticing how it smells like him—like bike fumes tangled in spearmint. "I thought you weren't coming home for a few days."

"Plans change." Ben looks toward the guy passed out on the floor. "Anyway, Adam arrived here just in time. I only witnessed the tail end of things, but you should've seen the way Adam pounded him."

"Really?" I ask, surprised at the news. Before I can probe any further, I hear police sirens outside.

Some medics burst in and assess the damage—to me,

to Rachael, to the guy. While Adam is questioned by the police, I'm placed on a stretcher with ice packs on the top of my head and ribs.

"I think someone's already called your parents," Ben says, kneeling down by my side. "They'll probably be meeting you at the hospital."

"Will you come to the hospital, too?" I ask him.

His eyes look slightly redder than usual, and there's a spot of blood on his lower lip.

"Ben?" I ask, trying to sit up, noticing that he looks almost as pain-stricken as me. "Is everything okay?"

"Adam will go with you," he says quickly, quietly, avoiding the question—even though the answer's obvious.

"What happened to your lip?" I ask.

He licks the spot and then wipes it with a finger. "I bit it by accident on the ride over here—too much anxiety, I guess."

"Why won't you even look at me?" I ask, desperate for a connection.

But then Adam busts into the conversation: "We're heading to Hayden General. Ben, will you be coming along?"

"No," Ben says, finally looking at me. I can see the conflict in his eyes. He leans in to kiss the side of my mouth, and I can taste the blood on his lip.

"Are you sure?" Adam asks. "There's plenty of room in the ambulance. . . ."

Ben nods, *un*sure. But he shakes Adam's hand and tells him to take good care of me. And then he watches us go.

Dear Jill,

I feel like I've been put through hell. The police searched my apartment, questioned my father, and checked out my car. They're asking me if I was the one who did the hit-and-run on Debbie Marcus a few months back, but they'll never be able to prove it.

I want you to know that I never meant to hurt Debbie that night. I'd been following her, watching as she walked home from a friend's house, making sure that she got there safely. The problem was she kept stumbling out into the street, not paying any attention to where she was going.

She wasn't killed. A coma isn't death, so I don't understand why they're making such a big deal of it. Plus, I know for a fact that Debbie is out of the coma, which is why I've moved on to bigger and better things.

Like you, Jill. The cops say that you refuse to talk—that I've done that to you. They don't understand that you're choosing to remain silent to protect me, which only makes me love you more.

They asked me all kinds of questions—how I met you, what my intentions were, why I was forced to tie you up like that.

I tell them the truth: that, as with Debbie Marcus and some of the others, I saw something in you that reminded me a lot of myself. And so I watched you and studied you and learned all of your habits. I wanted to show you how beautiful you really are, because despite what anyone says, you deserve to be loved—to be my Jill forever.

I know that when you start speaking again, you'll tell the police all this, which is why I've been writing it down for you, documenting the beginning of our love story together, so you'll know just what to say, and remember how good it really was. It can be that good again one day. I promise it can and it will.

Always your love,

Jack

Dear Jack:

I have no idea who he was. But he saved me. From you.

I watched from the doorway as he smacked, punched, and threw you against the wall. You fought back hard—I'll give you that—but you were no match for him.

And when it was over—when you'd finally passed out—the boy made direct eye contact with me. He removed the rag from my mouth and asked me if I was okay.

"Yes. I mean, I think so," I told him.

But it was her that he was really interested in: the girl who was lying unconscious on the floor. Her eyes were swollen, and there looked to be a trail of blood running from her nose.

The boy wiped her face with a rag. And then he kissed her, and held her, and ran his hand over her cheek, finally grabbing his cell to dial 911.

He was wearing gloves, which I thought was weird. Maybe he was concerned about his fingerprints, from breaking in. But once he hung up, he removed the gloves, took the girl's hand, and placed it on the front of his leg—as if it were some magical hot spot that would make her better somehow. Tears welled up in his eyes as he apologized for not getting there sooner.

"I'm so sorry," he just kept saying.

And suddenly I felt sorry too.

Apparently it was the anniversary of something tragic that'd happened. I couldn't really hear him clearly, but I was pretty sure he'd mentioned visiting an old girlfriend's grave.

"You deserve someone better," he told her. "Someone who'll be open and honest; who won't be afraid to share everything with you." He draped his sweatshirt over her, kissed her behind the ear, and then promised to love her forever.

A couple minutes later, another boy came in, all out of breath. "Is she all right?" he asked.

The boy who saved me stood up, wiped his tearful eyes, and told the other guy to sit with her until she woke up. And then he went to find scissors for me. He cut me free and brought me out to the sofa. "My name's Ben," he said. "And help is on the way."

When the girl finally did wake up, Ben allowed the other guy to take credit for saving her life. I wanted to ask him why, but I haven't been able to speak.

That's what this letter is for. My therapist says that I need to tell my side of things in order to regain my voice. She suggested that addressing my thoughts directly to you might help provide some closure.

So far, it hasn't done the trick.

Never your Jill,

Rachael

EPILOGUE

*I*T'S BEEN TWO WEEKS since Adam saved my life.

And two weeks since Ben walked out of it.

I'm back at school, bandages and all, but Ben's taken a leave of absence—his second one since arriving in Freetown last fall.

Meanwhile, Ms. Beady is up my butt, making sure that I'm truly okay to resume my classes, and offering to have one of her infamous tea sessions with me (whereby we sit in the cushy chairs in her office and she pretends to know what's wrong with me). But I've decided that, as far as Ms. Beady is concerned, I'm boycotting tea altogether.

Luckily, Danica's sister is okay. She still isn't speaking, but her physical wounds have mostly healed. I ended up having to lie to her father, saying that I'd seen someone whom I believed to be Danica (obviously, Danica's twin sister), being followed by a dark sedan on more than one occasion.

"It was the only logical explanation I could think of as to why I'd been so convinced that Danica was in trouble," I explain to Kimmie and Wes. "Short of telling him the truth, that is."

"And we all know the truth is the last resort," Wes jokes.

It's a Saturday afternoon, and both he and Kimmie have come over. While Wes rifles through my desk drawer, allegedly searching for a stick of gum, Kimmie sits beside me on my bed, giving me her version of therapy, in the form of a manicure, using black-and-white nail polish.

Danica's coming over, too. She called me just a little while ago, saying that she wanted to stop by.

"And how were you able to explain that you knew where Jack lived?" Kimmie asks.

"That's where Wes's high-speed chase story came in," I explain. "When, on a whim, we decided to follow the sedan in question. Only, instead of admitting that we lost the guy, I've been telling people that we followed him to his apartment."

"I actually like that version of the story much better," Wes says, his ego inflating before our eyes. "And while you're at it, be sure to tell people that not only did I get us across the train tracks just in the nick of time, I also managed to jump a bridge just as it was opening up for a boat to pass through."

"Right, I'll be *sure* to tell them." I roll my eyes.

"And what about the timing of things?" Kimmie asks. "The reason you had such an urge to leave the hospital to go find the damsel in distress—"

"Okay, well, thankfully, no one's asked me that yet."
But I suspect it may one day come up, especially since I
told the officer at the hospital about my premonitions.

"I didn't even know that Danica had a twin," Kimmie
says.

"*No one* knew Danica had a twin," Wes says, correcting
her, having finally given up on his gum-searching. He's
now using one of Kimmie's nail files to scratch his near-
nonexistent facial scruff.

"But that's obviously why I felt so connected to her,"
I tell them.

"And it's obviously what the 'there are two' clue was all
about," Kimmie adds.

Rachael didn't go to Freetown High. She and Danica—
a.k.a. Dee, according to those closest to her, which now
includes me—moved here in the sixth grade, started at
the same elementary school together (on the other side
of town), but then parted ways to go to different schools,
shortly after all the harassment started.

It was that first year, in the sixth grade, when Rachael
began skating with some of the Candies; when they told
her that she was worthless and talentless, because they
were jealous of her skill; and when they barricaded her
in the girls' locker room so she'd miss the tryouts for the
skating team.

The Candies were punished for the incident, but
Rachael decided to give up skating altogether.

"What happened that day didn't *make* Rachael
depressed," Danica explained on a visit to my house right

after the incident at Jack's apartment. "It just shined a spotlight on her already depressive thoughts."

And just knowing that—how unhappy Rachael was, even when she was much younger—brought everything full circle for me. Rachael's depression was most likely the reason the voices in my head had been so dark and self-loathing all the time.

But now that the danger's over, I haven't heard those voices again.

"Anybody home?" Danica asks, poking her head in through the open door. She steps inside, armed with a box full of treats from the Press & Grind. "Your dad let me in."

"Great," I say, perking up, glad that she's been feeling comfortable enough to come around on occasion. She's even ventured to have lunch with us a couple of times at school.

"Are you sure?" She looks at Kimmie and Wes. "Because I don't want to interrupt. . . ."

"Not at all," Wes says, eyeing the box of treats.

Danica sets the box down on my lap. "Double-dip chocolate cookies," she says. "They always make me feel better."

"Thanks," I say, noticing how cute she looks in a hooded pink rain jacket with matching rubber boots. Her hair is tied into two tiny pigtails, and a silver heart necklace dangles around her neck (instead of the sea glass pendant that she once borrowed from her sister). "Have a seat," I tell her. "We were actually just talking about you. Or at least about the whole Jack incident."

"Unfortunately, I can't really stay." She looks down at her watch. "My dad's just doing a loop around the block."

"Well, at least tell us how your sister's doing," Kimmie says.

"Better, I guess." She shrugs. "I mean, I think it helps that she's been writing about what happened. When you look into her eyes, you can see that she wants to talk—that she has a lot to say. Initially, her expression was pretty lifeless."

"You know what's really weird?" Wes says, unable to resist the box of cookies. He opens it and helps himself. "For all the time I spent at the Press & Grind, I never even noticed your sister worked there. I mean, not that I even knew the girl, but I was pretty sure I could ID all the employees."

"It was a relatively new job," Danica explains. "My father thought it'd be good for her—thought it'd help her gain some self-confidence—and the guidance counselor at Humphrey said it was fine. Rachael was originally only supposed to be working in the back."

"But then she quickly got promoted to the front," I point out.

"Right, which is when *I* got hired," Danica says. "They needed someone to take her place baking treats."

"And that's when she met 'Jack,'" I add.

Danica nods, tension visible in her jaw. "I really wish she'd told me about him."

"Do you think that's why you were getting harassed at school?" Kimmie asks. "Because of your sister, I mean, and her history with the Candies?"

"Guilty by association." She nods again. "Only, the difference between Rachael and me is that she actually cares what people say." Danica looks away, leading me to assume that Rachael cared a little too much.

A little too deeply.

Which was probably just one of the reasons she'd found Jack so appealing. Instead of making her feel as if something were always wrong with her, he made her feel like everything was always right.

"Rock-out Mama?" Kimmie offers, holding up a bottle of coral nail polish. "This is what always makes *me* feel better."

"Excuse me?" Danica makes a face.

"That's the name of the shade." Kimmie giggles. "I bet it'd look pretty stylin' with that supercute outfit of yours. Interested?"

"I actually have to go," Danica says. "I just wanted to say hi and drop off the cookies. Another time?"

"Sure," Kimmie says.

I get off the bed to walk Danica out, giving her a lame-o hug at the door, so as not to smudge the polish on my fingernails. "Thanks again for stopping by," I tell her. "Come visit whenever you feel like it."

"I will," Danica says.

And I happily believe her.

"Do you think we freaked her out?" Wes asks when I return to my room. It appears he's eaten over half the box of cookies.

"I think she's just leery of trusting," I tell him, returning to my spot on the bed. "But she's definitely coming around."

"And considering what happened to her sister," Kimmie says, applying Rock-out Mama to one of her pinkies, "it probably takes more than our mere presence to get her freaked."

"You know what's *really* freaky?" Wes segues. "The fact that the psycho in question was the same guy who was after Debbie Marcus."

The whole fiasco with Debbie Marcus happened at around the same time that I was getting stalked. But instead of taking her seriously, people chalked her stories up to pranks and practical jokes, concluding that Debbie had gotten paranoid as a result.

But there was obviously a lot more to it.

"Actually, it's not nearly as freaky as the fact that Camelia decided to go to the psycho's house without even calling us first," Kimmie says.

"I already told you guys, I didn't have my phone."

"And you've obviously never heard of a *collect call*," Wes says.

"Nor have you heard of nine-one-one." Kimmie's barbell-pierced eyebrow rises high. "Because I hear that's free as well."

"What's going to happen to that freak-o, anyway?" Wes asks.

"Word's still out," I say. "Those other two girls, whose pictures were part of the Jack and Jill shrine, never reported the fact that he took them to his apartment for photo shoots. And, unfortunately, they're still not willing to talk, so no one's sure how they escaped or if they even had to."

The police said that Jack had been described by neighbors and former classmates as a loner. He ended up dropping out of school and changing his appearance so he could feel as if he fit in. He targeted those he believed to be "lost souls" in hopes that he could heal himself by healing them—by making them his partners, while at the same time boosting their self-confidence (and "taking their pain away").

"I'll bet his dad knew what he was up to," Wes says.

"Because where family's concerned, there's only so much you can hide, right?" Kimmie asks, painting a giant capital *F* on my thumbnail with the white polish.

I bite my lip, knowing she's talking about what happened a few days ago, when Kimmie and I took a walk to China Moon.

It was late afternoon, so the restaurant was pretty dead, but there was an overly amorous couple in the corner booth. Kimmie and I tried to kill time while waiting for our order by making fun of the couple's audible kisses and the way at one point the girl actually sat in the guy's lap. But then the guy got up to pay his bill. And we were able to see his face.

It was Kimmie's dad, cheating on Tammy the Toddler with some girl he'd recently met.

"I never told you this," Kimmie confessed after a full-on scene at China Moon (as a result of which we've been forever banned from the place), "but I knew my dad had been cheating on my mom. It's sort of why I hate him." She wiped her purple-shadowed eyes on her anti-D scarf. After that, we went back to my house, and Kimmie opened up about her family, really talking about how she felt and what she feared. It was nice to be able to be there for her— to be able to reciprocate her friendship in spite of all the chaos going on in my life.

While Kimmie paints capital *F*'s on all of my finger-nails, Wes gives said *F*'s a curious look. "Do you really think Prana Mama will approve?" he asks.

"FYI: the *F* stands for 'fearless,'" Kimmie says, "because that's what our dear Chameleon truly is."

"The ovaries of a champion," Wes agrees. "And the snout of one, too." He gestures at my nose. It's still slightly swollen from falling on my face at Jack's apartment, but luckily, it isn't broken. "And fearlessness such as yours," he continues, "is just one of the reasons I've brought you a long overdue present." He pulls his poetry journal out of his bag. "I'd love your honest—and fearless—opinion."

"You got it," I say, knowing that in showing me his work, exposing another side of himself, he's being fear-less, too.

"I'm sure your Neanderthal of a dad loves that you're writing poetry," Kimmie says. "Does he still plan on having the Audi painted pink?"

"Are you kidding? No matter what he says, he'd rather die than see me in anything pastel, vehicles included," Wes says.

"Did he report the vandalism on your car?" I ask.

He shakes his head. "Now he thinks I deserved what happened, that people are saying someone like me doesn't deserve to drive a car like mine—that the car's way out of my league and people are disgusted with my ways."

"What ways?" I glance down at his poetry journal, excited to finally *get him*, and still wondering if it wasn't indeed Jack who keyed his car.

"Not being more like him, I guess." Wes shrugs.

"More grotesque, sluggish, and stupid, you mean?" Kimmie asks.

"Camelia?" Mom says, interrupting us. She raps lightly on the door (the lock of which has recently been removed). "I'm heading to the hospital to visit Aunt Alexia, but your father will be home."

Both my aunt and I have been meeting with Dr. Tylyn regularly—not together, just on our own. My parents have been meeting with the doctor, too, trying to comprehend fully just what I'm dealing with as far as my psychometric powers go. That's one of the few blessings that's come out of all this—my parents have actually bonded over my gift.

And luckily, I wasn't punished after everything that happened. Initially, my mom accused me of not keeping her in the loop (once again), but the truth was, at some point, she stopped being able to be in it. Her behavior at the hospital was a direct example of that: of her regressing back to childhood, to everything Aunt Alexia had been dealing with. She couldn't handle the idea of my following in my aunt's path.

My dad, on the other hand, seemed a bit more reliable. And so I tried to open up to him on more than one occasion, though it was sort of like part of him didn't want to know the truth, either—didn't want to accept the possibility of my mother's biggest fears coming true.

For now, the most important thing I want both my parents to know is that I've chosen to handle things differently from the way my aunt has.

For as long as I possibly can.

Before Mom leaves, I grab Miss Dream Baby from my closet. After Aunt Alexia was admitted to the hospital, I retrieved the doll from her room, cleaned her up, and wrapped her in a silk-trimmed blanket. "Can you give this to her?" I ask.

"Sure," she says, giving me a puzzled look. But still she doesn't question it.

A moment later, I hear the familiar engine rumble of Adam's car pulling up in front of our house.

"You're not planning to have a party here, are you, Camelia?" Mom asks in a lame attempt at sarcasm—as if having three people over makes a party.

"Wes and I should probably go anyway," Kimmie says. "I've got some design stuff I want to finish up for Dwayne."

"Sketch class," I say, knowing that I need to get back to it if I ever want to finish my bowl.

Both Kimmie and Wes give me hugs good-bye, and then my mom walks them out, warning me not to let Adam stay too long. "School tomorrow," she reminds me.

Even though it's barely three p.m.

As expected, Adam's been great since the incident, calling me daily, coming by my house, surprising me with Mexican takeout one day and tabloid magazines the next.

While Dad does some work at the dining room table, Adam and I move out onto the back patio, where the signs of spring are definitely present. Mom's tulips have sprouted in the garden, and the buds on the cherry tree have already started to bloom.

We sit on the porch swing, facing one another. Adam's brought along the most delectable hot chocolate I've ever tasted—so rich and thick I can actually stand a piece of biscotti in the center and it won't even lose a crumb.

"You don't have to bring me treats all the time," I tell him. "It's nice just to see you."

"So, no more hot chocolate and biscotti, I take it?"

"Well, I wouldn't exactly go that far."

We drink our hot chocolate and make small talk about school. But I can tell there's something more pressing on his mind: his shoulders are tense, his face looks slightly peaked, and he keeps shifting against the bench as if he can't quite get comfortable.

"Is everything okay?" I reach out to touch his forearm. He looks more fearful than I've ever seen him.

"There's something I need to tell you," he says.

"What is it?" I ask, expecting the worst.

"It's about Ben."

"*Ben?*" I repeat, surprised to hear his name brought up.

Adam looks down into his cup. His wavy brown hair is ruffled slightly by the breeze. "You should know that he's been calling me every day to see how you're doing—if your wounds have healed, if you're getting on with things . . ."

I nod, thinking how, like me, or perhaps *because* of me, Ben also got the sense that Danica, or someone connected to her, was in trouble, which is why he tried to spend time with her. "Where is he?" I ask.

"Back home. That's where he was just before the attack. This is a really tough time of the year for him— the anniversary of Julie's death."

"Anniversary?" I ask, hating myself for not knowing that fact, for not figuring out the dates and putting two and two together.

"Yeah. It was the weekend when all that stuff went down with Jack—when he asked me to keep an eye on you."

"I really wish he'd told me," I say, disappointed that, once again, Ben hasn't wanted me to be there for him.

"I was going to mention it," Adam says, "but then Ben asked me not to . . ."

"Did he say anything else? Anything about why he was already on his way home that night?" I've gone over the scenario several times in my head. Ben's hometown is more than three hours away. He supposedly called Adam to check in around seven, and then showed up at Jack's house sometime after eight.

"He said it was just a coincidence that he decided to cut his trip short."

"Really," I say, suspecting there's a lot more to it—that Ben must have sensed I was in trouble somehow, and that

that was the real reason he decided to come back early. The anniversary of Julie's death must've been beyond difficult for him, must've reminded him of what he feels he's capable of—which is why he pushed me away at the labyrinth.

I zip up my sweatshirt, curious as to whether Ben misses it, or whether he even remembers that I still have it. It's the same sweatshirt I was wearing that night at the labyrinth—the one I woke up with after being knocked out at Jack's apartment. I can't help wondering if it carried my vibe—if that's how Ben knew I was in trouble and where to find me.

"Ben didn't really talk much during our last conversation," Adam says. "Except to say that he's working on things, working on himself, and that he'll be back soon enough. But bottom line, he really cares about you."

"And why are you telling me all of this now?" I ask.

"You mean, why am I burning away any shred of hope that I might actually have of being with you?" he asks.

"Okay . . ." I feel myself smile.

"Because, like you, I don't want any secrets."

"Well, I'm glad you told me," I say, thinking how hard the truth must've been for him to say. But how refreshing it is to hear.

"So, is there anything else I should know about?" I ask. "Any skeletons in your closet, or other secrets I need to know?"

Adam hesitates a moment, as if there might indeed be something else on his mind. But then he unleashes a tiny grin. "No more secrets," he says.

I move to sit closer to him, almost unable to fully fathom the idea of a relationship without any secrets—a relationship where I don't have to overanalyze every single solitary syllable because I'm trying to guess the truth.

I rest my head against his shoulder and glance down at the capital *F*'s on my fingernails, knowing that I *am* fearless. And so is Adam.

"So, what now?" he asks, followed by an angst-ridden breath. "Do you want to dump hot chocolate over my head for not telling you everything sooner?"

I hold my cup high, as if ready to call his bluff. Adam closes his eyes in anticipation. But instead, I kiss him full on the lips, reminding myself that I have choices.

And I'm happy to be choosing him.

Look for the final book
in the Touch series,

DEADLY LITTLE LESSONS